THE LAST SUTTEE:
A Novel

Madhu Bazaz Wangu
2017

Cover Design: Jenny Quinlan
ISBN – 13: 978-1974362462
ISBN – 10: 1974362469

OTHER BOOKS

Fiction

The Immigrant Wife: Her Spiritual Journey
Chance Meetings: Cross-Cultural Karmic Collisions and
Compassion

Non-Fiction

Images of Indian Goddesses
A Goddess is Born
Hinduism
Buddhism

CDs

Mindful Meditation for Writers: *Body, Heart, Mind*
Mindful Meditation for Writers II: *Walking Through the*
Forest, Awakening the Senses, Mountain and Lotus, Animating
Seven Energy Chakra

Foreword

On the morning of September 5, 1987, I was going through the Hillman Library card catalogue at the University of Pittsburgh when a friend stopped by. She told me something I would never forget. She said that an eighteen-year-old Indian woman, named Roop Kanwar, had immolated herself on the pyre of her dead husband. I was dumbfounded. *Suttee* in the twentieth century? It couldn't be. But *The New York Times* confirmed the news. The ritual, known as *suttee*, was witnessed by the townspeople and thousands more came to see it from nearby villages and towns. When the news was leaked the following day, the town was swarmed for days by Indian and international journalists. I was stunned and speechless, my legs laden with lead. At that frozen moment, the seed for this book was planted.

The kernel stayed dormant, but the incident continued to sear like a wound at the back of my mind. The distress was raw, but I was not yet emotionally ready to write about what had happened and how it had affected me. In the ensuing years, I trawled libraries, bookstores, and the Internet, learning about the history of *suttee* and the cultural and religious traditions in which it is rooted. I studied records of the shrines dedicated to women who had committed *suttee*. I read the history and mythology of the namesake goddess, spelled Sati. Critically and carefully I analyzed the photographs of Sati temples and studied the engravings, drawings, and paintings of the goddess Sati and the *suttee* ritual that had been made by British, European, and Indian artists and travelers.

Suttee is a centuries-old Hindu ritual. This ancient belief still persists in some remote corners in India. The belief is if a widow cremates herself with her dead husband, the couple will live in heaven as they did on earth. Furthermore, such a sacrifice guarantees a place in heaven for seven generations for both sides of the family.

The ritual is rooted in the myths of two goddesses: Sati, Shiva's wife, and Sita, Rama's wife. Here are summaries of the myths:

> **Goddess Sati** *is the daughter of the high priest Daksha. Shiva, the world renouncer, is so awed by her yogic skills and asceticism that he grants her a boon. Sati asks to marry him. He agrees.*
>
> *Daksha dislikes Shiva. He finds Shiva unconventional and unkempt. Despite her father's opposition Sati marries Shiva and they live in his mountain abode in Himalayas.*
>
> *Daksha plans a great sacrifice. He invites all the important divine beings, except Shiva. Sati feels disgraced by the way in which her father has treated her husband. On the day of the great sacrifice, she throws herself in the fire pit meant for the sacrifice. And burns herself to death. When Shiva discovers what has happened to his wife, he is outraged. He pulls out Sati's half-burnt body, holds it on his shoulders, and in anguish and lamentations whirls*

around the world.

Goddess Sita *is an ideal Hindu wife. Her husband, Rama, is the center of her life. His welfare, reputation, and wishes are most important to her. One day, the demon king Ravana abducts her and takes her to his golden palace. He lies to her that he has killed Rama. Sita is horrified. She moans and tells him that it must have been her fault that her husband was killed. She warns Ravana she could burn him to ashes with the fire of her chastity, but she won't because she did not have her husband's permission.*

In the end, Rama defeats Ravana and brings Sita home. There he severely tests her loyalty because she has spent days under the control of another man. Sita is shocked at such an accusation. She protests her innocence. She says she has remained wholly devoted and completely faithful to him. Rama persists.

Grieved by his false accusation, Sita asks for a funeral pyre to prove her innocence. A pyre is built, and Sita stands atop it with hands folded. Agni, the god of fire, refuses to harm her because she is innocent and pure. She returns to Rama unscathed. Yet he banishes her to a forest.

Sati and Sita are faithful and chaste wives, and they are devoted to their husbands. The lives of these goddesses are defined by their husbands. Although their dedication and chastity are exemplary, they pay a heavy price for being wives. In both myths, fire plays an important role. Whereas Sati voluntarily kills herself, Sita is saved by *Agni*. Their god/husbands are alive when the women jump into the sacrificial pit or on the funeral pyre. But ordinary women's lives are no myths. When a woman is forced into being a *suttee,* neither her husband nor the god of fire will save her.

The *suttee* ritual was outlawed by British Raj in 1829. The ritual was described as "heinous rite" when cases surfaced about widows being tied to their husband's pyre even after being intoxicated with *bhang* or opium. Many reports of widows escaping and being rescued by strangers were also recorded. Still, more than a century later, scattered instances of the custom have been reported, such as Savitri Soni's in 1973 and Charan Shah's in 1999.

The most notorious and controversial case, however, was of Roop Kanwar. Indian people either publicly defended Roop's action or declared that she had been murdered. Following the outcry that followed Roop Kanwar's *suttee,* the government of India enacted the Rajasthan Sati Prevention Ordinance on October 1, 1987. The law makes it not only illegal to commit *suttee* but also illegal to glorify the ritual or coerce a woman to commit *suttee.* Glorification includes erecting a shrine to honor the dead woman or converting the place where immolation took place into a pilgrimage site. Derivation of any income from such activities is also banned. The law makes no distinction between a passive observer and an active promoter. Everyone is held equally guilty.

The seed for writing a book inspired by Roop Kanwar's *suttee* finally sprouted in November 2009, when I wrote its first draft as part of National Novel Writing Month (NaNoWriMo), a nonprofit internet organization that supports writers in an effort to complete the initial draft of a novel in one month.

It would take me seven more years to finalize the draft.

The story continued to incubate. I developed the characters, sketched the settings, wrote the narrative and dialogue. But to birth a healthy novel and bring it to life, I had to experience the environment in which Roop Kanwar was born, lived, and died. I needed to converse with the people who allowed it to happen. I wanted to know the antagonist and protagonist's viewpoints.

I visited India for a month in 2013 for that purpose. I went to the small towns of Deorala, where Roop Kanwar committed *suttee*, and Jhunjhunu, home of an imposing marble temple dedicated to faithful women who sacrifice their young lives immediately after their husbands' deaths. The visit stirred feelings of remorse and wonder. Why did people celebrate sacrificial death? How does blind faith hide behind the stunning structure? Domestic and temple architecture, middle and high schools, ancient mansions with bedroom walls made of mirror-mosaics (some now converted to five-star hotels) were breathtakingly beautiful. The local flora and fauna were intriguing, and men and women's attire colorful. I fell in love with the place. But I wasn't there as a tourist. I was there to fulfill a quest, to do something about an event that jolted the core of my being.

Meeting with the people of Deorala opened my mind to the fact that a community's worldview can be so different from my own. Yet my sorrow and awe about Roop Kanwar and my feelings about other widows like her were not alleviated by talking to Roop's father-in-law, her brother-in-law and his wife, or their neighbors. Nor did I blame them after visiting her neglected and unkempt *suttee* site. However, the visit helped me better understand the point of view of the town residents. A magnificent temple dedicated to the goddess Sati, which locals honor and regard highly, further clarified their worldview.

My interview with Roop Kanwar's father-in-law took place in the verandah outside the room where Roop lived with her husband. This was the room where she dressed herself in bridal attire and decked herself in jewelry before following her husband's dead body to the cremation site. The room has been turned into a shrine, and Roop has become an *ishtadevi*, a manifestation of Narayani Satimata, a local goddess higher in the pantheon of the thousands of village goddesses of India.

When I asked to go to where Roop performed *suttee*, her father-in-law declined to walk along, but he did ask other men to take me there. I treaded the path that evidently Roop Kanwar, most probably intoxicated with *bhang*, walked with the help of two women. They followed her husband's litter, which four male relatives carried. I was told a lamenting crowd of men, women, and children followed the dead body and Roop as they headed toward her husband's funeral pyre.

Facing the desolate ground where the ritual had taken place twenty-six years earlier, I shed tears of pain for an eighteen-year-old who didn't know better, and who no one came to rescue.

The characters in this novel are fictional, but the setting is historic. Writing it does not feel like redemption, for I still ache for the women of the world who are engulfed in outmoded traditions, who are uneducated and dependent. Women with so much potential to offer their families, their communities, and, most importantly, to themselves.

Undoubtedly, the world over, women have made tremendous progress. Yet, the path to elevating women's social status has many roadblocks, and the process is slow. I sincerely hope *The Last Suttee* not only helps remove a block or two but also adds substance to the process of change.

Madhu Bazaz Wangu
Wexford, Pennsylvania, USA
August 2017

Chapter One

The Little Orphan

A policeman holding a little girl's hand walked inside a building marked SAVE GIRLS SOULS ORPHANAGE. He walked to the front desk. The receptionist, Christina, greeted him with a smile and said,

"May I help you?"

"Would you admit this girl?" he said.

Christina hesitated a few moments, then said, "I'm sorry sir. You'll have to take her to *Aasra* or *Sneh Sadan*. At present, we don't have a room to accommodate her."

The policeman, who was looking at the girl, jerked his head towards the receptionist and said louder than was necessary, "No vacancy! Is this a hotel? What sort of orphanage are you running if you can't admit one little orphan?"

"A very well-run place, sir!" Christina said, pointing at the award plaques hanging on the wall behind her. "We take good care of our residents; unfortunately, that's the reason I cannot admit her. Rooms are crowded. Currently we have four to a room. Not a single space is available."

"Where is the director?" The policeman looked through the window of the room marked *Director's Office.* "What is her name?"

"Ms. Kumud Kuthiyala," Christina said calmly. "She should be here soon. Please take a seat in the reception room."

"Do you know what sort of vultures lurk in the city for a girl in her situation? You'd have to admit her… just for a few days…. until I…"

"My heart goes out to her, but the director can't do anything about it either. I assure you." Christina had strict instructions not to admit someone unless they could provide a bed and some privacy. "Would you like a cup of tea, sir?" she asked.

He shook his head. "No. I'll wait." Reluctantly he sat on a wooden bench against the front wall, his back straight and his legs stretched out. The girl stood next to him with her head bent. He pointed to the seat next to him, but she didn't move. He gently pulled her to the seat and made her sit. She sat at the edge of the bench, her hands cushioning her bottom.

At that moment, Kumud Kuthiyala entered wearing a crisp cotton peach-colored sari. She was about to turn the knob to her office door when she noticed the policeman and a little girl sitting on the bench. She walked towards them.

"I am Kumud Kuthiyala, the director here. Can I help you, officer?" She said.

She looked like someone in authority who would not mind changing the protocol. "Yes, Madam, you certainly can. This girl was brought to the police station early this morning. The inspector told me to bring her here. But your receptionist tells me you have a policy of not admitting more than a certain number of girls."

"Yes, that is correct," Kumud said.

The girl's face triggered an image from Kumud's past. In her ex-husband's neighborhood, a woman had died giving birth, as had the newborn. Her widowed husband had handed over his little daughter, Parvati, to Kumud for safe keeping until he could make some arrangement for her. Taking care of Parvati for a week had been a bright spot in an otherwise depressing and lonely year for Kumud. The memory stirred a tender feeling in her, and she smoothed the girl's hair.

"I don't know where else to take her," the policeman said, his broad shoulders slumping.

Kumud crouched, facing the girl and holding her hand. The director tucked unruly curly bangs behind her small ear and asked, "What is your name, child?"

Kumud looked into the girl's eyes; they were beautiful, penetrating.

"Alka," she said softly.

"A perfect name for a girl with black curls!"

The girl nodded. "That's what my mother says," she said.

"You look hungry," Kumud said, standing. "Let's get something to eat." She asked the policeman to follow her to the office and instructed Christina to ask Radha, one of the caretakers, to bring two breakfast plates.

"No thanks. I have had my breakfast." the policeman said to Christina as they entered the office. He pulled out a chair and helped Alka sit on it and then sat next to her. Kumud unfolded a file, took out a form and asked, "Where did you find her, Mister. . .?"

"Tipnis. A construction worker brought her to the police station."

"A construction worker? And where did *he* find her?"

"In Kalaba. In a decrepit building that was set to be dismantled years ago. But you know how government works, slower than a snail. Homeless people began sleeping there. Yesterday, when it was finally time to demolish the building, the workers found her sleeping behind a door. She told them her mother had gone to get food."

Just then Radha, a woman in her late seventies entered with a breakfast plate. Her hands trembled as she placed the tray in front of Alka. Yuna Li, the previous director, had hired Radha when the founder of Save Girls Souls Orphanage (SGSO), Nari Millwalla, was alive. In the ensuing twenty years, Radha, once energetic and efficient, had become slow and enfeebled. The passing years had snatched her strength and agility. Kumud knew she needed to hire a younger woman but didn't have the heart to let Radha go.

Radha asked if they needed anything else.

"Would you like a cup of tea or coffee, Mr. Tipnis?" Kumud asked.

He politely declined. Kumud shook her head and Radha left.

Alka gulped down the milk and ate a piece of toast.

"She must be famished. I don't think she's eaten for a day or so. I offered her biscuits when they brought her to the station, but she refused," he said.

"Wonder why her mother did not return?" Kumud said, more to herself than to the police officer.

THE LAST SUTTEE

Moving closer to Kumud, the police officer whispered, "We found the body of a beggar woman, a hit and run, on the side of the road, about a mile from the building. Perhaps that is why."

"Oh, Ma!" Kumud cried out and pressed her palms to her eyes. When she opened them, Alka was munching on a second slice of toast. After finishing the bread, Alka picked up the glass, tipped it between her lips and emptied the glass of milk.

"More milk?" Kumud asked, and the girl nodded yes. On the internal phone line, Kumud rang Christina for another glass of milk. Tapping her fingers on the desk trying to think of some way to admit Alka. She turned to the officer and said, "As our receptionist informed you, Mr. Tipnis, we don't have a single bed available. I feel bad."

"Why can't you let her sleep on the floor? It is better here than *Aasra* or *Sneh Sadan*. Those orphanages are terrible," he said, his forehead furrowing.

"Thank you, but we must follow our founder's policy. We aren't permitted to change or modify it," she said hesitantly.

"I guess I could drive her to the orphanage at the other end of the city, but that one is also a madhouse!"

Radha entered the room quietly and handed a second glass of milk to Alka, then cleared the tray from the table.

Christina peeked in the office and said, "Madam, the caterer is here!"

"Oh, I almost forgot!" Kumud said, looking at her wristwatch, then at Alka. "Finish your milk. The policeman will take you to another place for now. I'll try

5

my best to bring you back here. Okay, Alka?"

Looking a bit confused, Alka got up and held policeman's hand. The bangs behind her ear came loose, and the memory of Parvati again stirred in Kumud's heart.

"I'm so glad we met," she said to Alka. "Let me walk you to the door. I'm sorry, officer!"

"Thanks anyway, madam."

At the door, Kumud watched as the policeman and Alka walked away. Her gaze followed them as they entered the parked Jeep.

When Kumud turned back towards her office, she saw Veena's wedding caterer waiting on the bench. Veena was Kumud's first ward at SGSO. She was getting married to her sweetheart, Vinod. The wedding would be the orphanage's first big event under her directorship.

"Why so sad, Kumud Madam?" the caterer remarked. "Veena Bitiya has not left yet. A few more weeks before she goes."

Suddenly, Kumud remembered that Veena was getting married, interviewing for jobs and would be leaving the orphanage soon.

"Please wait, I'll be right back!" She said to the caterer and ran out of the room.

A few minutes later she returned holding Alka's hand.

"You are a fortunate little girl," the caterer said to Alka. "Out of hundreds of girls like you in this metropolis, you are lucky to have been brought here at the moment when another girl is about to leave."

Chapter Two

The Wedding

Kumud's flat was on the topmost floor of the SGSO main building. A terrace extended from the back of the flat and overlooked a public park. The park was the only green patch on the vast sandy shore that locals called the "lungs of southern Ambayu." Palm trees lined the road leading to the park and swayed perpetually in the salty, humid breeze. Red-lipped blossoms of *amaltas* welcomed people of all backgrounds—Hindus, Parsees, Muslims, Sikhs and foreigners from various countries. They came to cool their perspiring skin, stroll, walk, or simply enjoy the setting sun simmering on the western horizon.

The orphanage was located on Mumbai Hill, a wealthy neighborhood in southern Ambayu. The building was a century-old Victorian house built during the British rule. Its fifteen rooms housed forty-five girls, one director, one doctor, and several *chotti ma*, "junior mothers." Kumud was like a mother to the girls, and Dr. Shekhar Roy, almost like a father.

Shekhar had been a tremendous support to the

girls since he started working as a resident doctor at the orphanage. He lived there in an apartment at the back of the first floor. His small clinic was behind Kumud's office. He was not only the doctor for the young girls but also a mentor and a male role model. Part doctor, part psychologist, he counseled them about their emotional problems as well.

From childhood to adulthood Shekhar Roy had not faced many wants. He was raised in comparative luxury and with his parents' love. He studied at one of the best medical colleges, did his internship at another, and then a residency. He had not paid much attention to how blessed his life was until he accepted a job at the orphanage.

Shekhar loved Kumud. So much so that he wanted to marry her. He had expressed his feelings openly to her, but even though she admired and cared deeply for him, she was not ready to make a commitment. Still, when he touched her arm or back with his large, strong hands, gooseflesh rose on her skin.

Karmic coincidence had brought Kumud to SGSO. The orphanage was founded by Nari Millwalla. He was the multi-millionaire industrialist whom Yuna Li, the director before Kumud, had nursed during last years of his life.

Nari Millwalla would not have flourished in Ambayu if his Zoroastrian descendants had not fled from Muslim persecution in Persia in the eighth century and settled in the metropolis Ambayu. They worshipped Zarathrusta. In India their ethnic group was known as *Parsees*. By interacting freely with various races and cultures, their ethnic group prospered and became

THE LAST SUTTEE

affluent and thus magnanimous.

Kumud was a drop in the river of the people who had coalesced in Ambayu and made it a vibrant cosmopolitan metropolis. The orphanage reflected that mingling: Nari Millwalla, a Parsee; Yuna Li, Chinese; Kumud Kuthiyala, runaway from Rajasthan; Shekhar Roy, from East Bengal; and the young resident girls from different Indian states. SGSO Center was a miniature India.

Nari Millwalla was the owner of Jute Mills. He had dedicated his life to his business, transforming it from a single, small-scale mill to the major jute industry—Paymaster Jute Mills. He lived in the Victorian mansion in the wealthy neighborhood of Mumbai Hills, but preoccupied with work, he never spent much time there. Only later in his life did he regret not marrying or fathering children.

During the last years of his life, the nursing student Yuna Li ministered to his needs with selfless care and concern. He became quite attached to her and hired her full-time. She left school and lived in his mansion. Soon Nari Millwalla learned that Yuna Li's parents had once owned a successful shoe business in India. After retirement, as they were returning to their mother country, their plane crashed, making Yuna Li an orphan. Nari Millwalla adopted her, and in his will left her the fifteen-room mansion. His last wish was that the mansion should be converted to a girls' orphanage and named it Save Girls' Souls Orphanage.

During the last years of his life, Nari Millwalla often had heart-to-heart conversations with Yuna Li. He would tell her about his struggles and how his hard work and devotion had helped him succeed as a businessman. Months before his death, Nari Millwalla said to Yuna Li, "I am well respected and admired in the community, still I feel an emptiness inside me. They admire me for my wealth." With tears in his eyes he continued, "I've everything, yet I don't feel fulfilled. If I had married and fathered children, perhaps I would have been a happier man."

Yuna Li, seated on his bedside helping him eat lunch said with affection,

"You fathered me. I was an orphan, you made me feel like your daughter."

"You are more than my daughter, Yuna!" He said patting her head.

For a few moments, both were quiet. When Nari was done eating he said,

"For the past year, I have used only this room. What is the use of a mansion? Why don't we turn this mansion into an orphanage for girls? Perhaps by becoming father of helpless and destitute girls would give meaning to my life." His eyes lit up as he said it. With sudden rush of emotions he said to Yuna Li, "Perhaps this was meant to be the true purpose of my life!"

"Such a noble idea." Yuna Li agreed.

"Call my attorney! I want to add this to my will."

Yuna Li got up to make the phone call.

He called after her and said, "Yuna, I want you to be its first director."

Yuna Li accepted Nari Millwalla's offer and helped him realize his path to bliss.

The orphanage was a ten-minute walk from the

THE LAST SUTTEE

Waterfront Park, a mile of greenery on the ocean front. The park, historic mansions, iconic monuments, and newly constructed high-rise buildings on the Mumbai Hills overlooked the deep blue Arabian Sea and offered a magnificent view against the brilliant blue sky.

One of the important monuments visible from the Park on the shore of the Arabian Sea was *dakhmas*, the Tower of Silence. Here Parsees of Ambayu disposed of their dead. Vultures circled above the tower. When Nari Millwalla died at age eighty-nine, he was laid atop the Tower to be recycled back to the elements, lest his rotting flesh contaminate the earth and water. Only Parsees parted with their dead in this manner. Nari Millwalla's corpse was carried on a litter by four men dressed in white. They had placed it on the highest circular stone plinth enclosed by a brick wall. His clothes were slit with scissors. After the ball-bearers left, vultures swooped and devoured the whole body in half-hour, leaving nothing but the skeleton. On the third day, the bones were cast into the central well where they crumbled away. Dust to dust.

If he was still alive, Nari Millwalla would have been proud of the way Kumud was managing his orphanage. This was Kumud's fifteenth year there. Veena, the bride-to-be had been her first ward.

Recently one morning Veena had come to Kumud's office and said, "Ma, I have to tell you something."

"What is it?"

"I don't know how to say it." Veena looked uneasy.

"Whatever way you feel comfortable."

"I want to marry my classmate Vinod!" she said in one breath, then stared nervously at Kumud.

The news astonished Kumud; anxious thoughts flooded her mind. *When had this little girl matured into a young woman? Why didn't I see this love affair developing?*

She got up, walked closer to Veena, gently pushed up her chin and looked into her eyes. She said, "And who is this Vinod you're in love with?"

Veena flushed and smiled quietly.

"You have my blessings, Veena, but before I give my consent, I want to meet this young man."

Kumud wanted to know what sort of person Vinod was, his character and family background. She also had heard that if Vinod was unable to obtain a job in Ambayu, he planned to move back to Chhattisgarh, hundreds of miles away from Ambayu. There he would live with his parents after he and Veena married. Kumud did not like the idea of Veena living so far away.

"No wedding before I meet this young man!" she repeated.

"Tell me when and where and I'll obey!" Veena answered eagerly, though still a bit shy.

Later that day Kumud talked to Veena's friends. Sarla, her best friend, confirmed that for the past year Veena and Vinod were rarely seen separately. In classrooms, they sat side by side and at lunchtime, instead of eating, they gazed into each other's eyes.

"They are meant for each other," the girls claimed. Even during exam month Veena spent her evenings with him, they said, and when she returned home she made excuses of being 'at the library studying.'

Kumud learned that Vinod was born and grew up

in Chhattisgarh, a small town near Madhya Shahar, whose boundaries touched *Neela Nagar*, meaning blue town. Neela Nagar was frequently in the news for smothering female infants, marrying girls to much older men before they reached puberty, and sacrificing widows to immolation, *suttee*. Thoughts of Neela Nagar, entrenched in archaic and cruel rituals, floated her mind. Even the mention of it made her shudder.

An evening tea was arranged.

When Vinod arrived, he thanked 'Kumud Ma,' as she was affectionately called, for going to the trouble of inviting him to her home.

What a pleasant young man! Kumud thought as they sat talking in the living room.

"Tell me something about your family," Kumud said after she and Veena finished serving the tea.

"We live in Chhattisgarh. My father is a landowner. I'm an only child so my parents are very possessive of me."

"Didn't they mind you coming to Ambayu to study, so far away?"

"My father minded very much! I joined college against his wishes. My mother, married at eight, is unlettered. Yet she wanted me to get college education."

"A sensible woman!" Kumud said.

"But in our house, her opinion does not matter. My father wanted me to tend fields, oversee farmers, and not come here 'just to study.' He has remained cold and distant for the last four years, but, to be fair, he supported my studies financially."

"That was generous of him," Veena commented.

"Yes, but he set a condition. I was to marry a girl

chosen by my parents. 'After all,' my father says, 'marriage is an alliance between families of the same caste. A marriage outside the clan is taboo. It disrupts tradition.' If I married an outsider, he says 'it would throw our family customs and tradition into disorder. An educated girl from a different caste or sub-caste would be worse.' He and my mother are afraid that her unfamiliarity with the local culture and customs, her inability to get along with the older women of the family, and her refusal to be subservient to them could jeopardize everything'," Vinod said, trying to meet Veena's gaze.

She looked uneasily at the floor.

He turned to Kumud, and said, "I don't agree with him. If I did I wouldn't be so candid about it. I don't know how my mother is different, or why she consented to my coming here for education."

Kumud liked Vinod for his open, honest attitude. He went on to tell Kumud that when he first hinted of his interest in Veena to his father, he immediately nullified what Vinod said. He wrote back that they had already chosen a girl for him. He asked how I could betray them. Did I not remember my promise? He wrote, 'The girl we chose for you is of the right caste and from a well-established family. We would be shamed if you disobeyed us. How are we to save face? Besides, the girl we chose would make you happier. Who knows which caste the girl you mention is from, what sort of family, what traditions her family follows?' But I remained adamant," Vinod said, looking lovingly at Veena, making her blush. "They have stopped objecting. I am sure they will give me their consent."

"Oh, good, I am glad." Kumud said and asked abruptly, "How many people will be attending the wedding?"

"Maybe twenty to thirty."

"Would they expect any dowry?"

"I hope not. I don't think so."

"Will both your parents attend?"

"I am quite sure they would," Vinod said. "My marriage is a turning point in their lives too. We want their blessings." He again looked at Veena, who nodded in agreement.

"More importantly, being their only son, I do not want to deprive them of the pleasure of participating in our wedding. I am rather old-fashioned that way." He paused a moment, then added, "Last week, I posted another letter to them explaining my feelings. I expect a positive response."

Kumud blessed him as he prepared to leave. Later she said to Veena, "He seems like a nice boy, honest and confident, sincere. Let's wait and see what his parents say."

The following week, Vinod received an offer for his first job with a small architectural company in Ambayu. Veena was still interviewing. A few days later, Kumud invited Veena and Vinod for dinner. This time she asked Dr. Shekhar Roy, the resident doctor, to join them.

Shekhar suggested they go out to eat and offered to make dinner reservations. The evening was pleasant, as the four laughed and chatted about the significance of marriage and the pleasures and perils of starting a family. When the evening was over, Kumud and Shekhar walked home. Both agreed that Vinod was intelligent and personable. Shekhar thought Vinod rather old-fashioned, but Kumud reminded him that Veena was not a feminist type either.

"They are meant for each other!" she said, and Shekhar did not disagree.

A few days later, Vinod informed them that his parents had accepted his choice, though reluctantly.

On the eve of Veena's marriage, she looked lovely in a plain orange salwar-kameez embroidered with silver blossoms and a matching chunni. A professional henna applier was too costly for the orphanage, but Veena's friend Sarla did a good job painting the bride's palms and feet. Veena's colorful hands showed off the ring Vinod had slipped on to her finger a day before. The girls also applied henna designs on each other's palms.

In addition to limited funds, the orphanage had limited space. Kumud and Shekhar had made a selected list of SGSO's close friends and well-wishers. The groom's party would stay at a bed and breakfast motel, a mere twenty-minute drive from the orphanage.

"How thoughtful of his parents to bring only thirty guests to the wedding," Kumud said to Shekhar.

"Most grooms' families bring hundreds of guests, irrespective of the financial situation of the bride's family," Shekhar agreed.

On the wedding eve, Veena looked even more beautiful in a crimson Banarasi silk sari (Kumud's gift to her) with gold zari border and pallu showing dancing peacocks. Simple gold earrings and a necklace adorned her face and neck. Alternating red glass and gold bangles jangled on her wrists. Moments before the guests arrived, Kumud stopped to look at the bride. Alka, the newest and the youngest resident, was dressed in a red frock and sitting next to Veena. The seven-year-old gazed open-mouthed at the colorful balloons and streamers decorating the lawn and building. Alka's wide eyes and faint smile were reminiscent of Veena's when she was brought to the orphanage. Then, she too had not experienced much gaiety or pomp in her abused young life. Alka's story was not so different from that of Veena's.

Kumud kissed Veena's forehead. Smiling demurely, the bride hugged her back. When Veena first arrived at the orphanage, fifteen years ago, she was a physically abused and emotionally unstable young girl. Kumud found it difficult to communicate with her. Under Kumud's steady guardianship, the girl struggled and fought back, but eventually she started to listen and learned to trust Kumud. And now, Veena had blossomed into a sensible young woman. She had done well in school, graduated with flying colors in the major of her choice, and was now marrying the man she loved.

Kumud remembered as if it were yesterday, when she had just arrived at the orphanage and Yuna Li handed seven-year-old Veena into her custody. Yuna Li wanted to see if she was capable of handling a traumatized girl like Veena.

Veena's head was shaved, her eyes flashed with anger, her fists balled. She was not easy to care for. She was ready to pounce on anyone who stood in her way. Veena had tried to flee her cruel aunt's home several times, but every time the authorities brought her back.

Much later, when Veena started sharing her experiences with Kumud, she explained how she had been repeatedly starved and abused, but there was no one to listen to her gripes. The last time she ran away she had felt dizzy close to SGSO, a passerby found her unconscious on the roadside and carried her to the orphanage.

Kumud was with Veena when she woke, dressed, ate, studied, and played. She neither criticized nor judged Veena or ask her prying questions. She felt the girl's suffering as if it was her own. Because of Kumud's steady attention and caring, Veena began to trust her a little.

At first, when Veena came to the orphanage Kumud had to pay extra attention to her personal hygiene. Veena avoided taking a shower even when her skin and hair turned stinky. Other girls complained about it. It took several weeks of shampooing, conditioning, and combing sessions before Veena's hair was finally clean.

Yuna Li watched how tenderly and attentively Kumud taught Veena to follow daily routines: to make her bed, take a bath, wash her clothes, sweep and mop. Soon, Yuna Li gave Kumud full responsibility for the girl.

Kumud clearly remembered how one morning, soon after Veena had become her ward, she had washed her hair.

"May I oil and comb your hair?" Kumud asked.

Veena neither answered nor looked at her. She sat hunched, hugging herself. Gently Kumud opened Veena's arms and lifted her chin, "Give me a smile," she said.

Veena frowned and slumped into a crouch.

Kumud moved behind Veena and straightened her

shoulders. Then she began combing her hair.

"Oooouch! Why? But why do you have to comb my hair every day?"

"So that you are clean," Kumud said.

"What is the point?" she whined.

"You mean why, in addition to keeping your head free from lice and smell, and scratching the whole day?" Kumud said as she continued to comb through and braid the hair.

"Who are you?" Veena shot back. "Why should I listen to you? I was better off with my aunt."

Just then Yuna Li walked into the room, and Kumud silently greeted her.

"Because she loves you," Yuna Li addressed Veena.

"How do you know she loves me?" Veena asked.

"Because she cares for you as if you were her own daughter. Because I watch what she does for you," Yuna Li said. "I wouldn't care for someone who is rude to me and is not thankful for what I do for them. Have you ever thanked Kumud Ma for what she does for you? Don't answer me. Just think about it."

Veena looked at Yuna Li with piercing eyes and lowered her lids.

Kumud and Yuna Li exchanged glances; Kumud continued braiding Veena's hair. She knew that several times earlier Yuna Li had said something similar to Veena without any results.

But slowly, with time, Veena began to pay attention to what she was being told. Still, she continued to rebel and defy Kumud but Kumud continued to give her tough love.

One late afternoon after school hours the girls were playing in the back lawn. Veena came running to Kumud with a bleeding knee and bruised face. Kumud was instructing a handyman about a clogged drain. At once, she turned to see what was wrong.

"Poor, dear! You hurt yourself!" Kumud said to the sobbing Veena. She excused herself from the handyman, held Veena's hand, and led her to nurse's office.

Veena wiped her eyes and asked, "Are you angry? Will you lock me up in a dingy dark room?"

"Why would I lock you up?"

"Because I was bad!"

"Were you bad?"

"I screamed at a girl, so she kicked me and I slipped."

"I will never ever lock you up. You are hurt and we need to go to nurse's room so that she can make you feel better."

Veena looked surprised. "My aunt used to beat me until I was unable to get up from the floor. . . Then she would drag me pulling me with my braids to a dark wet room and leave me there for days."

Kumud stopped. Stooped to hold the little girl's hands between hers and kissed them. "That's why you are with me now," she said, squeezing her gently on the shoulders.

Veena cried, the way she had never cried before. Kumud let her. When Veena's cries quieted down, Kumud rubbed her back and said. "Let's go to nurse's room."

Veena was now sobbing and in between her sobs

she said, "Then she would come back and make me remove my clothes. . . she would touch me at places. . . and. . . ." She could cry no longer.

Kumud's heart bled. She wiped her eyes and nose and entered the nurse's room. There she helped Veena sit on a chair.

Whenever Kumud felt agitated she went for walks in the park. The incident with Veena had distracted her the whole day. By the time she finished her work the sun was set. From her flat, she briskly walked to the park. There she sat on a rock, facing the skyline of her neighborhood, with her back toward the Arabian Sea. Vultures were hovering over the Parsee's burial place, Dakham, where Nari Millwalla's last rites were performed. *No matter what kind of life one lives, it eventually ends.* She remembered Nari Millwalla's conversations with Yuna Li on his death bed. She briskly walked back to the orphanage. Instead of returning to her flat she went to Veena's room. She was doing her homework.

"Is your hurt better?"

"Yes." Veena said.

Kumud patted her head and said, "I am happy to hear that. Can I ask you something?"

"What?"

"Can you let me be your mother?"

Veena just looked at her.

"I would love to have you as my daughter. Would you let me?"

Veena was chewing the end of her pencil. She placed it on her notebook and turned to Kumud. They tightly hugged one another. And not a word was said further.

From that day on, Veena accepted Kumud as her own.

That year on the day of *Deepavali*, the festival of lights, a feast was prepared. The girls sat around nicely set tables. Each table seated nine girls and an adult. Veena was sitting at Kumud's table. Kumud served each girl a plate filled with delicacies. When Veena's turn came, her eyes widened.

She said, "For me too? What did I do to deserve this?"

Kumud realized her feeling of worthlessness and self-loathing. She smiled tenderly at her and said, "You very much deserve it. You deserve it for behaving like the Veena we love, for being yourself."

Slowly, Veena began sharing her intimate experiences with Kumud. By the time Veena was an adolescent, Kumud had helped her understand the significance of self-worth as she tutored her in reading, writing, sciences and mathematics. By the time she was in high school, Veena had become a confident and diligent student who took pride in working hard.

As time passed, Veena's rebellious nature and hardheadedness rechanneled itself into creative work such as sketching and drawing. Kumud admired and encouraged her creativity. Kumud's attention and care fructified. Not only did Veena's grades improve she also tutored younger girls in math and English. She graduated from high school with excellent marks in drawing and mathematics. She wanted to become an architect. And now she had a degree in Architecture and Urban Planning.

Kumud's years of caring and attention had grown

into genuine love for Veena.

On the wedding day, the blue sky was dotted with timid white puffs of cloud. A long table was set on the back lawn with plates, napkins, silverware, and glass jugs of lemonade and orange juice. The guests arrived. Kumud and Shekhar warmly greeted each one of them. Many were the philanthropist friends of Nari Millwalla. Others had been well-wishers of SGSO who continued to support it even after Nari Millwalla's death. After all, SGSO was doing a fine job of helping destitute and oppressed girls to become educated and independent women.

Vinod's family and friends, mostly men and a few women, arrived. They were dressed in traditional wedding attire. Vinod introduced them to Kumud, Shekhar and several other guests. Vinod's father and uncle chatted with Shekhar while Kumud smilingly stood next to him. The groom's guests were treated with special attention.

An atmosphere of festivity and excitement filled the air as the girls, from little Alka to young Sarla, dressed in their finery, greeted the guests.

The party was warming up with such tasty tidbits as *aloo* and cheese *pakoras, mirch samosas, papads*, hot tea, and Coca-Cola. The sun peeked through for a while then vanished behind encroaching dark clouds. Blue-black clouds weighed down with rain moved in, pushing away the timid ones. Suddenly, the sky thundered and it began to drizzle. Before a downpour, the girls swiftly escorted the guests indoors to the assembly hall.

Shekhar, foreseeing the possibility of a rainfall, had

cleared the space in the hall and decorated it with balloons and festoons of colored paper. Long tables covered with white sheets and set with serving dishes were set against the long wall. As the guests streamed in, dabbing damp hair and faces, the aroma of delicacies teased their nostrils. Several girls stood behind the tables, ready to serve.

Dinner was announced. The line moved slowly from platters of mutton curry, makhani chicken, brinjal with potatoes, spiced okra, channa and fried bread, and moong dal to steaming rice and tandoori roti. Some guests reminisced about beloved Nari Millwalla and the early years of SGSO.

Kumud stood with one of the benefactor, an elderly couple. "This mansion was a quiet, desolate place when Nari lived alone, especially after he fell sick," said the elderly woman.

"But Yuna Li brought the house back to life," her husband reminded her.

"It was because of Yuna Li's selfless care for him that Mr. Millwalla turned the mansion into an orphanage." Kumud said, trying to make small talk.

"Yuna Li was something else! It was her compassion and tremendous effort that transformed this place into what it is today," he said.

"Don't forget her," the wife said pointing to Kumud. "She is continuing the tradition beautifully."

"Of course! Here's to you, dear Kumud, and to the first wedding at the center." The old man chuckled, patting Kumud's back.

Kumud led them to the dessert table. The couple said they were stuffed but could not resist sweet balls of juicy gulab-jamun and rounds of jalebi. Kumud left them only after they took their first bites.

In a corner, at the opposite end of the dinner buffet, a priest had prepared a pit for the fire-ritual. Vinod and Veena wanted a traditional wedding. The priest had fasted the whole day to purify himself for performing the ritual. After consecrating the space, he constructed an enclosure with terracotta bricks. He had stacked twigs at the center of the pit that would be lit. For the wedding ritual the bride and the groom would deposit spoonsful of ghee, grain, and *durba* grass into the flames. At the end of the ritual they would be pronounced husband and wife.

Kumud checked with the priest to see if he needed anything. He was ready. She went to the kitchen to see if the servers and escorts had eaten. Gratified, she returned to the hall for the ceremony to start. The sumptuous dinner was now over. She watched as the guests were served *paan* and *supari*.

By now the guests, including the local philanthropists, had blessed the bridal couple. The elderly had excused themselves and left. Kumud accompanied some of them to the main entrance and thanked them for their gracious presence. Vinod's family and many locals interested in watching the ritual were seated either on the carpet or on chairs. The wedding ritual was about to begin.

The groom sat cross-legged, facing the fire-pit and the priest. Then came the bride, accompanied by her friends. Sarla helped Veena sit to the left of Vinod. The girls sat behind the couple. At the front of the hall, closer to the main entrance, a group of Vinod's family members had gathered in a circle, conversing amongst themselves.

As Kumud watched, a sense of gratification overcame her. She was exhausted but happy. Her body relaxed as she watched the bride and groom sitting together. The priest lit the twigs. He invited the dancing flames to implore Agni, the god of fire to witness the ceremony. He poured a spoonful of ghee onto the flames and recited the first sacred *shloka*. The flames burned as hot and fresh as Veena and Vinod's love. The smell of ghee and herbs and smoke added ambiance to the ceremonious space.

Kumud turned her gaze to the couple facing the flames. Love stirred in her own heart. Veena deserved everything good life had to offer. She had brought her up like she was her own child. Now she was crossing over to the next phase of her life. The thought that Veena would live with Vinod, a man whom she did not yet know very well, made her feel a bit anxious. *He is a good man. They will make a good life together*, she consoled herself, curbing her pangs of separation. *May her life be better than mine!* Kumud inhaled and exhaled deeply.

Something caught her attention. Vinod's uncle was whispering in the priest's ear. This gave her pause, but then she spotted the caterer, who was looking for her. Kumud led him out of the assembly hall and into her office. There she handed him a check and thanked him for the tasty food and good service. She hurried back to the hall.

The priest was sitting with his hands in his lap.

She saw Vinod's Uncle approaching her. "I have asked the priest to stop the ritual," he said, "Could I speak with you, Kumudji?"

"Certainly! Is everything all right, Chachaji? Did you and your guests enjoy the dinner?"

"Yes, yes everything is fine! But before the ritual begins, before the groom and bride circumambulate seven times around the fire and make the wedding vows final, we want to make sure that we are on the same page."

"Same page?"

"Yes, agreement."

"What agreement?" Kumud was confused.

"Surely, you must be jesting."

"No, I'm not. What agreement are you talking about?"

"Vinod's father wants to make certain we are on the same page about the transaction," he said.

"What transaction are you talking about? Come to the point, Chachaji," Kumud said confidently.

"Agreement, transaction, it is all the same. These terms mean the same thing when it comes to marriage. Come on, Kumudji," said Vinod's uncle, who seemed to speak with the authority of a family spokesman.

"Please state clearly what you are trying to say. What do you expect from me?" Kumud said, though by now, to her amazement, she understood that Vinod's family was asking for a dowry.

A few other men had joined them in their conversation.

"Haven't you heard of the tradition of dowry?" someone cried mockingly.

The uncles and cousins agreed in nods and grunts.

"Yes, I have! Dowry is not a tradition. It's a blemish on the sanctity of marriage, and if you haven't heard yet, it is illegal, punishable by law," she said.

The uncle, wearing traditional attire for the occasion, a turban, kurta, and pajama, did not respond.

"Why doesn't Vinod's father talk to me himself? Where is he? Where is Vinod?" Kumud asked, irritated.

The uncle pointed out Vinod's father to her. He was standing at the back.

"I would rather talk to the man of the house!" Vinod's father said loudly as he came forward.

"Understand this," she said to Vinod's father," her face livid with anger. "I am Veena's father and her mother, so I am the one you need to talk to."

The silence deepened. No one budged.

Her heart sank.

"Hasn't Vinod told you that Veena's parents passed away many years ago? Did you even know she is an orphan? Didn't Vinod tell you?" She turned to look at Vinod, who was no longer seated next to Veena.

"We knew. He did tell us. Come now, you didn't think you were going to get away without a dowry. We are the boy's family. We expect at least one million rupees and a car. Nothing less!" Vinod's father blurted.

"One million. . . we have no such money!" Kumud said.

"We know you don't. But we also know you can get it. How about your wealthy patrons? After all they don't want bad publicity. Do they? Do you?"

Kumud saw Vinod emerging from the mumbling group to stand next to his father. Though taller than him, he looked shorter because his shoulder sagged.

Her breath slowed when Shekhar walked towards her.

THE LAST SUTTEE

"What is going on?" he said.

Kumud, tight-lipped, was looking hard at the male members of Vinod's family.

"They are demanding dowry," she told him.

"What?" he asked, clearly agitated.

She looked at him. "They want dowry or they will leave."

"Let's not spoil this auspicious occasion with something as unpleasant as bridal money," Shekhar pleaded to no one in particular.

"Come now! We are only asking for what is traditionally due a boy's family," Vinod's father responded.

"No such thing. Your son loves Veena. She is educated and capable of earning money herself. He will be taking her home after a beautiful celebration and ceremony. Isn't that enough for you people?" Shekhar said.

"My son is a fool! I did not mention dowry to him because I was afraid he'd elope," the father said, violently shaking Vinod's arm. "We had offers from rich families with dowry in cash and worldly goods. But no! The fool wants a love marriage! None of the boys in my family married for love! This one turned out to be a damn fool! You can very well afford a dowry. Your patrons are filthy rich," he said, stomping his foot with finality.

"Vinod, are you going to stand here and listen to all this?" Kumud chided.

Vinod looked helplessly at Kumud. "Just give him what he wants," he pleaded.

"What? What did you say?" she gasped.

She looked around. All the girls were behind her,

their mouths slightly open, their eyes glued to her. The groom's family stood before her. Everyone was waiting for her to say something. Her eyes closed for a moment.

Opening them, she said to Vinod's father, "Respectfully," she looked at the groom's party, "I have nothing against you. But I don't believe in buying a groom for my child. Even if I had the money, which I don't, I wouldn't waste it on dowry. I beg you to reconsider what you are asking and allow these young people to marry. The decision is yours."

The men were stunned. Dumbfounded, Vinod's father glared at her.

Kumud continued. "If you have nothing else to say, you may leave and take your spineless son with you!" She was aware of the consequences of what she had said. No one would ever marry a girl rejected by her groom on the day of the wedding. The news would soon spread like wildfire.

Veena watched the drama from a distance.

"Who are you to cancel the wedding?" Vinod's father screamed, spit lacing his chin. "We want to hear it from the man of the house!"

"Maybe you did not hear me the first time. I said that I am in charge here." Kumud's lips quivered but she continued. "If you don't want your son to marry my daughter, please leave!" She turned to look at Vinod. She wanted him to say something, anything, to her, to his father. But he said nothing. He simply stared, his face pleading with her to relent.

"Do you realize that no one will marry your bastard daughter if we leave? You will be put to shame in your community?" Vinod's father said.

"How dare you talk like that about Veena!" cried Kumud. "And don't worry about my shame! Just leave! Please go!"

"Whore!" someone yelled, and the groom's party headed towards the door.

Vinod did not move, as if his legs were cemented to the ground. His father pulled his arms, but Vinod did not budge. His uncle grabbed his arms from behind, and the two men dragged him toward the exit.

Kumud approached Veena. "I'm so sorry my darling!"

Veena walked a few steps away from the ritual fire pit and stopped. Her arms crossed over her chest she glared at Kumud. "I hate you!" she yelled. "I hate you as much as I hated you the day I was brought to this damn place! Don't ever talk to me again!" She ran to the staircase, and several girls followed her.

Everything seemed to have occurred at the speed of light. Guests were stunned, speechless. They had witnessed an unfortunate event with far-reaching consequences. Uttering words of regret to Kumud, they nervously shook their heads and said good-bye with folded palms. One by one they left, talking to one another in hushed tones.

"So, sorry it turned out this way!" Shekhar said, gently rubbing Kumud's back.

Together they sat in front of the fire pit, the flames extinguished, and the firewood a heap of smoldering ash. The priest packed his paraphernalia, and Shekhar paid him. He offered sympathy and was gone.

Whenever Kumud's spirits were low or she felt dejected, Shekhar was the one who made her feel better, even cheered her up. They may not be a couple but they were meant for each other.

"A young girl's dream turned to ashes!" Kumud said with her hands between her knees.

Several girls came and sat nearby. One walked over to them and said, "Kumud Ma, are you all right? Can we get you something? Can we do something?"

Kumud looked at her affectionately, smiled faintly, and shook her head.

"Thank you my dear. I'm all right. All of you go to your rooms and rest. Tomorrow is a school day." The girl nodded and prepared to leave with her companions.

"You know what would be nice?" Shekhar said to them. "If you go and cheer up Veena."

"Don't *you* want to talk to Veena?" Shekhar asked Kumud after the girls were out of sight.

"Her dream is demolished. Do you think she wants to talk to me? It will be some time before she is ready to see me. Did you see how she reacted when I tried to console her?"

"That was a passing sentiment. She is badly hurt," Shekhar said.

"I destroyed the wedding day of two people in love."

"What could you do? Considering the situation, you handled it well . . . I think Vinod's family planned it that way all along. They were desperate for a dowry. I would have said the same thing you did. Don't fret over those close-minded, uncivilized men—greedy minded misogynists!"

She turned to look at him. "Not evil, Shekhar. Ignorant, simply ignorant. Ignorance is like a dark cloud that hides the sun's light."

"You are right!" Shekhar said, putting his arm around Kumud's waist, hugging her warmly. "When you talk to Veena, tell her how Vinod reacted and listen to what she says. For what it is worth, I want you to know that I am proud of how you handled the situation. You saved Veena from a life of torment and misery."

"Saved her?" Kumud cried. "I wish for once, just once in my life, I could save someone. . . ." With her arms wrapped around her bent head, Kumud sobbed.

Shekhar did not try to stop her. He gently rubbed her back and patted her head. She put her head on his shoulder. They sat quietly together for a few minutes. They could hear distant sounds of girls talking.

Finally, she wiped her eyes with the pallu of her sari and put her arm around his waist. She looked at him and said, "Shekhar, I would like to go home now." She let go of him, got up, and walked to the staircase.

Shekhar bid her good-bye and went to his flat at the back of the building.

Chapter Three
Reconciliation

Tossing and turning, Kumud was haunted by the emotional intensity of the previous night. Her whole body sought physical release from the unhappiness her words and action had caused. Her love was the only endearment Veena had experienced until she met Vinod, but now he had broken Veena's heart. To divert her mind, Kumud decided to work at the office.

There was nothing on her agenda for the day. If events had happened as planned, they would have been celebrating a simple farewell brunch for the newlyweds. She directed the staff to restore the building to its usual setting and called the caterer and some friends, who had missed the wedding ceremony, to let them know about the unforeseen changes. She sat behind the office desk for a long time, contemplating previous day's events, and tried to decide how to restore the orphanage to normality. Finally, taking a long and deep breath, she steadied herself to go to Veena.

From the corner of her eye, she saw Veena standing at the office door. Their gazes met, and Veena came running to Kumud.

"I'm sorry, about how I behaved last night, Ma!" Veena said wrapping her arms tightly around her.

"Don't be sorry." Kumud patted her. When Veena let go of her, Kumud saw the girl smiling sheepishly up at her, her hair combed hurriedly, her eyes swollen.

"At first, I was very angry," Veena said. "But after going over last night's episode again and again, I reminisced about the years I have lived here. I realized that you have always wanted only the best for me."

Kumud held her hands and said, "I am not going to let anyone treat you disrespectfully. Our social system debases and devalues women. I've experienced it myself. A long time ago I made an oath to myself that I would never let a girl or woman be devalued or demeaned by ignorant minds."

"I know that. All the girls know that. That's what you taught us, gave us books to read about! If you had not talked to us about unlocking our minds to independence and freedom and gaining dignity and self-respect, I would not have understood your behavior. Last night I witnessed how closed minds work."

"Come and sit," Kumud said, pointing to the chair facing her. Then she closed the door and settled back into her chair. "Yesterday was supposed to be the happiest day of your life, but their blackmailing us for a dowry triggered my anger. I tried to be hospitable, but they were small-minded. I couldn't take it anymore."

"When I went to my room, I dumped my bridal sari and jewelry and pulled out my hairdo. It hurt but it helped me cry. I was furious—with you, with my situation, with Vinod, with the whole world! When he sat

36

beside me at the fire pit, I was ecstatic. I watched the guests reveling in my wedding feast. The gaiety in the air made me pleasantly feverish. But then someone ordered the wedding ritual stopped. Vinod was called, and he left without saying a word.

Radha knocked at the door and entered with two cups of tea. She greeted the two women and sympathized with Veena. After she left, Veena continued to tell Kumud what had happened the previous night,

"While Sarla and I were climbing up the stairs, she told me what had transpired between you and Vinod's father. I was aghast that Vinod did not stand up for me. I glanced at my henna-painted hands and feet and my wrists adorned with bracelets. I felt so low and discarded. I thought Vinod would return and console me," Veena said and began to cry.

"I thought so too. I expected him to stay firm," Kumud agreed.

"Then someone knocked at my door, but I had locked myself in," she said. "Sitting at the edge of my bed, I cried my heart out. After some time, I heard Alka calling my name and begging me to open the door. She said, 'Please Veena Didi, I am scared, let me in! Let me in!' So, I let her in. I put her to bed, switched off the light, and left the door open hoping for Vinod to come back. I put my head under a pillow and lay in a fetal position. I kept looking at the door off and on but Vinod did not come."

"I am so sorry Veena." Kumud said and waited.

"Then I saw Dr. Roy's silhouette. He had come to comfort me. He said 'things may seem terrible at this moment but they are bound to get better. The whole episode has distressed all of us especially Kumud. She will surely come to see you in the morning. Everything will be all right, trust me dear. It is all for the best.' He said and gave me a sleeping pill before he left.

Shekhar, as always smoothening wrinkles, Kumud thought.

"My sleep was fitful. When I woke up, I thought of Vinod's betrayal, his father's greed. Feelings of shame circled in my mind. What would I have done if I had married Vinod and later realized that his values and beliefs were no different from his family's? When it came to choosing between them and me, who would he choose? His father demeaned and cheated us, yet Vinod did not say a word. He has dishonored my love."

Kumud's eyes glistened with tears. "Come here!" she said.

Veena walked to Kumud and they embraced.

Kumud remembered, how years ago she fled her husband's home in the middle of the night to escape oppression and conservative minds. Her heart had pounded as though it would explode as she walked towards the bus stop. Her face was covered with the *Chunni* so no one would recognize her. From the town of Neela Nagar, she rode a bus to the Madhya Shahar Railway Station, vowing never ever to return. She didn't know how she had gathered the courage to flee the blue town and catch a train to the metropolis Ambayu and, eventually, a taxi to Save Girls Souls Orphanage. She had been assured that the orphanage was like a sanctuary. Perhaps the promise of a safe and secure place infused her with courage. At the orphanage—far from lies,

38

desperation, and repression—she vowed to help herself, and other girls and young women to feel safe and secure. Through years, she cultivated and strengthened her sense of courage. That fearlessness had helped her overcome many obstacles in her life.

"Hello ladies!" Shekhar knocked at the office door, pulling Kumud from her reverie.

Veena greeted him and thanked him for his support the previous night. She bid farewell to Kumud and left.

"How is she doing?" Shekhar asked.

"Boy, am I glad to see you!" Kumud said. "She is better than I expected." She told him about the conversation that had transpired moments ago.

"She has a good head on her shoulders," Shekhar said with a smile.

"That's for sure," she agreed.

When Shekhar left Kumud realized how talking to them had made her feel better. But she also knew how centuries of karmic coincidences had led her to SGSO center. If Yuna Li had not sympathized with her, if she had not hired her, if Yuna Li had not devotedly nursed the multi-millionaire Nari Millwalla back to health, and if he had not bequeathed his mansion to orphan girls, Kumud's new life may not have been revitalized the way it did.

Chapter Four

A Telephone Call

The following week Veena received a job offer from prestigeous *Ambayu Architects and Designers*. The news was something to celebrate, but after the failed wedding that took a year to plan, Kumud had mixed feelings about Veena leaving SGSO. She had found a reasonable one-bedroom flat that she could share with another young woman not far from the orphanage.

Kumud helped Veena settle into her new place.

The following month was comparatively quiet. Then one evening when Shekhar was at Kumud's flat, the telephone rang. Kumud picked up the receiver.

"Call from Madhya Shahar. Please hold!" the operator said.

Madhya Shahar? Who can this be?

"Hello! Hello! Who is this?" Kumud said.

"This is Guruji. Is that Kumud?" the voice said.

"Who? Guruji?"

"Yes. Guruji speaking."

"*Namaskar*, Guruji! I can't believe it's you after so many years! Is everything okay?" Guruji had been

41

Kumud's elementary school teacher. In the absence of a middle and high school in the blue town, he had encouraged her parents to move to the city of Madhya Nagar. It had been decades since she had talked to him.

"No, everything is not okay. Terror is upon our town! A young girl has decided to commit suttee. Her husband is critically sick. Kumud, you must come at once if you want to stop it from happening this time."

"A suttee! Where? When? Where are you?"

"I'm calling from Madhya Shahar but I live in Neela Nagar. I'll meet you there, just come. . . Hurry. . . otherwise it will be Sau Massi all over again!" Guruji said then hung up.

Kumud's mind went to Neela Nagar, where houses were blue and the goddess temples white. Where the swaying harvest of green moong reeked of burning flesh. Where a widow was forced to immolate herself on her husband's pyre, and then was celebrated as an exemplar of a faithful wife, *sativrata*, and of truth, *sat*. Staring into space, Kumud relived the nightmare in her mind.

Nine years old Kumud. . . Sau Massi behind the plumes of smoke. . . the blazing flames. Sau Massi struggling. . . men holding her down. Sau Massi shrieking. . . Kumud screaming. Mixed smells of marigold flowers and burning flesh entering her nostrils. The reverberations of the shrieks and screams blurring behind the deafening sounds of mourning women, crying children. . . Frenzied beating of drums and shouting of men. . .

Shekhar cleared his throat. "Kumud!" he called gently.

Her eyes met his, she shook her head and stood up,

THE LAST SUTTEE

"I must go to Neela Nagar immediately."

"What is it?"

"That was Guruji. He said, a young woman has decided to commit suttee in Neela Nagar."

"Wait a minute, suttee—self-immolation? Wasn't that outlawed a century ago?"

"Anything is possible in Neela Nagar, Shekhar! Laws of our country do not apply there."

"How is that possible? What about the police?"

"Police? They not only believe in this ritual, they openly defend it," she said and added, "He might call again."

"Who is Guruji?"

"My elementary school teacher. He said someone in Neela Nagar is planning to commit suttee."

"What makes him so sure?"

"I have to go, I must go." Kumud murmured to herself as if in a trance.

"I thought you detested Neela Nagar and would never go back."

"This is different."

Kumud stared in space, lost in the memory of a place and time that Shekhar wasn't familiar with.

"Kumud, I'm on call at the hospital, I have to leave." He stood abruptly. "I don't want you to leave, but you're the best judge of what you need to do. I'll see you later," he said and left.

Chapter Five
The Exchange

Kumud's heart was in turmoil the whole day. Sipping a cup of her evening tea, she stared at the Chinese silk scroll behind the sofa in her living room. She knew she could not bring Sau Massi back to life, but if she could save another tragedy from happening, she might be relieved of the nagging guilt, and heal from the emotional scar that Sau Massi's suttee had left.

Seeing the scroll always calmed her. The scroll's landscape was filled with spirit; the Chinese *Chi*. The small rectangle hung vertically and reflected the layers of silence, movement, beauty, and grandeur of nature. It simultaneously represented the present and infinity. The water that moved in the scroll's streams and rivers and the sap that coursed through its trees and bushes was the same as the blood that flowed through her veins. She heard her mother's murmur in the water. It echoed the voice of all mothers, grandmothers, and great grandmothers. The wind that sweetened the meadow flowers was their breath. It was their first cry as well as their last sigh.

Whenever Kumud was stressed, she allowed herself to walk mentally through the panoramic scenery of the temple in the hills after rain. By the end of her stroll, she felt one with the smell of pine, the sparkle of water, the dewy mist, and the hum of insects. Walking through it temporarily dissolved her problems. The scroll had become a portal of escape, of going within and finding her inner essence, her true Self—beyond the physical self to be "more than" herself.

Kumud's gaze moved from the hanging scroll, to the crystal vase on the center table. In the rush of the wedding preparations she had neglected to buy flowers for it.

Someone knocked at the door. She opened it to the scent of *sonttake* flowers. Peaking from behind the bouquet of white flowers was Shekhar's smiling face.

"I hope I'm not intruding," he said. "It is rather late in the day, but I wanted to say good-bye."

"No, no intrusion!"

"I know you well enough that you must have decided to go," he said, giving her the flowers. "The scent reminds me of you," he said, causing her to blush.

"Thank you! Would you like to come in?"

"Are you sure?" He stepped in.

She inhaled the scent and said, "Yes, I am sure! Sit down. I'll put these in water." She picked up the crystal vase. "I should have wished for something else."

He sat on the sofa. "Like what?" He was not sure what she meant.

"A moment ago, I wished I had flowers to put into this vase, and here they are!"

She returned with water-filled vase, now

embellished with white *sonttake* blossoms, and placed it back on the table.

"Wish for anything you want today, and it will be granted!" Shekhar chuckled.

"Stay for dinner."

"Don't trouble yourself. I merely wanted to bring flowers."

"I want you to stay. Please stay!" she pleaded.

"Well, if you insist," he said.

"Be right back," she said. After a few minutes, she returned with snacks and two glasses of cold lemonade. She served and sat opposite him.

"I have to ask you something," he said, moving uncomfortably in his chair.

"What is it?"

"We both know that you are leaving tomorrow, and this may not be the right time. But I have to say this."

"Say it," she said, knowing what he was going to say.

"Are you sure?"

"Try me!"

He took her hands into his. His expression grew tender. "Kumud, you know how I feel about you, how much I love you and how I want to spend the rest of my life with you."

She sat silently still. The room quieted.

Then he said, "I love you, Kumud. But every time I bring this up, you avoid talking about it."

She stared at him, her eyes damp, her lips parted.

He felt her resistance and gently let go of her hands. His shoulders stooped and he got up to leave.

"Please, let's not talk about love and marriage right

before I go!"

He turned to face her. "All right, then listen!" he said. "I am not sure if you will ever feel for me what I feel for you, but if I do not get an answer before you leave, I'm not sure if my feelings for you will remain the same."

It sounded like an ultimatum.

"Say something!" he said.

She silently adored him, but she stared blankly into space, as if she had lost her tongue. She felt deep regret. If there was to be a man in her life ever again, it would be him. The betrayal of men had left an open wound that smarted when she thought of being with a man. Men like Shekhar were hard to find—respectful, dedicated, genuine, and good-looking. She had not fully disclosed her past to him. She remembered the day several years ago when she unwittingly allowed him to glimpse into her past. She regretted it later. But if she disclosed everything, would that jinx his love for her? He deserved to know, but she was not yet ready to share her bitter past.

She heard the door closing as he left.

Is happiness an end in itself? Does it last forever? She had had no such experience. Her life experience was filled with guilt, fear, hate, and injustice. Momentary happiness peeked through in passing moments she spent with Shekhar, but unhappiness had become a constant mental static. Her life may have stabilized after coming to Ambayu, meeting Yuna Li, and being with Shekhar. But there was so much unfinished business from her earlier life. Could she be completely honest with Shekhar? If so, where would she start? She could think of no one else but him with whom she could share her life story, her life.

Chapter Six
The Discord

The next morning, Kumud was in her office making travel arrangements when she heard a gentle knock at the door. It was Shekhar. Closing the door behind him, he said, "Did you give some thought to what I said?"

Kumud hung up the phone and said, "Sorry, Shekhar, but I must go! If I don't act on Guruji's message, something that has haunted me all my life, made me feel guilty, gnawed at my brain will continue to torment me for the rest of my life. This is urgent."

"What is it? Tell me, is it something personal? I want to help."

She hesitated. The look on his face expressed deep concern. She forced herself to say, "I saw a woman burned alive while the whole town watched!"

"What? Who?"

"My favorite aunt, Sau Massi. I watched her turn to ashes."

"You watched a suttee alone?" His eyes widened in amazement as he sat on the chair.

"I was with my mother."

"She let you?"

"They wouldn't let us leave. There were men with swords standing guard. I was nine," she chuckled humorlessly. "Nine years old, trying to fight the whole damn town!"

"Where were the authorities? Didn't someone call the police? Investigate the case?"

"I don't remember much. Much later I read about it in newspapers and magazines. What I do remember is Sau Massi struggling to escape the flames. . . I run to help her. . . try to. . . but I am stopped. Young men pushing her back. Her collapsing. Smoke burning my eyes, suffocating me, the smell of burning flesh making me sick."

Shekhar looked astounded. He reached for Kumud's hand and whispered,

"I am so sorry! You couldn't have stopped it, Kumud! Do you feel guilty? Do you believe you could have stopped it?"

She nodded, "Yes, kind of."

"You were just a little girl!" He squeezed her hand. They sat quietly.

"Kumud, think for a minute. Even now, can you change the world single-handedly? Do you think you can change people's centuries-old tradition? And in just days? Besides, we are not even certain if this is real."

"Guruji's call is the clue that this thing is certain and can be stopped. Otherwise, he wouldn't have called. If I miss this opportunity to redeem myself, my life will remain guilt-ridden, incomplete. I can't let it happen again, Shekhar."

THE LAST SUTTEE

"How much do you trust this Guruji?"

"As much as I trust myself." Affectionate and wise, Guruji was an inspiring role model, a stern, yet caring teacher and disciplinarian. *Why would he call if my being in Neela Nagar was not essential?* "It is risky. I can't change the world. But if I am able to stop this suttee and return home, I know I'll begin to live again."

"Begin to live?"

"I mean a meaningful life."

"With all the good you're doing at the orphanage—your dedication, your authenticity, your love for the girls—if this is not meaningful living, then I don't know what is."

"But you haven't looked inside me, Shekhar. If you could you would know I carry a burden. I must lift this boulder, heavy with pain. I sense it every moment of the day. I want to free myself of this lingering pain. When I do, you'll see the difference." She was swept with emotions. "I carry deep scars within me, Shekhar, scars made from Sau Massi's suttee, my failed marriage, my unrequited love, Dev." She withdrew her hand from Shekhar's and sobbed.

Kumud's father had died at the end of her first year in college. By that time, she had developed a close friendship with Dev. He had consoled and comforted her during her grief, provided her strength. Because of his affection and concern, she could give emotional support to her mother. Dev was from Apna Gaon, a village in the vicinity of Neela Nagar. He lived with his mother and younger brother. That's about it. That was what Kumud knew about Dev.

She had mentioned him to her mother, but she never dared bring him home. Slowly, throughout their college years, their love blossomed. Although she commuted to college and he stayed in a dorm, they spent much time together. They studied, ate lunches that Kumud often brought from home, watched movies, and attended lectures and debates. Madly in love, they vowed to marry after graduation. But Kumud knew as little about Dev's family as he knew about hers.

One day, after they graduated, Kumud's mother said, "Why don't you bring Dev home before he leaves?"

"Really?" Kumud blushed. She was pleasantly surprised.

"You have been talking about him since your father passed away. I'm curious to meet him."

So Kumud gathered up the courage and brought Dev home. He arrived in the morning, stayed for lunch. They chatted over coffee and cake. He stayed until late afternoon, but he seemed distant when it was time to say good-bye. He was gracious and told Kumud he would stay in touch, but his cold demeanor confused her. Something had changed. He did not act like a man in love, even though she was still madly in love with him.

He did not stay in touch. All through the summer months, Kumud languished for him, but there was no letter, not even a note. She did not know his address. When she had almost given up that she would ever hear from him again, a letter, notable for its brevity, arrived. He was so sorry he had not written sooner. He apologized for not telling her earlier that he was an untouchable, from the Dalit caste. He knew it would be impossible for her to adjust in their tiny shack in Apna

THE LAST SUTTEE

Gaon. She was too good for him.

The letter made it clear that he wanted to end their friendship and wished her a happy life. Kumud cried bitterly. After giving much thought to Dev's life situation and circumstances, she replied to his note. She wrote that she would convince her mother, and if her mother disagreed, she would elope with him. They could move away to a big city. They both had college degrees; they could get teaching jobs.

Dev's reply came full of excuses. He wrote his parents didn't think their match made any sense. If he married her, they would disown him, and he didn't want that. It would be better if they went their separate ways. He concluded the letter by saying it was better if they stopped writing.

His last letter made Kumud angry. Perhaps there was someone in the village he loved. Perhaps his parents had found a girl for him. What a weak bastard he was for making her feel so miserable.

Feeling her daughter's pain, Kumud's mother made inquiries from Neela Nagar, but to no avail. A year later, a friend informed her that she had heard Dev was indeed from a Dalit family of Apna Gaon. She said it was better that Kumud did not marry him. If she had, it would have been a major distress for the rest of her life. It may have been painful at first, but in the long run, the decision was sensible for all. Kumud disagreed. If she had known his reasons for not making the commitment, perhaps she could have convinced him of the wrong-headedness of his decision. But he had shut all portals and not given her a chance to make it work.

Kumud's grief squeezed zest from her life. Like

tooth pain, her love for Dev subsided for a while until a grain of memory surfaced, or a memento from him. Then her longing for Dev erupted again.

She began teaching English at a local girl's school. A senior colleague, after observing the new staff member often melancholic, advised Kumud to keep a journal. The colleague shared how jotting down her feelings and thoughts in a journal had helped her cope with her husband's death.

Kumud followed the advice, and as if by magic, some of her sorrow lifted. And the passing time made new memories with new people, places, and events. Time healed Kumud and her pangs of love lessened. Teaching replaced the emptiness.

On rare occasions, Kumud's mother tried to cheer her up with talks of marriage. "So many proposals are coming," she would say. "You only need to say yes." Every time her mother brought up the subject of marriage, Kumud felt a tug at her heart. She was not interested. She had convinced herself that there could be peace in living to a ripe old age without a man.

That is, until Kumar. Kumar was from Sau Massi's neighborhood in Neela Nagar. For several months, her mother went on about Kumar. . . "Kumar this, and Kumar that."

"Kumar means prince, Mother!" Kumud made fun of his name.

"I don't understand this girl," her mother mumbled to herself. "What is the harm? I'm not getting any younger. My only desire is to see you settled before I die," she said. Kumud listened with a smug smile. "Why won't you let me die in peace? Do you want to remain a spinster? What is the harm in seeing the boy? For my sake, just meet him once. If you don't like him, we'll leave it at that."

Kumud felt empathy for her mother. "What is his full name?" she asked, out of sheer curiosity.

"Kumar Agarwal. He is the only son of a well-known *zamindar* family; they own land and the farmers."

"I never understood how anyone can *own* land and farmers."

"Be serious just once!"

"I was being serious. Are they related to Sau Massi's family?"

"Of course not! Do you think your own mother would betroth you to a family who believes in suttee?"

"So, what does Kumar do for living? Does he have a real job or is he living off farmers' blood and sweat?"

"He has no reason to work."

"What does he do all day?"

"His father manages the land and the estate, and he helps his father."

"So basically, the family lives off of others' hard work. You expect me to marry and live in Neela Nagar? Mother, have you forgotten why we left that town? Sau Massi was killed there. Female infants are poisoned there. Those who are left to see the light of the day have no school to go to. Remember, it took courage for father to move to Madhya Shahar? No one leaves that town. *And no one goes to live there.* How could you even think of making such a match?"

"You're not marrying the town, my darling! Guruji lives there! As do so many other respectable families, including Kumar Agarwal's. They believe in the same things we do. That's why the middleman sent me the proposal."

"Respectable families, Mother? Have you forgotten about the slow-boiling puss underneath? A mere pin prick can spread the stench of their rotten superstitions and taboos."

"Don't be so intense! Don't generalize! You're a teacher. You are supposed to grade one student at a time, not fail the whole class because of a few rotten children."

"There are not just a few rotten people in that town; there are a few normal ones and maybe one or two who think," Kumud said. But she also realized her mother was right. After all, her family lived in that town as did Guruji and several other like-minded families.

"For my sake, please just meet Kumar Agarwal once. If you don't like him, no harm done. No commitments. I won't bring up the subject of marriage again."

"A widow's life is hell," said her mother. "You are an educated woman, a teacher. You can transfer anywhere you want. You don't have to stay in Neela Nagar."

"Let me think about it, Mother."

Teaching children and being financially independent had taught Kumud that it was possible to shape her own life. She controlled the choices she made. True, destiny was beyond her control. But at its best, that chance was only fifty percent.

Time was the cure for pain of her unrequited love. Kumud had learned to live with it and absorb herself in her work and her friendships. Occasionally, she thought of Kumar. She wondered what kind of man he would be, what sort of husband he would make. She could refuse to meet him because he didn't have a college degree. But the values and beliefs of so many college graduates often were worse than men with only a school certificate.

Ultimately, her mother had her way. Kumud agreed to meet Kumar.

"Don't push me into marriage," she warned. She was not attached to any particular man, perhaps she never would be. But if Kumar was as great as her mother had said, an intelligent and amiable man, she may even like him. "I'll meet Kumar. That's it. Nothing more." She said without realizing that meeting him would change her destiny.

At their first meeting, Kumud's mother was present, as were Kumar's parents. The two of them met alone several more times. Kumar was the sweetest, kindest, and most considerate man she had ever met. Kumud agreed to marry him and move to Neela Nagar. They celebrated the marriage with as much pomp as Kumud's widowed mother could afford.

"No bus or train goes there. How will you travel from Madhya Shahar to Neela Nagar?" Shekhar sounded concerned.

"I'll hire a taxi and walk the last leg. Perhaps Mr. and Mrs. Chauhan can help. They still live in Madhya Shahar."

"Who are they?"

"They were my mother's neighbors until I moved back to Neela Nagar. They would arrange a reliable taxiwalla for me."

"How long is the last leg?"

"Several hours, I think."

"Is it safe?"

"It is safe, but remote. The path is mud-packed and sandy. They may have paved it by now. After all, it has been fifteen years since I've been there. But I doubt it. Modern Neela Nagar remains the same as eighteenth-century Neela Nagar. Time has stopped there. Nothing moves," Kumud said. "Changeless; sand covers everything—ground, buildings, minds."

Chapter Seven
Railway Platforms

The night before she left, Kumud asked the girls to gather in the assembly hall. Evening meetings usually were held for unforeseeable occasions. The girls were curious as to why they had been asked to assemble. When they arrived, Kumud was waiting for them. She motioned to them to sit and pay close attention to what she had to say.

"This is rather sudden, but I need to go away for a few days to Neela Nagar. You may not have heard about this town. It is near the city of Madhya Shahar." The girls exchanged questioning glances, expecting an explanation as to why she was suddenly leaving.

"Some of you may not know that I was born in Neela Nagar."

"Why do you have to go? Sarla asked.

"I have learned that a young woman has decided to commit suttee." Kumud heard a collective cry.

"I know. That's how I also felt when I heard. Sometimes a woman finds herself in between places—leaving home for college, getting married, moving to her husband's home. Exchanging one world for another. These are vulnerable times. Women are susceptible when these things happen. And it seems to me that the woman in Neela Nagar has lost her way."

"Will you help her?"

"I hope so. That's the reason I am going."

"Is she an orphan?" "Isn't her family there to help?" "If she has made up her mind, how can you change it?" The girls peppered her with questions.

"I'll try my best," Kumud reassured them.

"Has her husband died?" asked another.

"For her to make this decision he must be critically ill."

Kumud assured them that she would do her best to help the young woman understand the folly of her decision.

The girls wished her good luck.

On the morning of Kumud's departure, Shekhar said little, but his eyes begged her not to go. Yet she was resolute.

"I wish I could come to the train station, but I can't," he said.

"I didn't think you could or would, but thanks for your concern."

They hugged as if parting forever. He kissed her goodbye, then turned abruptly and left.

Kumud took a taxi to the train station. She followed the coolie, who scurried ahead with her duffle bag through the overcrowded platform. Once aboard the Ambayu-Madhya Shahar Express Train, the coolie pushed her bag beneath the lower berth. She paid him. He bowed and slinked off.

The train was scheduled to leave in a half-hour. The compartment had four sleeping berths, three still vacant. Through the window, she saw passengers bidding farewell to friends and relatives.

She sat at the assigned window seat, and put up the shutter. The evening sunlight glistened on the henna design on the back of her hands. Seeing it triggered thoughts of her squabble with Vinod's male relatives. Hurting for Veena's lost love, she wished she could wash it off. But henna faded very slowly.

She knew Veena's pain was more intense than hers. How brave Veena had been when she talked to her the following morning. Kumud deeply regretted how the well-planned event had ended, chaotically and disgracefully. She was determined to find a solution to Veena's problem when she returned to Ambayu. For now, she was needed elsewhere.

Guruji's telephone call had conjured up repressed memories. Feelings of revulsion and deeper guilt surfaced. The encounter with the dowry demanding father of the groom felt miniscule in comparison, and she pushed it to the back of her mind. The possibility of a suttee in Neela Nagar became paramount.

How she wished Shekhar could accompany her! She could not think of anyone in her life whom she loved as much as him. He said Guruji's call might turn out to be a prank, and she hoped he was right. But what if it was not? The town she was headed to was the only place where she could exorcise the ghosts from her past.

The train shunted, then began to move. It hissed

and thudded as if asking, *A suttee?. . . A suttee?. . . A suttee?* and glided out of the station. It picked up speed, and Ambayu receded into the past. As they headed towards Boriwali, she watched how twilight softened the edges and muted the colors of things. From Boriwali to Surat, from Surat to Ankleshwar Junction, the constantly changing panorama of the metropolis' boundaries passed by. Gradually, the view turned to village life, where nothing seemed to change.

Kumud closed her eyes. She remembered the year after Shekhar came to the SGSO center. On a rare, not-so-busy-day after lunch, the receptionist had left for the day as had the elderly helper and janitor. Radha was helping the cook clean up after lunch. Some girls were in the hall downstairs, some chatting in the corridors, and others studying in their rooms. Kumud decided to finish her paperwork on the back lawn.

Shekhar Roy was already at the table. Not wanting to disturb him, she turned to go back to her office. He had seen her coming and pulled out a chair. "You are welcome to sit. This table is meant for six people!" he said, piling his files closer to where he was seated. Kumud sat opposite him. Radha served them coffee, and they worked in silence for a couple of hours.

Shekhar stretched his arms above his head. He was ready to take a break.

Kumud glanced at him. He was smiling.

"Do you like working here?" she asked.

He said he loved everything about the place. They sat quietly for a few moments. Shekhar gulped down the last sip of coffee now turned cold, then he unexpectedly said, "May I ask you something, Kumud?"

She nodded.

"I have worked here for one whole year now. But we are so busy we do not know anything about each other. We hardly get time to talk."

"This is true," she agreed.

"Why don't you tell me something about yourself," he asked nonchalantly.

"What about myself?" Kumud looked at his face. It was gentle, charming.

"Tell me anything about your life. I notice you are a patient listener, but never talk about yourself."

Kumud gazed at the doctor, took the last sip of coffee, and after a moment's pause said, "What can I tell you about my life? Would you believe me if I say my life, like the lives of thousands of Indian women, is a miracle."

"I don't know. Why do you say so?"

"Because a woman faces elimination at every stage of her life."

His eyes widened and he leaned in closer. "Like what? I don't understand."

"Thousands of female infants, girls, young women are murdered physically or killed emotionally. With the death of every woman, a part of me dies."

"I'm aware of female infanticide, inequality, and discrimination against women, but that is true everywhere—not justified, but prevalent throughout the world."

"You are a doctor; you should know. What I just told you is neither news nor secret knowledge. Female infants are suffocated before they see the light of the day.

63

Brides are 'accidentally' burnt in kitchens because they do not bring enough dowry. Husbands abuse their wives emotionally and physically. Suttees are committed in remote towns."

"I know female fetuses are aborted. I have heard about unfortunate bride burnings. But the way you speak about such incidents is as if you have experienced the pain yourself. If I may be so bold to ask, have you suffered personally?" He said and waited patiently for an answer.

Kumud looked at her hands on her lap, then said softly, "I don't know why I am confiding in you. I've never shared the details of my life with anyone, Dr. Roy."

"Please call me Shekhar."

"Okay, Shekhar, I don't know why I am telling you this," she repeated. "Whatever it is worth, here it goes: 'It's a girl!' the midwife told my mother. She had delivered me moments ago. She was lying there exhausted. She raised her head to see her mother-in-law mashing oleander seeds into oil. *Not again!* The two before me were girls. My mother pleaded with her mother-in-law, *please don't force that paste down my baby's throat.* She turned and picked me up and held my naked body over her bare bosom, 'My baby! My baby girl! My Kumud!' she said.

"Her mother-in-law hushed her and in harsh tone said. 'Are you crazy? Don't name it!' My mother retorted, 'Why not? She is mine. This time, I won't let you silence her.' My mother sobbed and repeated, 'Please don't! Please!' At that moment, she felt intense pressure. She placed me beside her and bore down hard. 'She has a twin! Great God save us all, a fourth girl is coming!' my grandmother shouted. But it was a boy, my twin brother. She was elated. My mother said to her, 'You have your boy. Let me keep this girl. Please. Please.' Her mother-in-law thought for a moment and said, 'Okay.' And I was saved!"

"You have a brother?"

"Unfortunately, he died a few days after our birth," Kumud said.

"Sorry to hear that!" Shekhar became thoughtful.

After a pause he asked, "Did you have similar experiences later in your life?"

"Not in mine, but with women I knew—neglect, dowry deaths, *suttee*…"

Following their conversation on the lawn, Kumud avoided Shekhar for several months. Still, he remained eternally gracious.

One day, after the two of them had taken care of some official business, he thanked her. Then hesitatingly added, "Kumud, your aloof and blunt demeanor seems out of sync with your actions. You are caring and kind to the girls and always concerned about the staff."

He had caught her off guard, unexpectedly penetrating her stern exterior. She said nothing.

The next morning, he sent her a bouquet of fragrantly scented pink roses.

On another occasion he told her, "I am determined to help you eradicate the past monsters that inhabit your mind. You are a rare and precious find, a genuine human being."

Was he the one who would bring color back into her life?

Chapter Eight
Bridal Party

Shadows danced across Kumud's face. A babble of voices drew her from a nightmare. The train slowed at a station. The night's light filtered through the shutter. She opened her eyes and squinted at the opposite berth. It was still empty.

She remembered another ride, this time on a bus to Neela Nagar with Kumar. They were just married. Throughout the ride, Kumar spent time with his friends. He had hopped from one seat to the other. Was it not proper for him to sit with her in front of his elders? He was not shy during their rendezvous in Madhya Shahar. No one would have sneered at him for sitting next to his bride. They would surely understand that she was moving away from her maiden home and did not yet know any of his family members.

Intermittently, Kumar's mother or other women would ask if she needed anything. The only thing she wanted was Kumar to sit next to her. But it would not be proper to openly express that sentiment. She pulled a journal from her purse. Her last entry was about how hurt she had been when Dev rejected her love. *How fleeting emotions are. How impermanent life events.* Momentarily, she was overcome by completely different emotions triggered by a different person.

She turned the page and jotted down her feelings. Her eyes were on the journal, her head properly covered. If her pallu slipped, one of the women covered her head immediately. Another woman put two hairpins to keep the pallu in place.

It took them half a day to reach Kumar's home. Before the newlyweds entered the family threshold, Kumar's oldest cousin, Susma, adorned both bride and groom with yellow and maroon marigold garlands. Susma held a lighted brass lamp, vermillion powder, and sweetmeats. She applied the red powder to their foreheads, then moving the lamp in circles before them, fed them sweets. After completing the ritual, Susma led Kumud to a room adjacent to the kitchen. An area rug with two cushions facing the door was especially prepared for the bride and the groom to sit and receive their guests. Kumud settled comfortably against the cushions. Friends and relatives gathered before her as if she were a goddess. They congratulated her, showering her with blessings and gifts. They praised Kumud's favorite aunt Sau Massi who had committed suttee years ago. They slurped tea and munched treats as they talked about how fortunate Kumar's family was to have a daughter-in-law from the lineage of Saubhagya Satimata whose soul was filled with *sat,* truth.

"Where is Kumar?" someone asked. "Must be with his friend," someone else suggested. A third shrugged her shoulders. After a while the guests left, giving way to new arrivals. They knew one another, and chatted, laughed, slurped and munched together. Eventually, someone whispered, "Your daughter-in-law must be exhausted. Why don't you let her rest?"

The words were music to Kumud's ears.

Finally, Susma led Kumud to his bedroom. It smelled like Kumar. She inhaled and examined an old-fashioned king-sized bed with wooden posts, two cane chairs, and an armoire. She liked the dark warm hue of the furniture. The pallu, which had covered her head since morning, could finally come down. She removed the hairpins, wrapped the pallu around her waist, and tucked it into the side of her petticoat.

Early evening light filtered through the windows. The room was accessible from the front porch, and from the kitchen through the eating area to central courtyard.

A little girl sat on the bed, dangling her legs. She told Kumud that she lived in the neighborhood. She said Kumar was one of her favorite persons.

"That is good to know. Where is he?"

"He is not home," the girl said.

"Why do you like him so much?"

"He smiles all the time and gives us candies."

"Where do you think he went?"

"I don't know. Perhaps to meet his friend."

Susma entered the room to ask Kumud if she would like to eat dinner in her room or in the central courtyard where the guests were feasting.

Wasn't Kumar going to eat? Won't he join them? Join her? Why wasn't he home? She didn't dare ask these questions. A bride's enquiries as to the whereabouts of the groom were not only inappropriate, but also unheard of. Yet

Kumud could not resist. She said, "Shouldn't we wait for Kumar?"

"He may come late. You eat," Susma said.

"Where is he?"

"Most probably gone to see his childhood friend who is not feeling well and couldn't attend the wedding."

Couldn't he have waited until tomorrow? she wanted to say, but instead said, "In that case I'd prefer eating in my room."

Kumud had lost her appetite, and as she nibbled, two women who had brought her dinner silently watched her. She could hear guests jabbering as she put small morsels into her mouth. The sounds from the courtyard soon subsided as the guests, after consuming the sumptuous feast, grew exhausted from the travel, rich food, and long day. Most took their leave, although some family members and out-of-towners lay down wherever there was space to do so. Her mother-in-law and several other women came to Kumud's room, suggesting that she rest until her husband returned. The women giggled. One said, "Better rest now when you can. You will be up all night."

Kumud tried to smile, touching her mother-in-law's feet to bid her goodnight.

Left alone, Kumud pulled her journal from her handbag. Intense emotions churned. Journaling somewhat helped rid herself of these feelings. She dated the page at the upper right-hand corner and titled it, 'My Wedding Night.' She jotted a few lines but was unable to concentrate or write more. *Why is he not here?* She sat with her journal on her lap, thinking, analyzing, second-guessing her choice to marry him. Too late now, she said to herself, and closed the journal.

She forced herself to get up, and remove her jewelry. Carefully, she placed her earrings, necklaces, bangles, and rings into the box. She folded her bridal sari, blouse, and petticoat and placed the clothes, jewelry box, and journal on a shelf inside the armoire. She changed into nightclothes, selecting old pajamas instead of the negligee she had purchased for her wedding night. Again, she waited, this time with her feet on the other chair. She dozed for a few minutes, but was woken by the sounds of late night guests leaving, thanking the hosts, and saying goodbye.

It was past midnight. She heard the night watchman striking his thick stick against the pavements to the rhythm of his cries, '*Jagte Raho*! Stay Awake!' to scare the night burglars.

Her back ached. Too tired to wait any longer, she lay on the bed. She tossed and turned. Her heartbeat quickened when the thought that Kumar may have had an accident crossed her mind. She sat upright against a pillow. A chill ran down her spine. She got down from the bed, pulled a cotton shawl from her trunk, and wrapped it around herself. Dismissing any worrying about being in nightclothes, she opened the front door and walked outside. She heard crickets chirping. The breeze was cool.

From the pitch darkness came a voice, "What are you doing here? Let's go in?"

She yelped. She had bumped into Kumar.

"Sorry to have kept you waiting!" he said.

"Where were you? What was so important? And if it was, why didn't you tell me? Why didn't you tell me you'd be so late? I had such horrible thoughts." She started to cry.

Without answering, he squeezed her shoulders then followed her to the room. He changed into his nightclothes.

Sitting on the edge of the bed, she said, "Why did you behave like a stranger on the bus? You were like a different person from the one I thought I married."

He didn't answer. Instead he made a bed on the floor.

"What are you doing?" she asked.

"Please go to sleep. You take the bed. I will sleep on the floor," he said and left the room.

She pulled her legs up and squeezed a pillow against her chest, puzzled, wondering, longing, embarrassed for her wanting.

He returned with two glasses of water.

With her eyes downcast, she flushed and said, "You don't have to sleep on the floor. We are married now; we can sleep in the same bed."

"We both are tired. I know I am. Let's go to sleep." He placed one glass of water on her bedside table and plopped the other on the table between two chairs near the window.

She watched him set a pillow on the rug that he had laid on the floor.

"Kumar, come on lay down on the bed."

There was silence in the room. Then she heard Kumar whisper, "Kumud, I want to confess something."

"What?"

"I laid down with someone before returning home."

With a jerk, she sat up and stared at him in amazement. "You slept with someone else? You can't be a husband to *me*? What do you mean? Did anyone force you into this marriage?"

"Yes."

"Who?"

"I forced myself."

"You *forced* yourself to marry me? Why?"

"Kumud, this marriage is a sham. My whole life is a sham." He looked away into the night's darkness.

"Are you all right? Anything wrong?"

"No, Kumud, I'm so sorry. I am not what you think me to be. What people perceive me to be." He pressed his temples with his fingertips, resting his elbows on his knees.

"I just don't understand. What happened?" Her heart beat violently. *Did he hear something about Dev?* She went to him, rubbing his back. "What is wrong? Why do you consider your life a sham? Do you want to tell me?" she said softly, so gently that he looked to make sure she was not mocking him.

"You mean that?" he asked.

When she nodded, he said, "I can't be a husband to you, but I can and will be a good friend. Can you live with such an arrangement? I'm sorry, but you'll *have* to live with that arrangement."

"But why?" she said, pulling away.

"Trust me; it is not your fault. It's my fault. That's how God made me. I'm not attracted to women that way."

"Oh my God! You are gay. Aren't you?" she said bluntly, making sure she understood what he was trying

73

to tell her.

He nodded, and the hair on her skin rose.

"Then, why did you marry me? Why didn't you stay a bachelor?" she asked, even though she knew what the answer would be. Tears of anger and sorrow mixed with kohl in her eyes, streamed down her cheeks.

"I couldn't share it with anyone. In school, boys made fun of me, beat me up, called me *gandu*, 'man lover.' Since I turned eighteen, my parents kept bombarding me with marriage proposals. 'You're getting old,' they said, 'our only son. You are the son of the richest landlord in the district, and we need descendants or our name will disappear into desert sand.' They wanted me to continue the lineage. If they ever discover I am gay, they will hang me from a pipal tree. You don't know this town!"

Her legs gave out. She sat on the floor, her head on her knees. He did not console her, and at that moment, she didn't need consoling. She pitied him, hated him, hated her mother for suggesting him to her, and hated herself for agreeing to this marriage.

Each pore of her body ached. She took two tablets of Anacin with water and cried herself to sleep in the wee morning hours.

When she awoke, Kumar was already gone.

Kumud was walking out of the bathroom when Kumar's mother called, "Get ready, daughter-in-law. Have your breakfast! People will be dropping in to see our new daughter-in-law!"

Kumud stopped, nodded, and went to her bedroom.

What was she going to do? Run back to her mother's home and scream, *I told you so?* It was Kumar who had duped them, and deceived the rest of the world. Her mother did not know he was a fraud, *dagabaz*! Her heart filled with sorrow, her mind a whirlpool of guilt, anger, and shame. But there was no way she could tell anyone, including her mother. Her life had been turned upside down.

She herself could not accept the reality of what had happened. She wished it were a mere nightmare. But it wasn't. What was she going to do? What did women who unwittingly married gay men do? Kumud had no other home to go to, no job. She was alone with her awful secret.

Chapter Nine

A Woman Saint

A sudden knock at the door of the train compartment startled Kumud from her reverie. She opened the door. The co-occupants of the coupe had finally arrived. Against the corridor light she saw the silhouette of a young woman in a salwar-kameez. They greeted each other, and the woman stepped aside to allow a coolie walk in with two metal trunks on his head and a bag in each hand. He dropped the handbags on the opposite berth and gingerly lowered the trunks to the floor, sliding them with his foot below the lower berth. The young woman paid him. A woman with a serene face, seemingly in her eighties, appeared at the door. She was draped in a white sari and wore a necklace and bracelets made from brown *rudraksha* beads.

The young woman opened the shutters that overlooked the platform. Suddenly, women and men swarmed to the windows, all trying to say goodbye in unison to the elderly woman. She had to be a saint of some repute.

The younger woman thanked the people, some by

name. The older woman patted heads and hands and then settled onto her seat, a peaceful smile playing on her lips. The young woman sat beside her. When the train began to move, some of the well-wishers kept pace with it, waving and uttering farewells until the train sped away. Their voices receded into the distance. Both women leaned back into their seats and closed their eyes.

Once again, Kumud lay under the white sheet, trying to get back to sleep, for she was only midway in her journey. In Madhya Shahar she was to meet Mr. and Mrs. Chauhan, who would help her get a taxi to the outskirts of Neela Nagar. Her heart beat faster at the thought.

Kumud watched the young woman prepare the older woman for bed. When the woman completed her task, she climbed to the upper berth, covered herself, and switched off the light. The train's movement rocked them all to sleep.

Kumud awoke to the shrieking train whistle. She looked at her watch. It was six-thirty in the morning. She sat up and saw the young woman washing her companion's feet over a circular metal tray. An empty water jug stood nearby. The woman gently shook one foot and then the other, wiping each with a small towel and putting on her sandals. She was the elderly woman's *cheli*, a saint's disciple.

The saint adjusted her position. Her eyes were closed, her shoulders covered with a saffron-colored shawl, her torso still, her feet firmly on the floor. She held her hands in a meditative gesture. Turning to Kumud who was about to go to the toilet, the disciple put a finger to her lips for her to be quiet.

Kumud nodded and left the compartment. They

were traveling through Madhya Pradesh; a six-hour journey was still ahead.

The disciple followed Kumud out of the compartment.

A young boy leaned against a window, his feet firm on the shaking floor. He held four ceramic cups from his left fingers and a dented aluminum teakettle in his right hand, steam escaping from its spout.

"Snake, madam, snake? *Chai garam?*" he hawked.

"Snake?" Kumud asked.

"He means snack!" The young woman snickered.

"No snake for me! I would like a cup of chai!" Kumud said, holding a window bar to stay erect.

"A cup of *chai* for me, too!" the disciple said.

They paid for their teas and introduced themselves to each other. The woman's name was Uma, and indeed she was the chief *cheli* of her Guru known as Tapasvini Ma. Ma was well known in central India, especially in the states of Rajasthan, Uttar Pradesh, and Bihar.

Uma seemed friendly, and Kumud wanted to know many things.

Hesitatingly, she said, "Do you mind if I ask who your guru was before she became Tapasvini Ma?"

It was as if Uma had been waiting for Kumud to enquire about her guru.

"I am used to people asking me such questions. I don't mind. Let's sit there." She pointed to two empty seats, and they sat facing each other.

"Ma's mother had tried to conceive a child for many years without success." Uma began narrating Tapasvini Ma's life story. "One day a holy man came to her home in search of food. She served him with such devotion that he blessed her with a boon—she would give birth to a beautiful girl who would grow up to be an extraordinary person. After one year, Ma was born to that family, who lived in a small town in the state of Bihar. They named her Suman.

"Suman was precocious," Uma continued. "Her parents, orthodox Brahmins, taught her to renounce selfish thoughts, not indulge in unnecessary action, and keep away from town gossip. She was clever and quickly learned cooking and household chores from her mother. With her father, she attended gatherings of spiritual teachers and saints who passed through their town. She wanted to follow their path, but her parents expected her to marry and have children.

"Suman grew to be petite and pretty with expressive black eyes and shiny black hair. At the suitable age of sixteen, her parents chose a man and married her to him. Her husband worked as a secretary to a middle school principle and believed women belonged to the kitchen. Whatever she believed was fine with him, as long as she prepared tasty meals and kept his home clean and orderly. He showed off her cooking skills by often inviting friends to their home for good food.

"Suman dutifully fulfilled her wifely obligations. She remained in the shadow of her husband by keeping to herself and not talking much. Her needs were limited, her emotions under control. She was never angry or hateful and got along well with neighbors and friends. Years passed, but Suman could not conceive. She devoted her leisure time to reading scriptures and helping neighbors in need."

Kumud listened attentively sipping the tea.

THE LAST SUTTEE

Uma continued, "In the third year of their marriage, Suman's husband passed away suddenly. She mourned for him. She continued to live in the same house for the next twenty years. During those years, she kept up with the study of the epics, *Mahabharata* and *Ramayana*, the scripture, *Bhagavad Gita*, and hagiographies of saints. She practiced meditation and yoga daily. Neighbors and friends to whom she had served meals and helped began to call her Ma, spiritual mother. For decades, they had watched her living a life of a renunciant so they added the prefix, Tapasvini. She was only in her thirties but accepted the new title with dignity.

"As a young woman, she wanted to follow a spiritual path that would befit a holy woman. Reading hagiographies had taught her that if she desired to experience *Brahman*, the ultimate source of spiritual power in the universe, she must know who she truly is and how to connect with her authentic self.

"The practice of meditation and yoga strengthened her inner voice and made her experience the divine space within. There were moments when in stillness, silence, and solitude she could transcend the physical and sensory world and yoke herself to the universal power. But she wanted to experience that spiritual intensity of the saints she had read about. So, with tremendous courage, at age thirty-eight, she cut off her hair, draped herself in white, smeared the exposed parts of her body with ash, and severed all familial and social links. It was then that she decided to leave her hometown."

"More *chai*, madam? *Snake*, madam?" the boy interrupted. He was back with freshly brewed tea, steam pouring from the spout of the worn kettle. He pointed to their empty cups.

They let him pour more tea and paid him a little extra this time. When he left Kumud said, "Then what happened?"

"Well, when her neighbors and acquaintances heard the news, they were shocked. They tried to stop her. Where did this quiet, sweet housewife get the courage to sever all connections to her past? Her neighbors asked, 'Where will you go?'

'I don't know,' she replied.

'How long will you be gone?'

'I don't know,' she repeated.

'Don't go!' they pleaded. But she was adamant.

"She took a bus to the holy city of Hardwar. From there she began a pilgrimage on foot to the seven *Shakti Pithas,* places where in ancient times goddess shrines had been established. Resolutely she kept going, whether she had bed to sleep in or food to eat, whether she was alone or alongside other renunciants, men or women all in search of self-realization. She had moved beyond comfort, appetite, and gender. Courage, attention, and determination were her tools and her teachers. They deepened her meditation and states of quiet ecstasy."

By now Kumud had an image of Tapasvini Ma that she could relate to. She felt inspired by her life story and thankful to Uma for unreservedly sharing the inspiring story of her guru.

"Should I go on?" Uma asked when she saw Kumud's attention wander. After all she was the consummate *cheli* of an exemplary holy woman.

"Yes, please! That is, if I am not keeping you."

"No, you are not! I like repeating Ma's story.

Besides, she will be in meditation for at least an hour, if not more!"

"How long does she meditate at home?"

"For two to three hours! So, as I was saying," Uma continued, "at the end of her pilgrimage to the goddess shrines, Ma returned to the city of Hardwar and settled into a solitary life. One day while in deep meditation she had a vision of a home for destitute women. But who was going to finance it? After much deliberation, Ma got in touch with her old neighbors and acquaintances. They had not forgotten her kindness to the needy, her leadership qualities, and her work on their behalf. They volunteered to collect money. With that money, Ma purchased a small house in Hardwar and took in widows and destitute women. The women there knew how to knit, crochet, cook, and make toys. They had many talents. Each woman who had a skill trained the other women with her skill. In a year, all the women were cooking and cleaning and making crafts. They produced enough handicrafts and goods to sell and make a profit.

"By word of mouth, Tapasvini Ma's name began to spread throughout Hardwar. Rich merchants as well as common folks came to hear her sermons. They viewed her luminescent face and listened to what she was saying. Impressed, they donated to her cause. Eventually enough money was collected for construction of a multi-story ashram.

"Within a few years, Ma's vision became a reality, an ashram for women shunned by society. Widows, married women who were abused or cast off by husbands for not giving birth to boys, and pregnant unwed girls. Women who had nowhere to go came to the ashram and were accepted as sisters, as daughters. And that's how it all started."

"What does Ma teach in her sermons and talks?" Kumud asked.

"She teaches how to become self-sufficient and financially independent. Ma says everyone cannot be enlightened, but everyone can become independent. Personal uplifting requires effort and self-knowledge. She emphasizes the significance of work and dedication," Uma said, her eyes shining with enthusiasm.

"How and when did you join her?" Kumud asked, then realized her question was too prying. "I'm sorry! You don't have to tell me, if you'd rather not."

"I don't mind," said Uma. "Ma spotted me begging outside the Kali temple she frequents. I had been widowed at the age of twelve and became a burden on my husband's family. They abandoned me at the Kali temple, and I had no way to return home. Ma brought me to the ashram, taught me to read and write, and encouraged me to study economics."

"Economics?"

"Yes, economics!" Uma smiled. "I was good in math. Now, I manage the ashram's accounting books. When I was in my twenties, Ma suggested I marry, but I chose not to.

"Let's go inside! Ma must be done with her meditation," Uma said.

Chapter Ten
A Saint?

Kumud saw the vast desert speeding by through the train window. Listening to Ma's life story had strengthened her courage. How fortunate that she had crossed paths with these extraordinary women!

The horizon was touched with crimson glow. Tapasvini Ma returned from the latrine to her seat. The train sped onward, and the compartment was filled with the sound of the reverberating floor and compartment walls.

"Ma, this nice woman with whom we spent the night is Kumud." Uma introduced her new friend.

Tapasvini Ma nodded.

Kumud folded her hands and with a slight bow said, "*Namaste*, Ma!"

Uma handed a cup of hot chai to Ma and sat cross-legged on the floor to massage her legs. Ma took a sip of tea. "Where are you going?" she asked. These were the first words she had spoken since boarding the train. Her voice was as melodious as her face was serene.

"To Neela Nagar."

"A holy town! I've been there, many years ago," said Ma.

"Do you have family there?"

"The whole world is my family, dear."

"But for what purpose did you go to that particular town?"

"The Elders of Neela Nagar invited me for a spiritual talk and *bhajan kirtan*, devotional singing."

"Oh!" Kumud said. In the silence that passed she watched Uma massaging Ma's feet. "I was touched by what Uma told me about your concern with and kindness toward helpless women, and how you have dedicated your life to their uplifting. I feel fortunate that a mere chance has allowed me to travel with you."

"My traveling with you is as much my fate as it is yours," Ma said, gesturing Uma to stop massaging.

"Uma also told me that most of the women you have in your ashram are shunned by society or forced out of their homes."

"Most of them were destitute, but many are there because they are barren. Their husbands readily remarried younger women so they could give them sons. Barren women are considered useless, another mouth to feed."

"Were these men sure the problem was with their wives? Did anyone examine them?"

Tapasvini Ma did not have an answer.

The more Kumud conversed with Tapasvini Ma, the more impressed she was with her ideas. Ma remained calm and relaxed even when talking about injustice and prejudice against women.

Kumud asked her to share her views about widows

remarrying.

"It is tragic when a husband dies before his wife," Ma said. "But it also gives the widow an opportunity for atonement. I myself was widowed at nineteen. But if a woman is widowed, what is the reason to remarry? Why not devote her life to doing something good, wherever and whatever she is capable of?"

"Perhaps many women do not have the determination and courage you had at a young age. There are so many reasons why women would like to remarry. What is the harm?" asked Kumud.

"What is the benefit? A better option is to follow the path of the goddess Sati. But how many women are so courageous as to become suttee?" Ma closed her eyes and exhaled.

"You approve of suttee?" Kumud's eyes widened and her jaw tightened. She could not believe what she was hearing. "You approve of a widow burning herself alive on her dead husband's pyre?"

"*Jai Satimata!*" Ma exclaimed, her belief matching her voice. She raised her arms and pointed her index fingers toward the sky.

"*Jai ho Narayani Satimata!* Victory to the goddess Narayani Satimata!" Tapasvini Ma repeated.

Kumud fixed her gaze on the woman who had dedicated her life to helping women.

"*Jai ho Narayani Satimata!* Victory to the goddess Narayani Satimata!" Uma repeated after her guru.

The shrill whistle of the train prompted Kumud to cover her ears. Minutes passed, and the two women looked at her.

"Suttee is an honorable tradition," Ma said,

breaking the strained silence. "Not many women believe in or have the courage to go through this ancient rite. I'm proud to be from a lineage in which two of my ancestors performed suttee. The first was Narayani Sati Devi's, performed four hundred years ago, and the second Kamala Rani, about seventy-five years ago. Two remarkable, faithful, and obedient women from my bloodline, unflinchingly sacrificing their youth and ending their lives with their dead husband's, so they could be together forever in heaven. They had accumulated *sat*, the power of purity and faithfulness throughout their lives. They voluntarily sat on the pyre of their husband's corpse. The women's purity accrued so much of the heat that the pyre combusted with their mere touch. Such women are not ordinary; they belong to the spiritual realm."

The more the female saint spoke about the merits of suttee, the less significant she became to Kumud. *Is this the same determined and courageous woman whose life story I have just heard? The woman who after her husband's death refused to follow Hindu Brahmin tradition? The one who had talked against dowry and gender discrimination? She was leading an ashram for destitute women. How could she revere the ritual murder of widows?* Unable to sit still, Kumud stood. She would leave the compartment and get some fresh air, but she had to ask one more question.

"Tapasvini Ma, do you condone suicide?"

"Why would you ask me such a question?" said Ma. After a pause, she added, "How can a person take their own life? The body is not theirs to destroy?"

"But isn't suttee suicide?" Kumud asked.

"Shame on you, young woman! Suttee is a sacred

ritual, not suicide! It's affirmation of a wife's unconditional faith and loyalty to her husband. Such a woman is a goddess in disguise: Steady in mind, steady in body."

"But what about the vulnerable young woman who realizes the inevitability of suttee, the way humans know about death? Society gives her no choice. She knows if her husband dies she is better off dying with him because she has no place in her family and no status in the community. If she did not kill herself by burning, her guilt and remorse will gnaw at her the rest of her life," Kumud said as her head throbbed.

"*Suttee* does not burn alone. Her husband's body is with her; his soul is hovering, blessing her resolve. His head, and at times his whole torso, is in her lap. The two are purified and consumed by the god of fire."

"But he is dead and she is alive! Don't you see? She can still sense, he can't."

"If her conduct in life is totally unblemished, she has no fear; she feels no pain."

"But that is not possible! Besides, how do you even know? No woman who performed suttee lives to tell us that! With due respect, you don't know. You didn't commit suttee!" Kumud blurted. Realizing she had insulted a saint, she gasped.

Ma stared hard at Kumud. Then she opened her lips to say something but instead she turned away and peered out the window.

On the outskirts of Ramganj Mandi a panorama of village life as old as eternal India came into view. Women walked gracefully, balancing firewood on their heads. Men of all ages were on their haunches, their bare bottoms in a row, defecating on the ground. To the men and women who lined the track, the passengers on the morning train mattered as much as the goats and sparrows witnessing the scene.

Chapter Eleven

The Last City

The train slowed, and, several signboards with the name Madhya Shahar, came into view. Two familiar words from the past seemed to be painted everywhere, on the signpost, on a brick walls and on vertical columns supporting the railway platform: Madhya Shahar, Madhya Shahar, Madhya Shahar. The train stopped with a jerk.

People pushed into the compartment, excitedly greeting Tapasvini Ma before whisking her and Uma away. Once outside, the crowd shouted, "*Tapasvini Ma ki Jai! Tapasvini Ma ki Jai!* Victory to Mother Tapasvini! Within minutes they were gone.

Kumud felt the familiarity of the place. She had spent her youth here, ten years of young adulthood. She felt suddenly exhausted. She stayed in her seat. No need to hurry. The tracks ended here. The train would return to Ambayu in the evening.

Only a scattering of people remained on the platform. Among them, walking towards the train, was a woman with salt and pepper hair, dressed in a crisp blue sari. She held a placard with Kumud's name. She didn't have to do that! *It was Amrita Chauhan!* Kumud waved and stepped down from the compartment carrying her duffle bag.

"Welcome, Kumud! Did you recognize me?"

"Amrita Auntie! You look as elegant as ever!" Kumud said delighted to see how vigorous her seventy-something neighbor from the past still was.

"Sweet as always!" she said.

Kumud placed her bag on the ground and, taking Amrita's hands in hers, looked a long time at her hostess. "You remind me of my mother. Seeing you has triggered memories of the two of you during my middle and high school years."

Amrita pulled her to her bosom and hugged her. As they walked to the parking lot, she said, "I too have fond memories of you and your mother. I'm glad you came!"

Kumud realized Amrita had no knowledge of the dire years of her life. During that time, Amrita and her husband, Amar, lived in Assam while Kumud taught school, married Kumar, ran away to Ambayu, and finally lost her mother. She threw her duffle bag in the trunk of the car.

Seeing Amrita in the driver's seat surprised her. Not many families in Madhya Shahar owned a car, and those who did either employed a chauffeur, or the men drove. As a girl, she had not seen a single woman driver.

"When did you start driving?"

"Oh, maybe six or seven years ago. Chauffeurs demand too much money. We hired one, but he was not dependable. Then we hired another; the same story. It was frustrating. Amar and I decided to learn to drive. At first, I hesitated, but after he learned he insisted that I learn too. That was one of the best decisions I have made. The freedom it gives me is priceless!"

Kumud nodded, *Yes, priceless freedom.* Amar always talked about self-reliance, independence, freedom. "How is Amar Uncle? Does he still travel a lot?"

"He is retired now—no more traveling. I accompanied him on his business trips to states with unique topography and enchanting landscapes. I started taking pictures. Amar bought me a nice camera on my sixty-fifth birthday. Some of the scenery is so breathtaking; those photographs still inspire me." She glanced sideways at Kumud.

"Can't wait to see them!" said, Kumud, the Chinese silk scroll landscape in her own drawing room passed through her mind.

They maneuvered through the main artery of the city. The buildings, painted various shades of pink, shimmered in the late morning sunlight. Kumud grew pensive, the view triggering memories of her childhood. She had mixed feelings about this road, this city. She remained quiet, then yawned.

"You must be quite tired."

"I am. But I'll be all right."

"Tell me about yourself!" Amrita said, "Where have you been hiding all these years? How did you end up in Ambayu?"

Kumud was not sure how much of her life her mother had shared with the Chauhans. She moved uncomfortably in her seat, unsure how to answer.

"You were not actually hiding, were you?

Undercover?" Amrita asked in mirth, gently patting Kumud's leg.

Kumud forced a smile. "Nothing like that, Auntie." She was quiet again, and Amrita did not push. Instead she said, "You must miss your mother!"

The traffic had cleared and Amrita sped up.

"Auntie, I would like to go to Neela Nagar right away." Kumud looked at her wristwatch, "It's only noon. Can I get a taxi now?"

"It is getting late, it's not safe in these parts. Leave early in the morning. Why are you going to Neela Nagar? Is it urgent?"

"I have an urgent business there, Auntie."

"I understand. In any case, Amar has engaged a taxiwalla for tomorrow. He is from Neela Nagar and knows everything there is to know about the town," Amrita said as she pulled in front of her pastel-pink home. "Here we are!"

The house peeked from behind dark green *gulmohar* trees with red and orange blossoms. They had grown taller and denser since Kumud had last seen them.

"*Namaskar*, Amar Uncle!" Kumud greeted Amar Chauhan at the front door.

"*Namaskar*, Kumud. *Beti*! Welcome!" He was casually dressed in kurta-pajama. His white moustache and beard added charm to the man who she remembered as clean-shaven and formal.

He insisted on carrying her bag inside. "You look like an older version of a girl I used to know," he said lightheartedly, gently patting her head.

In the drawing room, Amrita said, "Consider this your home, dear!"

THE LAST SUTTEE

Amar took her bag to the bedroom and returned.

On the central table, a tray was set with a pot covered with a tea cozy and pots of milk and sugar.

"You must be exhausted," Amar said. Facing him, Amrita sat next to Kumud.

Amar made tea while Kumud talked about her co-passengers, especially Tapasvini Ma. Amrita said she had read somewhere about a female saint. She wasn't sure if it was her or someone else. "There are hundreds if not thousands of wandering saints dressed in white or saffron, both female and male."

As they drank the tea, a maid brought a plate of assorted biscuits and salty *kachoris*. She greeted Kumud, served the snacks, then placed the plate on the table before leaving.

Sipping tea, they chatted about their retirement and Kumud's work at the orphanage. The Chauhans were keenly interested in the work she did with the girls. Amar talked in words; Amrita expressed herself in images. He was now professor Emeritus at the University of Madhya Nagar and she, a well-respected photographer.

Amrita excused herself to instruct the maid about dinner.

The telephone rang. "Feel free to walk around the house, Kumud!" Amar said before picking up the receiver.

Photographs and paintings from the Chauhans' travels hung on the wall. She paced through the rooms, each decorated tastefully and emitting a sense of prosperity. Yet the spaces felt cozy. Mementoes from the couple's travels were also on display, especially in an antique cabinet: a bronze Nataraja from Tanjore, walnut carvings from Kashmir, a Mughal miniature painting, a wicker boat.

Leather-bound books with gilt lettering lined a glass-covered bookshelf. There were also photographs of Professor Chauhan speaking, Mrs. Chauhan receiving an award, and the two of them meeting dignitaries. The pictures were positioned among the awards and medals arranged on a table against a wall. Kumud had never seen such a collection of art works, books, and awards under one roof. But here it was, a cultural mélange of the educated couple with taste and style had collected throughout their lives.

The décor inspired her to make changes in her own flat. It was good to be surrounded by art and good taste, Kumud thought. Such objects reflected the cultural ethos of the people who made the crafts. The creative process had transformed every object, even the unappealing and grotesque had achieved a level of the sublime, beyond human categorization. The kind and quality of one's surroundings certainly affected one's mental faculties. Her attention was drawn to a beam of light filtering through a window. She peeked through. A tiled courtyard lined with flowering plants came into view. This was the center of the house, and the inner windows opened into it. The Chauhan's home was typical of the domestic architecture of the city and reminded her of her childhood home.

Amar had hung up the receiver. Kumud walked back to the drawing room.

"You know, Kumud, when Amrita told me you were coming, I said to myself, 'I know that name.' Then I remembered," he said, pulling a booklet from the shelf,

"'*Reasons for Banning the Inhuman Suttee Ritual* by Kumud Kuthiyala,' he read.

"Where did you find it, Amar Uncle?" Kumud exclaimed.

"From someone in Neela Nagar." He grinned.

Kumud flushed. Completely taken aback, she said, "But I remember them burning all the booklets!"

"I know, I was there. There are as many inhabitants of Neela Nagar for suttee as are against it." He put on his glasses, cleared his throat, and read: "Listen to this. Neela Nagar is a town of general malaise, like so many towns in Bengal, Punjab, Rajasthan, and Sindh (now in Pakistan). Under British rule, the prosperous Hindu families who lived in these towns stopped patronizing religious images. Instead they spent money on rituals. They stopped recognizing education as a necessity, especially for girls. Flashes of talent and brilliance in young people passed unnoticed. Slowly, ugly elements of society reared their heads: Female infanticide, dowries, and the suttee ritual gained strength." Amar raised his gaze to look at her.

"I don't remember much of what I have written. It seems like someone else wrote that stuff," she said. "What I do remember from my research is that the ritual of suttee had become popular in places where the British establishment provided jobs for Indians. Upward social mobility! With their surplus income, the urbanites who left their villages and small towns in search of new opportunities lost a good deal of their social standing and religious values. They compensated for that by reviving emotionally intense rituals, irrespective of their effect. I think the revival of the suttee ritual provided them a sort of mock allegiance to their birth places?"

"I agree! They were seduced from their land by money and city life. The British could have done something about the ritual, but they didn't. Non-interference was their motto. During a suttee ritual, they stood guard and watched," Mr. Chauhan said. "Out of respect for social and religious liberties—but also afraid that they might face unrest and rebellion—British thought it prudent not to attempt to change Hindu customs and traditions."

"What sort of diplomacy was that! What made me crazy was when I learned that when a rare and remarkable officer tried to prosecute the family members of a suttee, his superiors thought it was unjust. To add salt to the wounds, the family of a suttee was neither disgraced nor shamed by their community. On the contrary, they gained social status and were applauded and honored by their neighbors. If a widow wavered from committing suttee at the last moment, the family was ruthless with her." Kumud was agitated.

"The ritual is very rare now, child, almost unheard of, though it survives because of orthodoxy and greed," said Mr. Chauhan, his brows narrowing thoughtfully. "Economics is also a motive. Family members see a widow as a threat because she has a good chance of inheriting property. The safest and most sanctimonious way of avoiding this is for families to persuade the widow to 'blaze a path of virtue' by committing suttee."

"Uncle, have you read this booklet recently?"

Amar Uncle nodded yes, "Why?"

"Then, you may remember reading that when the

THE LAST SUTTEE

British finally asked Brahmin pundits to compose a document of Hindu Law for local use, the pundits made sure the suttee custom was given full veneration and the government would protect their right to perform it. In eulogizing suttee, one pundit wrote that 'if a woman lost nerve at the critical moment, she could recover her purity by undergoing a severe penance'. But Uncle, if you met a woman undergoing such a penance, you'd know she'd prefer becoming a suttee."

"We did meet such a woman," he said with a twinkle in his eyes. "Anyway, I can assure you no one has read this booklet in Neela Nagar. No one would have cared to read it, even if it had been translated into Bhojpuri."

Amrita was back. "Thanks to Kumud's Guruji! He insisted on teaching English to his students. I wonder where he is now. Are you going to see him?"

"Of course!"

Amrita said, "Do you know a new school building is scheduled to be dedicated sometime this year?"

"After all these years!" Amar added.

"That's great news! I'll see it tomorrow."

"Talking about suttee, the ritual recurs every now and then. Each time it is kept top secret. Sometimes we find out about it, sometimes we don't. But when we do, it is too late," Amrita said, rubbing her forehead. "Madhya Shahar has had a history of suttee, but that has changed significantly since independence."

"Why doesn't Neela Nagar change? Why is it stagnant?" Kumud asked.

"Because it remains aloof. Aloof and at a standstill. As if it has shut down its senses. Deaf and blind to the changing world," Amar said.

"Uncle, Auntie, I must tell you something!" Her voice lowered she looked at each of them and said, "I've reason to believe that a young woman is going to become a widow soon, and she has decided to commit suttee. I must stop this murder and mayhem somehow! But I don't know how. I can't let it happen again. This is my urgent business I was talking about, Auntie !" Kumud was overcome with emotion.

For a few long moments, the three seemed lost in their own worlds.

"Dear girl, once the floodgate of intense frenzy opens, you cannot stop it, not alone. The widow's in-laws, the town Elders, especially Jabbar Singh, the close-minded families... even the police. They all conspire in the ritual. They will brainwash the girl. She will be drugged before it begins," Amar said.

"I know Uncle, I'm aware." She stared at him, determined not to be discouraged.

Their eyes met. "However," he said, "if you can change the young girl's mind, convince her the folly of her belief, make her understand the uselessness of the ritual you might make sense to her. But make sure you do it *before* her husband dies, that way you may be able to nip evil in the bud." He placed Kumud's booklet on the table and took the last gulp of tea.

"But the situation could be complicated," Amrita said.

"Complicated? How?" Kumud asked.

"The girl could be a staunch believer, perpetuated by folksongs, folktales, and her upbringing. Perhaps her husband's family members are patrons of Narayani

Temple. The young woman may believe the miracle of the ritual must be celebrated, not banned. The only way out is if you, as Amar said, if you can change the girl's mind. Convince her that her ultimate sacrifice is futile," Amrita said passionately.

"It's all in here!" Amar Uncle said to his wife, patting the booklet on the table.

"Wouldn't it be great if we could introduce matriarchy or expose a matrilineal family system in Neela Nagar? It functions well in the states of Meghalaya, Karnataka, even Kerala. We lived in these states and watched it firsthand," he said.

The maid, smiling sweetly at Kumud, entered with a tray to collect the cups and the plates.

"Kumud, Gopi is from Neela Nagar," Amrita Auntie said, pointing to her maid. Gopi nodded and carried the tray back to the kitchen.

Making sure Gopi had closed the kitchen door, Amrita said, "Her story would be of great interest to you. Do you want to tell Kumud, Amar?"

"Tell me what?" Kumud looked expectantly at Mr. Chauhan.

"You narrate it well, you tell it," Amar said to his wife.

"Okay, I will." Amrita turned to Kumud. "When Amar was working on his doctoral dissertation about the landlords and the Elders of Neela Nagar, we went to the town to collect data. I assisted in his research. One of the Elders took a liking to him and invited us to visit their homes. We did not see many women outdoors. Then we learned that women were not allowed outside while their men were working in the fields. The women leave home only when visiting the temple, neighbor or parents. At home, they wear bells on their ankles and bangles on their wrists. The trinkets make sounds like the bells around the cattle's neck. This way they can be heard and watched wherever they are in the house.

"One day I got a glimpse of a woman dressed in indigo," Amrita continued. "Her face was veiled. Figuring she was a widow because of the color of her garb, I wanted to talk to her about her life. Amar had left the house to interview a family nearby. I piled up the scattered papers, and as I was leaving, I must have taken a wrong turn and ended up in a cowshed. I inhaled the stench of cattle dung and urine. There were two cows facing the back wall. Ten feet away, on the opposite end of the shed, was a wall with two small windows. Scant kitchen utensils were on a shelf, and clothes hung from the rope. In a corner, the woman in indigo was stirring a pot of steaming moong dal. The smell of piss and shit and boiling dal made me gag."

Kumud listened raptly. Amrita's lips trembled. "I asked her why she was cooking in a cowshed. She said she lived there! Moong dal was her dinner! When I asked her why was she living by herself, she told me it was an appropriate place for a polluted woman to live. 'Cows do not mind a widow sharing their quarters,' she said.

"I had seen widows with covered faces and wearing indigo, but I had never seen a widow living with cattle," Amrita said, her voice quivering at the memory. "I could not get that woman out of my mind. Widowed young, she was living in place unfit for a human."

"Not only her husband's family but also her own family shunned her. No wonder some widows prefer dying with their husband than living," Amar said.

"Do you know what happened to this woman?"

Amrita pointed to the kitchen.

"Gopi?"

"Yes, Gopi. The next day we returned to that house. While Amar talked to the men, I asked the widow to come live with us in Madhya Nagar. At first she panicked. She worried what her in-laws would say. I asked her why she cared what people, who treated her like an animal, thought. She said she would think about it. A month later, when Amar wrapped up his work and it was time for us to leave, Gopi agreed to come with us."

"What about her family? Why did they let her come with you?"

"Her in-laws worried more what people would say than about her. 'Your daughter-in-law ran away? What a shame!' But Amar and I insisted, then gave them some money," Amrita said.

Amar interrupted. "At first they totally refused to let her go! They said we had insulted them by offering money! They threatened to inform the Elders and report us to the police. Then, one of the sons said in a low tone, 'How much money?'"

Amrita cut in. "But his father snubbed him. No one asked her what she wanted to do. They didn't even call her from her cowshed. They were only too happy to be rid of her! It was more difficult for her to leave than it was for them to let her go."

"'The townspeople would gossip about us,' they said. Then the eldest son said if she left, she could never return. The mother said they had lost their son, and now we expected them to lose their daughter-in-law," Amar added.

"She was not sorry about losing her daughter-in-law. She was worried who would do all the chores Gopi did," Amrita said. "Anyway, to make long story short, we were fortunate. She is a great help! She keeps the house in shipshape condition."

Gopi's story gave Kumud a good feeling. Amrita and Amar excused themselves to set the dining table. Kumud continued to sit mulling the story in her head. If Gopi had been raised elsewhere and was educated and independent, she could have moved to another state, found worked, and lived on her own. Why don't parents educate their daughters to make them self-reliant? Why don't they teach them to be more concerned with their own well-being instead of centering their lives around a man?

Amar returned and asked Kumud to follow him to the dining room. They walked through the outer corridor and into a dining room with a table that seated eight. Gopi had set three elegant places. Amar asked Kumud to take a seat on his left while Amrita sat on his right. He sat at the head of the table. After they were seated, Gopi wheeled a buffet cart to Amar's right, so he could plate the food.

"Thanks for all this," Kumud said as Amar handed her a plate with corn roti, *brinjal aloo sabzi*, a flavorful concoction of eggplant and potatoes, a local specialty that reminded Kumud of her mother's food.

"Gopi does most of the cooking," Amrita said. "Did you cook anything today?" she asked her husband.

"I cooked *brinjal aloo*," he said.

Kumud tasted the dish and complimented him on

it.

After the meal, Amrita took the leftovers to the kitchen, and Gopi collected the dirty dishes. Amrita returned with a plate of fruit and nuts. She peeled the apples while Amar smoked a cigar, filling the room with its sweet aroma.

"You see, Kumud," Amar said, "one of the reasons communities like Neela Nagar continue a tradition such as *suttee* is to get rid of the widow. And if she does not commit suttee, they hide her. They suppress her freedom so they can keep an eye on her. Unguarded, she may become a threat to the family, sexually dangerous and economically useless. Better to discard her or hide her. If she rebels against self-immolation, which most women do, so be it! The practice reflects a deep fear of the female gender."

"Women could rebel as a collective, but for that you need a courageous leader," Amrita added. "It is hard for women to take responsibility for their own lives if they are never given a choice about attending school, marrying, leading their own lives."

"It is essential that women have knowledge and are aware of everything that effects their lives, not only social and economic factors, but also religious practices such as *suttee*—its causes, history, and the reasons it is perpetuated," Kumud said. "That way they would understand the cause of this self-annihilating ritual. It may have made sense in medieval times for the protection of the women and to save their honor. The chief queen and her co-wives immolated themselves when news of a vanquishing king's death reached them. They killed themselves by fire lest the enemy molest and rape them."

"And as you must know, at times they performed group immolation, called *jauhar*. It is not clear how *jauhar* became the common people's custom and extended to ordinary communities like Neela Nagar," Amar said.

"That was then, but what I can't understand is why today a widow would want to commit suicide?" Kumud said.

"Good question!" said Amar. "I believe a woman who is brought up in an environment where there is an unshakable belief in a husband's superiority, in the wife's faithfulness, in a heavenly union, and in the miserable life of a widow, then the wife's emotional vulnerability at the time of her husband's death causes her to do whatever her upbringing says she should do."

"Is the mind so fogged from sorrow that a widow doesn't jump away from blazing fire? Where is self-preservation?" Amrita asked.

"They are heavily drugged, and thus unable to escape the flames," Kumud said wearily, thinking of Sau Massi.

"This brutality cannot be stopped until the whole community comes together to eradicate it." Amrita said.

"Who is going to stop it? Elders believe in it as do so many of the local people. The town police force is made up of locals. Their mental setup is the same. And politicians? They are silent for the sake of votes and dismiss it as an internal matter," Amar said.

"And what do intellectuals do, Amar? Write about it, discuss it, and then forget about it?" Amrita sounded angry. "We don't have the courage Kumud has." Then she turned to Kumud and said, "Come Kumud, let me show you to your room. Tomorrow is going to be a long day."

Amar nodded. Then pointing to Kumud he said with confidence. "If anyone can initiate something to stop this crime, it will be this young lady."

Kumud laid down and closed her eyes but could not fall asleep. She felt distressed and frustrated. Instead of lying there, she should be on her way. but a bus service nor a taxi was immediately available.

She turned toward the window and saw Gopi sitting in the courtyard under a tree. She felt a special connection and wanted to talk to her.

Seeing Kumud walking to her, Gopi adjusted her sari over her head and stood up.

"May I get you something, Bibi?"

"No thanks! I came to talk to you. Would that be okay?" Kumud said. "I hear you are from Neela Nagar."

"I was born there," Gopi said. "Having lived in Madhya Shahar for so many years, I now consider this my home. I do not want to say that name. That was a different world, a bad dream. I have not uttered that name aloud since Bibi and Babu brought me here."

"Do you remember anything about that town?"

"I remember the houses painted blue and the white huts of Apna Gaon across the river. From the village, we had a view of Chamunda Devi temple on the peak of the hill. Do you remember that temple?" Gopi asked.

"Like yesterday!" Kumud said.

"You could see the whole world from Devi temple!" Gopi said excitedly.

"Do you ever want to go back?"

"To hell? Go back to hell? No, Bibi! In that town, I was almost driven to begging. They were afraid of my shadow. If Amrita Bibi and Amar Babu had not brought me here, I don't know what I would have done. I tried to end my life so many times. But I didn't have the courage to hang myself, jump in a well, or set myself on fire. I wanted to die. I was nothing. What use was my life? The easiest way to die would have been to swallow arsenic, but I couldn't find it either."

"Tell me about the day you finally left."

"The day I met Amrita Bibi, she suggested that I leave with her right away but I didn't. Many weeks passed. I had time to think. Then one day she appeared against the light of the window out of nowhere. She appeared like the manifestation of Chamunda Devi! She made me aware of my own abilities. She said I must have been a good cook, that I must have embroidered beautiful blouses and odnis.

"Instead of treating me as a wretched widow, they treated me as a human being. I became a woman again. Living in that shed had made me think of myself as worthless, but by bringing me here and giving me a decent place to live, they made me realize that I was as worthy as anyone else!"

Chapter Twelve
The Egalitarians

Early the next morning, Kumud walked into the kitchen. Gopi had already made a fresh pot of tea. She handed Kumud a steaming cup and said Amrita Bibi was waiting for her in the bedroom. She tasted the sweet tea and carried the cup to the bedroom.

"Did you rest well?" Amrita asked. "Are you feeling ready for your mission?"

"I've been ready since I left Ambayu. Did you sleep well?"

"Like a log!" Amrita was standing next to a pile of folded clothes on the bed. "Did you know your mother and I borrowed clothes from each other?"

Kumud nodded. "I could tell when she wore yours. They were more stylish and warmer in color."

"Your mother tended to wear greens and blues even for parties," said Amrita, picking up a lemon kurta, intricately embroidered near the sleeves and neckline with boughs of pomegranates, with matching churidaar and dupatta.

"This is for you."

"This is beautiful!" She held the kurta against her front and turned to look at herself in the mirror behind her.

"These outfits are for you!" Amrita said, pushing the pile of clothes towards Kumud. "You would look conspicuous in jeans--or any western clothes. In Neela Nagar, try to wear Indian clothes."

Kumud hesitated. "I should have thought about this. I didn't even bring saris." She stared at the stack.

"Consider these your own." Amrita rested her palm on the pile and became thoughtful. "Perhaps you find these old fashioned, not your style."

"Not at all, Auntie. This is so generous of you!"

"You will stand out like a sore thumb in western clothes!" Amrita said. "Everyone will stare at you. Don't ask for undue attention. Even with kurta and churidaar you will be noticeable in a crowd where women wear lehenga, kurta, and odni, their faces veiled. Jeans and T-shirts are considered men's wear. Dressed like that, you will intimidate women and offend men. These outfits will easily fit in your duffle bag. Pick what you like."

"Thank you, Auntie! You are right. I should have thought about that. Do you think someone might recognize me in these clothes?"

With only a slight hesitance, Amrita said, "You mean because of Kumar?" Then she paused. "Kumud," she said, "We know about him and completely understand your leaving him. Besides, No one will recognize you. It has been so many years. . . And if they do, so what?"

Kumud didn't respond, but felt relieved that she didn't have to explain that part of her life to this wise couple. She nodded with thankful smile.

"So, with Kumar gone," Amrita continued, "no one knows or remembers your entire story."

"Oh, they know! How can they forget me leaving my sick husband behind?"

"Kumar's parents have passed away, his best friend is dead. Who else did you know during the ten months you were married?"

"Intimately? No one," she said, and her anxiety subsided a little.

After Kumud selected a few sets, Amrita put the rest back in her closet. Kumud noticed the ethnic clothes hanging there.

"Which states did you visit with Amar Uncle?"

"Mostly Meghalaya, Karnataka, and Kerala," she said, feeling nostalgic. "Amar was there for gender studies. I was there because of him. Once we settled in a place, I began to collect the local attire. Their clothes fascinated me, as did their jewelry. I photographed the people against local landscapes, in their ethnic garbs and embellishments. I was also interested in their gender equality. You would be interested to know that male and female roles are reversed in those societies."

"Does that work?"

"Amar has written a paper that was applauded by academia."

On the wall behind Amrita, Kumud saw a hexagonal painting made of smaller hexagons. In the center was an image of black Kali surrounded by images of six other goddesses set neatly against the sides of the central image. The hexagonal unit of seven goddesses mesmerized Kumud. She wanted to understand what the images meant. On the other hand, she never needed to understand the Chinese landscape in her flat that made her feel emotionally inspired and empty of anxious thoughts.

"Bedazzling images, aren't they?" Amrita said.

Kumud carefully looked at Kali's gruesome appearance—her rolling eyes, disheveled hair, and arms carrying ghastly objects. She had seen the images of Kali before, but her mind had become jaded to them. This image stood out from the others. "Why does she look unlike other goddesses? Dancing so frantically?" asked Kumud.

"Kali, one of the many forms of the great goddess, is the personified anger of woman and low castes. As an older woman, I see myself in her image. She opposes timidity and passivity. She teaches that fearlessness and determination are within us, waiting to be cultivated and transformed into action. Demons of desire, delusion, arrogance, greed, and fear replicate themselves endlessly—these demons are not only outside us but also within us. She demands that we vanquish them."

"How?"

"With courage and fearlessness, but also patience. She mocks the oppressed and underdogs who do not stand up for their rights. She challenges them to fight frantically for their freedom," Amrita said. "I've tried to express this in my photographs. I too must 'dance' frantically and voice my anger. That's why I put Kali's image in the middle."

"That is so powerful!" Kumud thanked Amrita for her words of wisdom and continued to stare at the images. Then she said, "I should get ready now."

THE LAST SUTTEE

"Yes! Taxiwalla should be here at ten."

"Do I have time to talk to Uncle about the matriarchal communities you visited?"

"Ask him for the short version, otherwise...." Amrita said with mirth and winked.

At the breakfast table, Amrita said to her husband, "Kumud wants to know about the paper you wrote about matriarchal and matrilineal communities."

"What about them?"

"The basics Uncle. How are these communities different, and how do they work?"

"Matriarchy is an ideal, just as patriarchy is these days. If you replace men's positions in current societies with women, you have matriarchy. Let's face it, this social structure will never be as universal as patriarchy. Even if it happens, it would take centuries."

"We don't want matriarchy to replace patriarchy" Amrita interjected. "No one wants to live in a social system where men are undermined as much as we undermine women in the present system."

Kumud nodded in agreement.

Amar said, "In a matriarchy, women are chief decision makers and take a stand in almost all spheres of life—political, judicial, and economic, including family inheritance, which favors men. On the other hand, in matrilineal societies, amongst whom your auntie and I lived in Meghalaya, Kerala, and Karnataka, the laws of inheritance favor women. They make decisions about major issues within the family, but they are not decision makers in the public domain."

"That's similar to patriarchy, where mothers and wives make most decisions within the home," Kumud said.

"And now listen to this, Kumud!" Amar said with zest, "The daughters of the Garo and Khasi tribes in Meghalaya become heiresses by default. They choose their own husbands and are free to work outside their homes. The Nairs and Ezhavas in Kerala are also matrilineal by tradition. At one point in history Kerala was completely matrilineal, although the system has declined somewhat. The difference is mindset of the people. If everyone within the society believes that women can do what men can, it makes a huge difference. This is different from the patriarchal system, where that idea rarely occurs."

"How has that tradition benefited women in Kerala?" Kumud asked.

"It has subverted many social evils. Women are not judged by what they wear. The men respect them for who they are. The dowry system is looked down upon; no *purdah* system is imposed. There are no restrictions on women's physical movement or attire, and there is no bride burning, female infanticide, or social stigma about widows re-marrying." Amar went on, "Sharp contrast to Neela Nagar."

"It is as it should be!" Amrita looked at Kumud.

"Absolutely!" she said.

"They view women the way they view men, as individuals. It is as Amrita said, the way it should be."

"Then why is this system declining?"

"These societies exist in a patriarchal country. Our culture sends silent messages reinforcing the patriarchal ways through the media. As a matter of fact, cultures throughout the world have homogenized into overwhelming patriarchies."

"If in patriarchal societies women get a raw deal, men in hypothetical matriarchal societies will also get a raw deal? Wouldn't they?"

"I can assure you that men will never let that happen! Prevailing patriarchal systems treat men as supreme and offer them full responsibility for the welfare of the family and the community."

"My question is why did patriarchy become dominant?" Amrita asked.

"She would know this," Amar said, pointing to Kumud.

"I know a little, such as how in the very early ages men were unaware of their share in procreation. They saw women as the sole actor in the drama of the miracle of birth. Woman was the primordial goddess, the Great Mother. As the physiological facts about paternity were understood and recognized, world religions assigned male partners to women, as sons, fathers, or husbands."

"I may add," Amar said, again taking over the conversation, "that the mystery of the fertile womb was feared, not revered, as some have written. Men were terrified and in awe of such biological functions as menstruation, pregnancy, and parturition. Childbirth was thought to have polluting effects. Numerous rules and prohibitions were created to counteract the potential danger. Homes and towns were divided into sacred and profane sections. Women's access was restricted to certain places at certain times."

"Because a man cannot create a new life the way a woman can," said Kumud, "This produced anxiety—the fear, the terror, the awe—which makes perfect sense."

"But the way men exploit feminine power is unjust and unfair," Amrita said.

Kumud couldn't help interrupting. "Nature made men and women, and we must accept that as it is, not abuse one another for being who he or she must be."

"Humans are exploitative by nature, Kumud!" Amrita said.

"But we can learn and change, the way you two have incorporated a matrilineal system into your own household!" Kumud smiled. "I remember this house being strictly patriarchal, now it is matrilineal." She looked at both of them for a reaction.

"That is a big compliment," said Amar. "I'm glad you noticed. But you too had something to do with it."

"Me? How?" Kumud was genuinely surprised.

"Your Amar Uncle was touched by your thesis. He suggested I read it too. I did and loved it! He had underlined some of the pages that had deeply touched him," Amrita said.

"Which page?"

"Read to her, Amar, the way you read to me," Amrita said to her husband.

Amar opened the booklet at the page he had earmarked and said, "You have quoted a priest from the ancient scripture *Atharva Veda*, instructing a widow on the pyre of her dead husband." He read, "'Get up, O Woman to the world of the living; thou liest by this one who is deceased; come! To him who grasps thy hand, thy second spouse, thou hast now entered into the relation of wife to husband.'

"Evidently during the time of Vedas, a widow sitting by the corpse of her husband was a symbolic rite.

The priest instructs her to rise and go forth with her new spouse to a life of 'progeny and property.' In that era, only after the widow departed was the pyre set ablaze.' When I read that, an insight came to me! Neela Nagar had turned a symbolic rite into a barbaric ritual. If this were true, I thought, then so many of their customs must be local—not much to do with ancient scriptures. That was the beginning of my awakening."

"I'm glad something worthwhile resulted from my thesis," Kumud said.

"This is good work, Kumud. You should be proud!" he said. "The fact is that my mindset and my paradigm regarding women slowly reformed while we were living within matrilineal communities. But your book gave me the final push. It helped me step up to the second stage of our marriage. In an egalitarian marriage, the two are one in spirit."

"But in Neela Nagar it is reversed. When a man stops breathing, his wife is forced to stop breathing too. Isn't she?" Kumud said.

They both nodded.

Chapter Thirteen

The Taxiwalla

"Kumud! Taxi is here!" Amar called from the porch.

The taxi driver loaded Kumud's stuffed duffle bag into the trunk and opened the backdoor for her.

"Goodbye Uncle and Auntie! It feels like I was with you for a month! Thanks for everything!"

Amar hugged her tight. "We enjoyed having you, dear! Remember there is a difference between writing and fighting. Make sure Guruji and his allies are there to help you," he said.

Amrita smiled nervously feeling anxious about Kumud's trip to Neela Nagar. "There are many good people in that town, but they will not talk. I hope they open up to you. I don't want to discourage you, but your being alone worries me."

"I will not be discouraged, Auntie. Trust me. I'll do whatever I must, even if I die doing it."

"No one is going to kill you! And don't say that," Amar said. "Your Auntie is already a nervous wreck!" He hugged her again and blessed her solemnly.

She kissed both on their cheeks and turned towards the taxi.

"May Lakshmi, the goddess of good luck, be with you all the time!" Amrita said aloud as Kumud slipped into the backseat.

"Stay with us on your return trip!" Kumud heard her say as the Taxiwalla closed the door. Rolling down the window, she said, "Visit me in Ambayu!" and waved good-bye. She grinned at the thought that her acquaintance with the Chauhans had been renewed and enriched.

She drew in a deep breath and settled into her seat as the driver adjusted his rearview mirror.

"Ready, Madam?" he asked in English with a heavy Indian accent, looking at her through the mirror. His smile showed teeth stained with betel juice.

"Ready," she nodded. His face made her nervous. The whites of his piercing eyes shone from a pockmarked face, his hair dyed orange with henna. *Will it be safe riding alone through the desert with this man?* Watching both Amrita and Amar waving good-bye lightened her anxiety. The taxi turned around, and thoughts of a possible suttee in Neela Nagar came flooding back to her.

Two houses down, along the main road, was where Kumud had lived as a young woman, and then with her mother after her father passed away. A large family lived there now, Amrita had said the previous evening, five sons and one married daughter. "Everyone is busy with work. No longer do we have time for the neighbors," she'd said.

Kumud did not like the dingy pink paint or the

barren front yard. The trees, bushes, and climbers her mother had so lovingly planted had died or were cut down.

The city streets buzzed with activity. A river of men, women, and children crowded the footpaths. On the main street, trucks, scooters, taxis, rickshaws, and cars sped past like scurrying mice. Stores displaying steel and brass pots and pans buzzed with customers, as did stalls with tie-dyed shirts, dupattas, and saris. Bland bamboo and burlap shanties held shimmering boxes of glass bangles and colorful braids hanging from hooks on bamboo posts.

Above the stores, people peeked from behind ornate window frames of the unpainted walls of old residential quarters. The building façades as well as the store's merchandise had an inherent elegance and artistry reminiscent of a culture steeped in tradition.

They drove through the city in silence, until sand dunes rose gently against the backdrop of the sparse landscape. Some foliage grew at the edges of the road. Bitter neem trees appeared on the horizon, and Kumud spotted a dense growth of *ankhda* bushes that bled milk.

Taxiwalla cleared his throat. "Come in ta-rain from Ambayu, Madam?"

"Yes."

"Ambayu! Big city. Me from small village, Apna Gaon, next to Neela Nagar. No ta-rain in Neela Nagar, no local taxi or rickshaw," he said and glanced at her through the mirror. "First time, Neela Nagar?"

"I lived there when I was little; I don't remember much," she said, unwilling to talk about her time there with Kumar.

"Visit relatives?"

"No... no relatives."

"Visit Narayani Temple? Worrrld people visit Mata temple."

"Yes, people all over the world come to see Narayani Temple!" Her mouth tasted bitter at that name. How else could she respond? Goddess Satimata was always on the minds of the people of the blue town. She wished they were not so devoted to her. She herself was not anti-goddess. Their hagiographies had taught her many aspects of femininity and being a woman, what she hated was how communities used female deities to justify their actions. During festival times, deep religiosity kept Neela Nagar humming with pilgrims.

"Worrrld people ask for boons," he said. "Mata fulfills them."

She forced a smile and then took out a book she was reading. She looked occasionally through the window at the sparse landscape, and then went back to the book.

"Scenery no good here. Near Neela Nagar lots of chillie fields. Only chillie fields important to Neela Nagar," he said, stressing and elongating the word chili. "Leather factory also very good for economy."

Kumud was aware how the economy depended on harvesting chili fields and manufacturing leather goods. The hot chilies were dried crisp in the sun and ground into powder, which was placed in polythene bags and packed into hundreds of thousands of burlap-sacks for export. The sacks were loaded on bullock carts and transported to Madhya Shahar, where they would be sent to their final destinations. But instead she said, "What about potters and dyers in your village of Apna Gaon? They produce blue pottery and tie-dye fabric. They contribute to the economy. Don't they?"

"Yess! Yess! But those things are made by lowly villagers. By Gaad, Madam, you know very much about this place!"

"As I said, I lived here as a young girl."

"You know Hindi?" He asked.

"Yes!"

"Then why I speak to you in English?" Then he said excitedly in Hindi. "If you lived in this town, that makes us siblings, Sister. Neela Nagar and Apna Gaon like siblings."

"I was wondering why you were talking to me in English," she said.

He said, "Sorry, sorry, too much CNN, Madam!"

"I understand." She glanced at his smiling face through the mirror. It no longer looked scary.

They grew quiet and rode silently for miles on the straight tarmac road. The noon sun made the sandy earth sparkle; strong winds shaped and re-shaped the sand dunes.

He continued in English, "Why you leave?"

"What?" she asked, raising her head from the book.

"Why you leave the town?"

"To attend high school." She said, "If it weren't for Guruji, I would never have studied further."

"Who? Guruji? Shantilal Sharma?" he asked, bemused.

"You know him?"

"Everyone in Neela Nagar knows Guruji. He

teaches at Neela Nagar School."

"Are you sure? He must be in his seventies," Kumud said.

"But very sharp—sharp as blade!" he said in English.

"Where does he live?"

"I don't know. I meet him on road or during festival time at Narayani Temple."

"Do you visit the temple often?"

"Yes, I am humble devotee!"

"I thought only women worshipped Satimata."

"No, men too, all castes and color! She inspires all with her *katha*. You'll see when you visit there."

A bus station came into view. "Madam, you stretch legs? I tell you Satimata *katha* after you eat something," he said, stopping the taxi in front of a roadside eatery.

She could hardly recall the story of Satimata that she had heard many years ago. The one thing she clearly remembered was that while Sati was the name of the goddess, suttee was the sacrificial ritual that the goddess had performed, the ritual that Kumud had witnessed when Sau Massi self-immolated herself.

Taxiwalla walked ahead of Kumud. He handed several coins to the toilet attendant to clean the toilet, and asked Kumud to wait. When the attendant was finished, he motioned to Kumud to use it. At the eatery, he ordered fresh roti and dal, and then sent the waiter to serve Kumud. He sat a few tables away from her.

When they were finished, he opened the door of the taxi. She thanked him and once again settled in the back seat to read. The engine revved, and the last leg of her journey began. They drove in silence for miles. Then he said, "Do you want to hear the story?"

"What did you say?" she said, narrowing her eyes.

"Narayani Satimata *katha*. Do you want to hear it?"

"Oh, yes! Of course."

"Do you know desires come true just by listening Satimata story?"

"Really!"

He cleared his throat and began in Hindi. "A long time ago there lived a very beautiful woman named Ganga Devi. She was devoted to her husband, Govinda Aggarsen. Her *dharma* was to be his faithful wife, *pativrata*. They were happy but for want of a child. For years they prayed to the gods, served Brahmins, and fed cows with the hope that they would be blessed with a child. Finally, on October 8, 1338, their prayers resulted in a boon. They had a baby girl. They named her Narayani.

"An exact date? Is this a historic event or the myth of the goddess?"

"Same thing! The story of this sacred woman is as real as the myth of the goddess Kali. Just listen, Madam," he said and continued. "It was an auspicious Tuesday, and the time was midnight. "Sister, are you listening?" he asked, looking at her through the mirror.

"I am."

"The face of the newborn reflected sheen. One night Ganga dreamed that the newborn was Devi, the great goddess herself, incarnated as her daughter. Govinda and Ganga imagined their child becoming famous and having millions of devotees.

"One day Ganga had a vision of a calf suckling milk from a cow. At that moment, she smelled milk burning. She quickly ran to the kitchen to check the milk pot. But the pot was cold to the touch. As she stood there wondering, a suttee flame combusted before her. When people learned of these visions, they knew that Ganga was going to give birth to an exceptional child.

"Narayani started school when she was five. Within a short time she memorized the four *Vedas*, *Bhagavad Gita*, and *Ramayana*. She loved listening to myths and legends about the god Vishnu. Her gurus were impressed with her understanding of scriptures and dedication to learning. At home, her father taught her fencing, shooting, and horseback riding. No one, not even the boys her age, could compete with her.

"Then a child-devouring she-demon heard about the beautiful and talented Narayani who was believed to be an incarnation of the goddess Sati. The she-demon arrived at the playground intending to abduct Narayani but lost her courage. Instead, she kidnapped and killed Narayani's best friend. Narayani confronted the she-demon. They fought, and the she-demon was blinded and fell unconscious to the ground.

"Narayani had magical powers and brought the demon back to consciousness and Kamala back to life. Hearing about her powerful miracles, the demon asked for forgiveness and promised that she would never again devour children."

Taxiwalla's story made no logical sense, Kumud thought, but it was intriguing in its mythic characters. "Is that the end?" she asked.

"Not yet, Madam. Once Satimata *katha* is started, it cannot be stopped or the narrator and listener will be cursed. So, listen! When Narayani turned thirteen, her parents began to search for a suitable boy. Messages were sent to nearby villages and towns, but in vain. Unable to find a match for their beloved daughter made them anxious. As you can imagine, madam, Narayani could not tolerate her parents' unhappiness. Using her magical powers, she helped them find a match for her. His name was Tanmandas.

"Narayani's parents sent a matrimonial proposal to the Tanmandas' parents, who happily accepted the offer. Hail to the woman who on the strength of her truth and inner beauty found a match for herself!" he said, excitedly.

"Wait!" Kumud interrupted. "Does this mean that if a girl finds her own husband the parents should accept the match?"

"No, Sister. Narayani was a goddess, not a mere mortal. It is different for mortals," Taxiwalla said.

"But what is the point of the goddess's myth if devotees don't or can't follow it as a model?"

"Madam what mean 'myth'?"

"Story, I mean Katha."

He continued in Hindi, "Listen to the story first, Madam! You'll know what to follow and what not to follow."

"Satimata's myth is to be followed selectively then?"

"If we could exactly follow the ways of gods and goddesses, then we wouldn't need them, would we?"

She remained quiet.

"Do you understand?" he asked.

She nodded.

"Okay, then. Narayani and Tanmandas were married with pomp. Narayani's father gave dowry, including elephants, horses, bulls, camels, and one thousand three-wheeled *chhakdas* and a white mare.

"The white mare was Tanmandas' favorite gift from his wife's dowry, so much so that men from other towns became jealous. They coveted the white mare. One day Tanmandas and his wife were riding in an enclosed *chhakda,* which was pulled by the mare. A jealous man lured Tanmandas from the vehicle, killed him, and took the mare.

"Narayani remained seated in the *chhakda.* She heard a fight, which was followed by an eerie silence. Peeking through the curtain, she saw the bloody body of her beloved husband. With the smoky fumes of her anger she was transformed into the battle goddess Kali. Her eyes were red, her black hair disheveled. To avenge her husband, she rode horseback, carrying a spear in one hand and a sword in the other. She asked her guard to take her husband's body to a designated place before sunset.

"She slew her husband's murderer, then returned to the place where her husband had been taken. The guard was there, collecting firewood for the cremation. She declared she would commit suttee, but must bathe first. A stream of water sprang from the ground in which she bathed her husband's body, putting the auspicious red mark on his forehead. Then she bathed and adorned herself.

"She bowed to her prostrate husband on the unlit pyre. She joined him on the firewood, taking his head in her lap and asking the guard to lay Tanmandas' weapons around them. Tears poured from the guard's eyes. He stood before the couple on the purified ground, his palms together as he honored the manifestation of the goddess Sati. Their gazes met, and Narayani nodded then covered her head and face with the pallu of her sari. She sang to her guard and devotee."

The Taxiwalla sang in a sweet voice.

Listen to me, my soldier,
Sat (truth) will be famous.
In each and every home, Sat will be worshipped.
The echo of Narayani's Sati manifestation will sound
everywhere.
You will be my first devotee

Listen to me my soldier
In three days, our ashes will turn cold.
Collect the ashes in cloth and ride the white mare.
Ride until she stops. Don't coerce her!

Where she stops, lay a foundation of a temple.
Don't enshrine my image, worship me in the form of
a trident.
During the dark half of Bhadon, celebrate a yearly
fair.
If you follow my command, you'll be showered with
blessings.

Listen, devotees of Satimata!
Whoever follows Narayani's command is showered
with blessings!

"The guard buried the ashes and the weapons and mounded dirt over them. The mound lit itself and its flames touched the sky. The fire's heat dried the guard's tears. People from nearby villages and towns saw the blaze and followed the light, bearing dried coconuts, rice, and clarified butter suitable for the god of fire. The cry "Hail goddess Narayani Satimata!" reverberated across the sky.

"The flame burned for thirteen days and nights. A melodious voice from the mound said, 'Pour water!' and people doused the mound with water. The fire was finally extinguished.

"Since that day, Madam, the fire of her truth and faith—Narayani Satimata's *sat*—continues to burn; it will burn for centuries. Narayani's miraculous sacrifice is followed the world over!

"Suttee ritual is only performed in Neela Nagar. Nowhere else in the world," Kumud tried telling him, but he ignored her and continued.

"Even now when people visit her temple they sprinkle water from the same stream that sprang on the day of Satimata's suttee. You can see it on the boulder inside the main chamber of the temple. They apply thirteen red marks on the trident and thirteen black marks on the eyes, and they offer rice, henna powder, red bangles, flower garlands, scented sticks, and a coconut divided into thirteen pieces. Then they say aloud, 'Victory to the mother of suttees! Victory to Narayani Satimata! Victory to the goddess Sati!' as they circumambulate around the inner shrine."

"Why thirteen?"

"One for the main temple on the top of the boulder and twelve for the suttee shrines on the side. You'll see for yourself when you go to the temple.

THE LAST SUTTEE

"Our traditions are safe here because no one moves out and hardly anyone moves in. The only flame in the world that remains lit twenty-four hours a day, seven days a week since that time. At no other temple in the world is so much clarified butter used as on the sacred mound. As if that was not enough, the water that streams from the ground has miraculous powers. It grants wishes."

"Do all your wishes come true?"

"Some do, some don't." Taxiwalla said and waved a pamphlet at her over his shoulder. "Here, Sister, take this! They hand it out free at the temple. It records pearls of wisdom from Narayani Satimata's *Katha*. Read it before you visit."

"Thank you!" Kumud took the slim volume from his hand. The images and colors were kitsch. She flipped through the pages and read one that caught her attention.

A woman doesn't have to immolate herself to be called Sati; the dedication and devotion towards her husband can win her the title of Sati.
Sati is the supreme title a society can give to a woman. Women of the world can follow their dharma and earn the title of Sati by being true and faithful to their husbands.
A female can only consider her husband her guru. No strange man can be her guru.
A married woman is like a saint. No man may lay his covetous eyes on her.
Narayani Satimata is against divorce and remarriage but shuns the caste system.
Marriage is not for enjoyment but for achieving a

possible suttee.
Sati is the one who walks a path of righteousness and
truth, not the one who immolates herself.

Kumud re-read the last line. She wanted to read it
to the Taxiwalla. but what would be the point? No use
arguing with a staunch follower. How did the
worshippers reconcile with what was written in the
pamphlet?
She read the last line:
Don't worship goddess images. Worship the trident.
The trident is a symbol of Satimata Shakti, the
feminine power.

Kumud closed the pamphlet and looked through
the window. It looked scorching hot. Chili fields lined
both sides of the road. The red chilies and green leaves
went on for miles under the blue sky, like colorful carpet.
Gazing at the vast landscape, Kumud remembered how
once, a long time ago, she and her mother had ridden a
bus from Madhya Nagar through these fields to visit Sau
Massi. She was excited at the thought of meeting her
favorite aunt. To curb her restless delight, she had
watched the colorful landscape and imagined she was
entering a fairyland.
Although the day had started with exuberance, it
ended in a macabre ritual. Kumud remembered the
mixed sounds of women singing and wailing, the smell of
burning flesh and marigold flowers, the smoky orange
and red flames against the green trees and evening sky,
and the pain in her heart and her mother's helplessness
and frustration. Her mother had held her hand tightly as

she tried to escape the scene. But young men carrying swords wouldn't allow them to leave. People pushed and shoved and children cried. The gruesome memories turned her hands and feet cold. She folded the pamphlet and shoved it into her purse. She rubbed her palms together and tried to warm the backs of her hands.

The tarmac road ended abruptly, and the taxi stopped.

"Sister, sadly my journey with you must come to an end here," the Taxiwalla said, opening her door. He pulled out her duffle bag and dumped it on the sand. "There is the school." He pointed to a faraway building that shimmered under the scorching sun.

Kumud paid him more than he had asked and thanked him for his company. He brought his palms together and said, "*Namaskar*, Sister!"

After the Taxiwalla drove away, she headed toward the school building, the duffle bag heavy on her shoulder. The afternoon desert sun scorched her scalp as she watched the taxi vanish in the horizon. Her fortuitous meeting with the Taxiwalla made her think of the people she had previously met by chance. Each one of them had either changed her life or given meaning to it—Dev, Yuna Li, Shekhar, and now Taxiwalla.

Chapter Fourteen

Town Under a Dome

The tarmac road appeared and disappeared amid the gusting sand. It bifurcated into two lanes, the northeast-bound to Apna Gaon, a village of low castes and artisans, and the west to Neela Nagar, the blue town.

Descendants of potters, carpenters, dyers, and criers lived in the village of Apna Gaon. Most were unaware of how much their ancestors prided themselves in exporting wares to Ambayu, Delhi, Madras and other booming metropolitan cities. Middlemen made money while the villagers remained poor. And yet they were satisfied as long as their skills provided them with the basic necessities of life and, a few believed, gave them inner strength. Practicing creative arts had steeped them with dignity and pride in their community.

Kumud remembered the village's whitewashed huts and well-swept courtyards shimmering under the sun. Palm and kikar trees added touches of greenery to the landscape. The village had spread beyond the boundaries of an ancient temple complex, now in ruins. The dilapidated soft stone monument enshrined a granite image of the great goddess, Devi. The image was preserved well in the temple's womb chamber, reminiscent of a glorious period when kings and queens worshipped here. The monument stood between Apna Gaon, where lanes were wide and open, and Chamunda Hill, which overlooked Neela Nagar with its narrow, zigzagging lanes. River Tapasya separated the hill, the village, and the monument from Neela Nagar. The Apna Gaon villagers who worked in Neela Nagar had to cross a narrow tightrope bridge to reach the town, although Neela Nagar's high caste residents hardly ever used this bridge.

Buffalo carts passing through the narrow tarmac lanes of Neela Nagar were often blamed for scratching the painted wooden windows when they were accidently left open. A handcart pulled by a man was easier to maneuver. Neighbors passed baskets of fresh bread or vegetables to one another through second-floor windows with a rope pulley.

The main market street was wider. A green grocer, shoe repairman, tailor, fruit seller, and spice vendor displayed their meager items in shops that resembled the cells in a beehive. On rare occasions young Kumud accompanied her father in the afternoon to the market. She saw flies buzzing and shopkeepers snoring. But in the evening, the place was alive with haggling customers, barefoot boys, men smoking hookah, and people eating paan and chatting in groups.

Girls or women were rarely seen in the market. During late afternoons, a woman or two could be spotted buying a spice or some vegetable, their faces and necks covered with odni. Most believed the women were better off in the confines of their homes, protected and safe.

In a shop of posters, an old man sold oleographs of gods and goddesses. They could be bought framed or rolled. The most popular poster was of the goddess Narayani Satimata dressed in her bridal attire and embellished with gold ornaments, seated on a blazing fire with the head of her dead husband in her lap. Above them was depicted the great goddess Devi, blessing the couple about to be engulfed by flames. Rays of light emanated from the palm of Devi's raised arm.

Kumud doubted that the town would have changed much from how she remembered it. Its skyline became visible through the haze. The blue sky above lidded the dry and airless town below like a vault. Kumud saw the silhouettes of the school building, and the Narayani Satimata Temple and the House where the Elders held their meetings. Kumud spotted the shade of a neem tree several hundred feet ahead where she would rest.

This was the town where she had lived with Kumar while his best friend, Ranju lived in Apna Gaon. Even fifteen years later she still could not imagine the two men as lovers. The day after her wedding her mother-in-law had instructed her of her responsibilities as a daughter-in-law. Kumar was an only child. His wife was expected to help his mother in the kitchen. A servant and a maid took care of most other household chores that left a couple of hours after breakfast and a few more after lunch free for Kumud.

In the first month of her unconsummated marriage, Kumud became amicable with women of the house and extended family. They taught her to embroider with pieces of glass and shiny beads on cotton blouses and long skirts. As they embroidered she learned that Kumar had refused to get married and even spoken against the tradition of marriage. His parents first pleaded with him, and then threatened to disown him. They said they would be disgraced if he were unable to continue their lineage. What about his religious duty to Hindu dharma, to uphold his duty as a householder? Not a day passed when they did not remind him of his responsibilities. His father warned. His mother pleaded. Finally, he succumbed to their demands and surrendered to their pleas and threats. The women also told her how almost every evening there were fierce arguments in Ranju's presence because he was like their son. They warned that Kumar's wife would be expected to serve Ranju as if he were her husband's brother.

"Kumar and Ranju are like twins," Kumar's mother had told Kumud the day she arrived. "You'll see when they resume their routine."

After Ranju regained his health he had continued his morning visits.

Six weeks after the wedding Ranju recovered and continued his daily visits to Kumar's home. He was like Kumar's shadow. Kumud, the new daughter-in-law, served him the way she was expected to. Soon she learned of Kumar and Ranju's love for corn or bajra roti, freshly baked. They ate it with generous helpings of butter and jaggery, the sap of a palm tree. As the final course, Kumar's mother served hot sugary tea before the two left for work.

Kumar and Ranju oversaw the farmers and field laborers throughout the different seasons of the year.

THE LAST SUTTEE

Twice a year, farmers tilled and sowed, tended the young crops, and harvested the yields. The two 'brothers' trotted on their horses, supervising the men and women in the fields, dismounting only when they spotted a problem.

During the day, the two men worked, talked, ate, laughed and returned home late. They were separated only after dinner when Kumar stayed home and Ranju went to his parents' place to sleep.

In Ranju's presence, neither Kumar nor Ranju said anything to Kumud. At dinner they talked about work, laughed, and exchanged glances. If Kumar complimented Kumud for a dish she had prepared, Ranju would interrupt and say that his mother made the dish differently. When Kumar asked Kumud about her day, Ranju interrupted and said, "Every day is the same for women, as it would be for her." Then he changed the subject. It was as if she was not there although she served breakfast, lunch and dinner.

When the family had siesta; Kumud read and wrote in her journal in the seclusion of her room. After dinner, Kumar slept on the floor and insisted she take the bed. During her sleepless nights, of which there were many, she wrote some more.

Kumud thought it best to remain quiet most of her day. She talked only when she had to and forced a smile if someone said something pleasant. She followed her mother-in-law's directions and did what she was told to do. She felt homeless, existing in a temporal limbo. But she did not want to return to her mother's home. That would cause her mother as much pain as it caused Kumud. And she did not know where else to go or what else to do.

Finally, three months after her wedding, Kumud visited her mother. There was no point in asking Kumar to accompany her. She had pretended with his family that everything was normal, but she refused to continue the charade with her own mother. She thought carefully about how to explain her situation to her. Would she even know the meaning of homosexuality? She may not even believe what she heard. There had not been a single instance when her mother talked to her about sexual matters.

She thought of these things as she was on the bus to her home in Madhya Shahar. How should she disclose Kumar's sexual orientation? How could she tell her mother that she had not slept with her husband? Would her mother think that something was wrong with *her*? Telling her that a man could like another man the way a man likes a woman may sound like nonsense to her. It seemed as if there was nothing Kumud could say that would convey her reality. Maybe she should say that Kumar was impotent. Her mother would understand, even accept that. But maybe not!

Standing in front of her mother's front door, Kumud hesitated. Mustering strength, she knocked, but no one responded. She rang the bell, wondering whether her mother had received the telegram telling her when she would arrive.

Then the door opened. There was her mother, standing with open arms and beaming with the joy at seeing her daughter for the first time since the wedding. Seeing her mother's face, Kumud began sobbing as her mother hugged her.

"Oh, my dear! I missed you too! I missed you, my darling. You don't know how happy you have made me by this visit. Where is Kumar?"

"He couldn't come. Busy time at the fields."

They went inside and sat at the kitchen table. Her mother handed Kumud a cup of tea. "Why didn't you hold off your visit until he had more leisure?"

"I shouldn't have come alone, then?"

"That's not what I am saying; good that you came, child! But after marriage, it is proper that your husband brings you here."

"Next time things will be different, believe me," Kumud said, and changed the subject. She did not yet have the heart to tell her mother the truth about why her husband did not accompany her.

"Mother, I miss teaching. I miss my friends and the children at the school. What would you say if I tried to get my job back?"

Her mother's eyebrows narrowed and she said, "Never joke like this. It is bad luck! You are talking as if you do not intend to return to your husband."

Silently, Kumud drank her tea. What should she say? Finally, she said,

"What if I told you that I liked my life as a teacher more than being married to Kumar?"

"Such are the sacrifices we women have to make. If it is your independence and spinster life you're missing, I understand, but wait until you have children. You'll forget the school."

"I doubt that very much," she said and left the table to unpack.

The first few days, Kumud pretended gaiety. She

talked about her days in college, asked her mother if she remembered Dev? Her mother remembered, but did not encourage any talk about him. They reminisced about Guruji and the one-room school. The third morning, when they had finished breakfast and were sipping tea, Kumud couldn't contain the secret any longer. She said, "Mother, what would you say if I ask to stay back for a few months?"

Her mother's expression changed. "Why would you do that? What would Kumar say? What would he do without you?"

"He has his family and his best friend, Ranju. Kumar loves Ranju very much. They are like twins."

"Are you jealous of his good friend? Well, that is normal. But no one can take a wife's place."

"He loves Ranju more than me, Mother."

"That is not possible. Ranju can't give him what you can, can he?"

"Yes, he can!"

"Now, you are talking nonsense! What is eating you, Daughter? Tell me, what is wrong?" Her mother became agitated.

"Mother, they are like husband and wife?"

"How is that possible?" Her mother looked appalled.

"It is possible! Everyone knows, but no one talks about it. Everyone pretends things are normal between Kumar and me. He meets Ranju behind closed doors."

"If people find out what they do in secret, you know what will happen to them? They will burn them alive!" her mother replied without remorse.

Slowly and carefully Kumud disclosed the details

of her unconsummated marriage. At first, the mother refused to believe her daughter. "What is wrong with you? Did Dev come to meet you in Neela Nagar?" She refused to believe that Kumar was homosexual. She turned on her daughter, as if it was her fault.

"What did you do to make him behave this way? Are you sure there is nothing wrong with you?"

Her mother's doubt hurt Kumud deeply.

She mumbled as if to herself, "I want divorce, Mother! I want a divorce!" She mocked her ninety days and ninety nights of wide-eyed, dumbstruck boredom.

"Divorce is for the people who live in fancy towns and fancy homes. Whoever heard of a thing like that in this town?" her mother responded.

"They will soon! Through my lawyer."

"Who?"

"Nothing, Mother!"

Her mother's only advice was to return to Kumar and bring him back to his senses. Kumud no longer felt at home in her mother's home, and she forced herself to go back to Kumar.

With a heavy heart, Kumud returned. Her husband had fallen sick in her absence. In the bedroom, she saw Kumar on the bed and Ranju seated next to him. With long faces, they acknowledged her presence.

"What happened? I have been gone only six days. How did you get so sick?" Kumar asked.

Kumar stared at Ranju gesturing him to speak, "A couple of days after you had left", Ranju said, "we were on our usual rounds when suddenly he had difficulty breathing. I took him to the town healer, *vaid*."

"What did he say? What is it?" Kumud asked

anxiously.

"He isn't sure yet, but he gave him powder for the fever and a mixture for fatigue. He said the night sweats should cure him."

"And what if they don't?" Kumud asked and looked at Kumar. He had lost weight in the short time she had been gone.

"Then we will take him to the hospital in Madhya Shahar." Ranju said. "I must go. I'll be back in the evening." He bid them goodbye. From that day on, Ranju came to greet them every morning and evening but entrusted his lover to Kumud's care for the day. He had business to attend to.

Kumar's mother came to check on him several times a day. She sat silently beside him, pressing his arms, and spooning him water. She entered with a sad face and left even sadder. The other women of the house hesitated to enter the room. Kumud didn't think Kumar was contagious; otherwise Ranju and she would be infected. She took over the task of keeping her husband clean, comfortable, and fed. Doing so, she wondered how she could ever leave a sick man.

One morning, when Kumud came from the kitchen carrying breakfast, Kumar was sitting up in the bed. His eyes were closed, and he gasped frequently to breathe. He had been restless through the night, so she allowed him to rest.

When she returned half-an-hour later, he was grinning.

"Why are you so good to me after what I have done to you?" he asked, scooting down to lay flat on the bed. "I wish there was something to eradicate whatever is sucking the energy out of me."

"Why couldn't the town *vaid* diagnose the disease?" she asked, without responding to his question.

"He has never seen symptoms like mine. He has no clue. He is going to talk to the *vaid* from the other villages and try and find a new powder and a different mixture."

"Why don't you see a doctor in Madhya Shahar?"

"What are doctors going to do that our *vaid* can't cure? Let us give him a chance."

"Doctors will run tests. They have better ways to diagnose an illness, like x-ray, CT scan, blood transfusion, perhaps some new drug."

"I don't believe in hospitals, and I surely don't trust doctors," Kumar said.

He had lost ten kilograms of weight and had suffered bouts of vomiting and diarrhea. His skin had pink and purple blotches around his eyes and mouth, but he had stopped looking at himself in the mirror and couldn't see the changes in himself.

The thought of divorcing him still floated in Kumud's mind, but she didn't have the heart to abandon a sick man. As she helped her mother-in-law in the kitchen or joined the women as they ground barley or wheat and cut vegetables, she thought of different ways to change her situation. But even if she could convince herself to leave, where would she go?

Kumar gave a crack-lipped smile. Kumud sat next to Ranju. "See this." Kumar said in a raspy voice as he pointed to lesions on his hand. Kumud wanted Ranju to convince Kumar to go to the Madhya Shahar hospital. Initially Kumar groaned at the idea but finally agreed to seek the advice of an allopathic doctor in the city.

At the hospital, doctors examined Kumar. Immediately they diagnosed his disease, an unknown virus that infected the immune system and was devouring his body. Unfortunately, there was no treatment; Kumar was dying. He was discharged with the advice that he would be better off at home. The three returned, and Kumud and Ranju made Kumar feel as comfortable as they possibly could in his own bed.

Because doctors were unable to diagnose Kumar's illness, Kumud occasionally heard the women of the house talk about Sati Saubhagya, Sau Massi. One afternoon, when female relatives and neighbors were chit-chatting in the central court, she overheard them saying how dedicated she had been to Kumar.

"She is the one who would bring *sat* to this family," Kumud's mother-in-law said.

"After all, she has the attributes of a faithful wife and Sati Saubhagya's *samskaras*," a friend said.

"Educated women no longer follow our traditions, but it seems she could be the one who would," an older woman said with conviction.

"You talk as if Kumar is going to leave us. Don't use heartless words." The mother-in-law said knowing that her son was going to die.

"But if he does it would be an honor not only for our family but for seven generations to come." The oldest in the group whispered.

The ground under Kumud's feet shook. She knew that if she walked in they would stop talking about suttee, for this had happened several times before. But this time when she joined them, they continued to talk.

146

THE LAST SUTTEE

"Daughter-in-law, do you know merits and benefits of becoming suttee?" the oldest woman asked.

Kumud did not respond. Fear shot through her spine and she excused herself.

The gnawing thought that she would be a widow soon and Kumar's family expected her to voluntarily commit suttee caused Kumud persistent and wearing distress. Hellish nightmares stole what little peace she had. She saw herself in bridal finery sitting on a pyre with Kumar's body in her lap. She awoke in a sweat and sat upright on the floor. *No one can force me to commit suttee! Can they?*

If she ran away from this, her values were at stake. But if she stayed, and even if she chose not to face Sau Massi's plight, a widow's life would be worse. These thoughts raged like typhoons in her mind. She would not commit suttee, and she would not live a widow's life. Then what?

Kumud was in the kitchen helping to prepare lunch when she heard a knock at the front door. Looking through the kitchen window, she saw the cleaning woman, who was sweeping the front verandah, stop and open the door. She said it was someone from the village who wanted to see Kumud.

Her mother-in-law raised her eyebrow. "Who can that be?" And without waiting for an answer, she turned to Kumud and asked sternly, "Who do you know from the village?"

"I don't know anyone from the village."

"What does he want?"

"We'll find out," Kumud said, and walked to the door. She sensed her mother-in-law and the cleaning lady watching her.

"Salutations, Mother! I am from Apna Gaon." He greeted Kumar's mother-in-law.

"Namaskar, Sister!" The visitor addressed Kumud, "Your mother is an old acquaintance of mine. She sends her greetings. I just returned from Madhya Shahar, where I paid her a visit. She sends you a box of sweets," he said.

It was Dev, and he was smiling.

He looked at her with the same trustworthy eyes, the same charm. . . as if nothing had changed since their day together at her home.

The mother-in-law reciprocated his greeting, then went back to what she were doing. Kumud greeted him with folded hands, trying hard not to touch him and cry. She said, "How kind of you to bring it here! Won't you come in?"

"No, thanks, I must return to my work," he said. He was about to leave when the mother-in-law shouted from the kitchen,

"Has the visitor left, Daughter-in-law?"

"No, he is still here!" Kumud walked back to the kitchen, handed over the box of sweets, and hastily said, "He is going back to Madhya Shahar. I'm going to write a note to my mother."

She returned to Dev and said, "Wait! Will you be going back to Madhya Shahar soon?"

"I go to the city often."

She whispered, "May I give you something for my mother? Please wait!"

She stepped quietly into the bedroom, careful not to wake Kumar. From the locked drawer of her closet, she pulled out the journal that she had written almost every day. She handed over the most intimate reflections of her married life to Dev, the man she had once loved and trusted.

"Please give her this note. . . and my love," Kumud said.

A squawking bird pulled her from her reverie under the neem tree. *Oh, how she detested Neela Nagar!* She collected herself after the mental spell, picked up her duffle bag, and tried walking briskly, but her sandals on the sandy earth made her steps heavy. The tarmac path, sometimes visible, sometimes hidden, slowed her pace. The swirling sand made the edges of her *salwaar* flare around her ankles.

Fifteen years ago, in the wee morning hours, less than a year after she married, she had run away from this town. At this very spot, she had ridden the bus to the Madhya Shahar train station. She had vowed that she would never return, even if it was a matter of life and death. But here she was!

Fifteen years! The town had betrayed her twice, first when she was made to watch suttee at age nine, and then again when she was twenty-two when she married Kumar. Not a single day had passed without her thinking of it. Her nightmares emerged from her memories of this godforsaken town. Dejected, exploited, and almost deranged, she had fled it the second time.

Stopping suddenly, she dropped the duffle bag, pulled out a straw hat and a pair of dark glasses from the bag and put them on. Then she marched on with the bag on her shoulder.

Chapter Fifteen
New High School

When Kamal looked up again, the Neela Nagar School was less than half a mile away. Sunrays burned her scalp, and sweat oozed from her pores. It dripped on her forehead and neck and down the small of her back. She stopped to wipe her forehead and neck with the end of her *chunni* and pat her back. She turned three hundred sixty degrees to absorb the vast empty space around her. It was hot. Her throat was parched. She coughed and closed her eyes. . . .

The flames are scorching her flesh. The sensation moves down her head, neck, back, legs. A crowd of petrified men, fossilized women, and bewildered children are staring at the flaming pyre. She smells burning flesh and smoke. She goes into a fit of cough.

She opened her eyes and thought of a drink of cool water from earthenware *mataka* at the school. Placing the duffle bag on her other shoulder, she thought of Shekhar; her home in Ambayu; the girls; and Veena's incomplete marriage ceremony.

In place of the one-room schoolhouse that Kumud remembered stood a rectangular compound with

151

numerous classrooms facing it. Kumud entered and walked toward the main office. The smell of pencils, books and chalk brought back so many memories.

Students were seated on the floor as teachers lectured and wrote on blackboards. One teacher waved at Kumud. Was that Guruji? She waved back, but upon a closer look, she saw it was just a friendly teacher. She walked through a row of amaltas trees that led to the principal's office.

With each step she felt closer to her childhood. She remembered graduating from sixth grade and telling Guruji that her father had asked for a transfer to Madhya Shahar. His eyes lit up, and he gave her a big smile. 'A door of opportunity has opened for you,' he said. 'You must make full use of it, finish your high school in that city, and then go to college.' That had surprised her. Was he not sad to lose her, 'his most cherished student—his right eye?'

After four years, when she was in tenth grade at Madhya Shahar High School, she heard that Guruji had left Neela Nagar. Where did he go? Why did he leave? No one could tell her.

It has been a long time. Will he recognize me? If he does not, no one else would either. She straightened her shoulders and picked up her pace. When she reached the principal's office, she recognized it as the original one-room school. She saw the wood-framed door. The year she left, it had been freshly painted. Weathered now, its green paint chipping. On both sides of the original one-room school extended more class rooms turning it into a rectangular building, with a playground in the middle.

Kumud stood outside the office door, removed

her hat and glasses, put them back into her bag and waited. The bright sunlight made the interior of the office look darker than it really was. Her eyes adjusted, and she saw a man with his back towards her standing in front of a filing cabinet.

"Guruji?" she called with affectionate respect, her chest heaving.

Instead a younger man turned towards her and asked, "Can I help you, Madam?"

"Oh! I apologize for barging in! Someone told me I'd find Guruji here. I mean, Mr. Shantilal Sharma. Does he still teach?"

"No problem, Madam! But Guruji has retired."

"Are you the principal?"

"Yes, I am! I'm Mohan Chand." He greeted her with folded palms. "Please come in, take a seat!" He pulled out a chair. "May I offer you some tea?"

Kumud shook her head. "May I have a glass of water?" she said.

Mohan rang the bell and a peon brought two glasses of water. Mohan watched as Kumud gulped hers down and quickly ask for another. Mohan said he wasn't thirsty, and she could have his water. She finished drinking the second glass of water and said, "I was very thirsty!"

"Have some tea! A cup of hot tea quenches thirst like nothing else!"

"No, thank you, but I'll remember that," she said.

"Madam, Guruji retired last year," Mohan said. "He is on the education board. Now I sit in his chair, unworthy of this position. No one can replace him."

"Please don't say that. They must have thought

deep and long before they handed over this job to you. Nice to meet you, Mohanji."

"You are generous with your words, Madam!"

"I used to be Guruji's student. Does he still live in the town?"

"Oh, yes! He's actively working towards the inauguration of the high school. You must have seen the new building while on your way here. Did you?"

"A high school building, I heard," she said.

At that one-room school, the highest educational level a student could reach was eighth grade. After that the boys worked in the fields or at the leather factory. The girls helped their mothers at home until a suitable match was found. A few ambitious parents who wanted their sons to study further arranged for them to complete high school in a neighboring town. Some fortunate families, like hers, who could get a job or had relatives in Madhya Shahar, moved there so their children could finish school and attend college.

"The new building is ready. We are preparing for its dedication. Soon, we'll have a proper secondary school where girls and children from Apan Gaon village can also attend."

"Good news! I didn't see it. Where is it?" Kumud was excited at the thought of a high school for girls and children of all castes.

"Behind this building, a five-minute walk from here."

"I must have missed it. I'll certainly attend the ceremony if I'm still here," she said and then asked, "Do you know where Guruji's lives? Do you have his address?"

THE LAST SUTTEE

"You won't be able to find his house even if I give you his address. There are no house numbers here. Everyone knows where everyone else lives—we are five thousand people in all. His home is about a fifteen-minute walk from here. I'll ask my peon to take you," Mohan Chand said, walking out of the office to summon him.

The peon, a slim young man in worn pajamas and kurta, was watering morning glory creepers outside the principal's office. Mohan Chand instructed him to accompany Kumud to Guruji's house and to carry her bag. He picked up the duffle bag, put it on his back, and led her outside the school gate.

Chapter Sixteen
Guruji

Kumud lagged behind the young man as he sped through the maze of lanes; she was simultaneously nervous and excited. He turned left, then right, but she did not recognize any of the houses. The lanes seemed wider than she remembered. When she asked the peon why nothing looked familiar, he explained that her family had lived in the older part of town; this neighborhood had been built after she left. Yet the color of the houses had not changed. They were painted blue, the color extracted from indigo plants locally grown and harvested. The color of the newer houses, with varnished wooden doors and windows, was still blue, which linked them with the old parts of the town. The peon stopped in front of a house with a painted red door. "Guruji lives here," he said.

"Are you sure?"

"Yes, he is the only one who has a red door!"

Kumud looked to her left and right. There was no way she would have found the house on her own. She thanked the young man and offered him a ten-rupee note. He took it quickly, nodded with a *namaskar*, and left.

Kumud knocked nervously, and a middle-aged woman opened the door.

"May I help you?" Dressed in a sari, she examined Kumud from head to toe.

"Is this Guruji's home?"

"Yes, it is! Who are you? How can I help you?"

"My name is Kumud Kuthiyala. I have travelled here from Ambayu to see Guruji."

"How did you find us?"

"I went to the school. Mr. Mohan Chand, the principal, sent an escort with me."

"Does Guruji know you are coming?"

Was she Guruji's wife? She hesitated to ask. If she were, she would know her husband had telephoned her. She seemed to have no idea who Kumud was.

"I was his student a long time ago. I got a telephone call from Guruji summoning me to Neela Nagar."

"He's had a busy morning and is taking a nap," she said politely. "Would you like to wait?"

"I'm sorry, I was unable to get in touch," Kumud said.

"I'm Shyamli, Guruji's wife. Please come in and make yourself comfortable. It is extremely hot outside!" Shyamli stepped sideways to let Kumud into the house, then quickly shut the door.

Inside, Kumud took off her sandals on the front verandah. The cement floor felt cool against the soles of her feet. When her eyes adjusted to the light, a staircase between two doors that faced the entrance became visible. She followed Shyamli into a room on the right. The four chairs and a sofa were set with cushions decorated with mirror-work. These were arranged around a table that was also covered with mirror-work cloth.

"You look hot and tired. What would you like to drink, a glass of cold water or a cup of tea?" Shyamli said.

"Tea, please!" she said, telling Shyamli how the school principal had said that 'nothing quenches thirst like a cup of hot tea.'

Shyamli smiled, nodded, and went to boil water. When she returned, she said, "That's what they believe here. But in Calcutta, they say there is nothing like water to quench your thirst."

"Are you from. . . .

"Do we have a guest, Shamu?" A familiar voice interrupted them from the other room.

"Come and see for yourself," his wife said and flashed Kumud a smile.

Hearing his voice made Kumud nervous. What would he say when he saw her? He had called her about the suttee, but would he recognize her?

"*Namaskar*, Madam," Guruji said to Kumud. He doffed his spectacles, cleaned them, sat down opposite her, and put them back on. His calming voice warmed her heart.

"Namaste, Guruji! You don't remember me. I was your pupil from first to sixth grade many years ago!"

"What is your name, child?"

"Kumud."

"Kumud? That sounds familiar." Kumud suddenly realized he must not be the one who had called her. Then who? Her heart raced, but she remained calm.

"Kumud Kuthiyala. When I was in sixth grade, my father got himself transferred to Madhya Shahar. When I gave you the news, you were happy. Your being happy about my leaving had made me sad. Do you remember?"

She could see that Guruji was struggling to remember.

"You came to my home to tutor me in math. You wondered how someone could be brilliant in history and geography and so dull in math... remember?" She looked hard at him, hoping he would recall something.

He gazed intently at her with a faint look of recognition, and then a look of pleasant surprise crossed his face. "Kumud! Yes, yes. Mr. Kuthiyala was transferred to Madhya Shahar. Your parents were happy, mainly so you could complete your secondary school education! Later, you went to Madhya Shahar University, didn't you?"

"Yes, that is correct. I finished my degree in English Literature," she said proudly.

"Oh! English! I recall everything now. How could I forget you?"

"Thank you, Guruji!" she said, bending to touch his feet as a gesture of respect.

"*Areee beti!* Oh child!" He said and patted her head.

She sat again, and the phone call returned to her mind.

"I have high regard for parents who make the extra effort to educate their children. In your case, it was your father who did not mind leaving and resettling in an unfamiliar town so his daughter could study further. Many years ago, now I recall, when I needed an example to illustrate the significance of the parents' role in their children's education, I narrated them your story. Tell me, what do you do? Where do you live? What brought you here?"

"I live in Ambayu and manage an orphanage now. Your phone call brought me here."

"My phone call? What phone call? I did not call you."

"You didn't? Then someone pretending to be you did. I feel like a fool now!"

"Why would someone call you using my name?"

"I don't know! Three days ago, someone pretending to be you called."

"What was the reason for the call?"

"He said, 'Terror is upon our town! A girl whose husband is critically ill has decided to commit suttee if he dies. You must come at once if you want to stop it from happening this time.'"

"I don't know anything about that. What made him think there was going to be a suttee?" Guruji asked, confused but concerned.

"Is a man in town on his deathbed? Perhaps his wife has decided to commit suttee." Kumud asked.

"I haven't heard of anyone being critically ill, but the town isn't as intimate as it used to be. Is that why you are here? There has not been a *suttee* in this town since that of the unfortunate Saubhagya. And I remember your mother telling me how deeply that affected you."

"But if it was not you, Guruji, then who would call me? How did this person know my telephone number?"

"Obviously, there is someone else in town who knows your feelings about this, but I can't think of who it would be."

"We don't have telephones here. Perhaps someone from a close by town called?" Shyamli wondered.

They brainstormed about who it might be, but could think of no one. Guruji said, "I will talk to the Elders in the morning; they are responsible for the town's affairs. They settle disputes. Do you remember?"

"Yes, I remember *Panchayat*, comprised of the five Elders." Kumud said.

"They are not necessarily wise or widely respected. The current head of the *Panchayat* in this town is Umraodeo, their youngest member. And the oldest is Jabbar Singh."

"In the morning, they may not be at their usual meeting place," Shyamli said.

"At least one of them is always there," Guruji said.

"How can this town let such a thing happen?" Kumud asked.

"We are remote, closed to outside influences and modernization. We are trying to change that," Shyamli said.

"There is God, glory, and gold in the ritual of suttee!" Guruji said. "If that telephone call has any basis, some townspeople and even a couple of the Elders, including the senior priest at the temple, would grab at the rare opportunity."

"If the news gets out, thousands of pilgrims and journalists will come here," Shyamli said. "Do you know that after Saubhagya's suttee, three hundred thousand pilgrims from around the country came to this town to 'pay their respects'? For them the suttee is tested by the god of fire and gets transformed into a goddess of truth, *sat*—pure, peerless, and powerful."

"What can we do? The town's passion rises when there is a possibility of a human transmuting to a deity, just like it did with Sau Massi," Kumud said. "And as it did with Narayani Satimata three hundred years before her," she added, recounting what she had learned from Taxiwalla.

"To the credit of Taxiwalla and those like him, their faith is not feigned," said Shyamli. "It is real. Thousands come to the temple. They believe. Gold or glory is not the first thing on their minds, it may be on the minds of the greedy half of Neela Nagar, but many townspeople have pure belief in the miracle and mystery of the goddess. They ask for boons and blessings."

"Their faith is real, I agree, but it is blind. As long as it is confined to worship and prayer, there is no harm. But when it turns into destroying life, it is blindness, and a crime. Shouldn't we open our eyes and ask why do we treat our women the way we do," Kumud said, louder than she intended.

"Change is not possible until our mindset changes," Guruji said pensively, as if he had thought about this many times before. "The mindset that causes such practices is embedded in the belief that women are manageable under a man's command—father, brother, husband or son. An unmarried girl or widow roaming freely instills a deep-seated fear. When this fear remains unexamined, it turns to hatred.

"When a man dies young, his unguarded widow becomes a threat to her husband's family. They are afraid they may not be able to control her urges. They are afraid her actions could result in chaos," Guruji added.

"When will this practice stop? How can we stop it?" Kumud asked.

"When people begin to think as individuals and not as a mob. . .."

"Sorry to interrupt," Shyamli said, "but the sun is about to set. Will you stay for dinner, Kumud?"

"I don't want to impose," Kumud said, standing. "Would you please direct me to the closest *sarai*, a traveler's inn? I have already taken too much of your time. I should leave now."

"Let me think," Guruji said rubbing, his forehead. "A sarai is not safe for a single woman."

"What are you saying, Guruji?" Shyamli said. She called her husband Guruji, meaning respected teacher, as she had been his student many years ego.

"How can we think of letting her go? You have come all the way from Ambayu; you are staying with us!"

Guruji added, "Shamu is right. It's not a good idea to stay alone in a sarai."

"Are you sure?"

"Yes, we are sure. You are on a mission, and we would like to help," Shyamli said.

"I feel like I would be intruding."

"Now you are talking like a person from Ambayu. We've an extra room upstairs. No intrusion," Shyamli said.

"We'd welcome your company," Guruji nodded.

"You two talk. I'll see to dinner," Shyamli said, as she exited into the kitchen.

Kumud realized that since leaving Ambayu she had done nothing but listen to advocates and critics talk about the suttee ritual. She had refreshed her understanding of the tradition, but what was she going to do if the young woman decides to die. She felt uneasy.

"One would think since suttee is against the law, people would fear imprisonment," Guruji mused.

"Kumud, I can't imagine watching a suttee while it was happening," Shyamli shouted from the kitchen. She came close to Kumud, and placing her hand on Kumud's shoulder said, "How horrifying it must have been for you!"

"Left me scarred for life," Kumud said looking up at her.

"We need to strategize," Shyamli said as she returned to the kitchen.

Kumud turned to her husband. "What should we do, Guruji?"

"I don't know. What can one do in a short period of time? Mindsets only change if a society is educated and interacts with outsiders. In Neela Nagar no one leaves and no one comes in except at festival times," he said, then added. "You left, and I did, too."

"Why did you return, Guruji?"

"I hoped to bring about change. Changing the attitude of a community takes time. I returned to build a school and a library for boys and girls. I placed my hope in the future generations of the town and village. I want them to choose change. Besides, this is my ancestral town. Nature has blessed it with a range of hills, the River Tapasya, and vast land, but we have blemished it with our evil ways."

"What are you thinking?" Guruji asked Kumud.

"I'm thinking about my girls at the orphanage! Just like you, I tell them that if they get educated, they will have the freedom to choose the kind of life they want. Education will give them the ability to think on several levels, and they will be comparatively free to make their own decisions. If this unknown young woman is widowed and chooses to live after her husband's death, she can demand the inheritance due her and move on with her life. Most widows don't even know they have a right to property." She stopped looked at Guruji and said,

"But you must already know this."

"Go on," said Guruji.

"An idea just came to me, Guruji. I think I should meet the town widows. I can't go knocking doors and asking people if a widow lives there but I can talk to them at the temple. Is there a day or time when they meet at the Narayani Temple?"

"But how would meeting them solve your problem?"

"I want to know about their lives, their concerns, desires, thoughts. I want to ask them about suttee, and hope that they will open up to me."

"That's a good idea. Perhaps they will know something about this young girl. There is no fixed time when the widows meet, but there are always some seated along a long corridor facing suttee shrines. At the Narayani Temple you'll recognize them in their indigo clothing."

"I know, thank you!"

"Why don't you go to the temple in the morning while I find out from the Elders if there is a young man critically ill."

Shyamli left vegetables and dal simmering in the

kitchen and rejoined the conversation. "He is such a doer. It is the reason I fell in love with him," she said.

"She'll be teaching at the new school," Guruji proudly said to Kumud.

"That's nice!" Kumud said.

"What about the local police? If this is true, can they help us in this regard?" Shyamli asked.

"Their thinking is no different from most of the townspeople. I experienced that first hand. When I heard about Saubhagya's intention to commit suttee, I called the chief of police. I urged him to take some action. At first, he dismissed me, and when he finally sent a handful of policemen, it was too late. One of the policeman who arrived at the suttee site, asked one witness if he had seen a woman burning! Afraid of the authority, he denied it, and the policeman reported that he found no witnesses to corroborate that Saubhagya's suttee actually took place," Guruji said.

"I remember my parents telling me that within two days national and international journalists rushed to this town. And thousands of people from the surrounding villages and towns had come to witness the ritual," Kumud said.

"Yes, when the news leaked, central government authorities came to investigate. All the male members of Saubhagya's family were charged with conspiring to commit murder. They were held for a while and then released. But that's about it. In my opinion, they were part of the conspiracy. They glorified her suttee by their silence and inaction." Guruji was getting emotional.

"But no one from the community spoke up. They were all murderers!" Kumud said.

"Not all families condone suttee, child. Narayani Temple has a sign condemning any celebration of the suttee ritual. In an effort to understand the landlords' point of view, I recall how, after independence, the government stole land from the landowners. Without the land, they lost their identity and wealth. Saubhagya's suttee gave them a tremendous moral and economic boost. It uplifted their place in society.

"The trust of Narayani Temple overflows with donations of the business men who leave town but are goddess' dedicated devotees. They return as pilgrims for her annual celebrations and visit local suttee sites," Guruji said.

"The open secret is that the women no longer have the courage to commit suttee," explained Shyamli. "In olden times, when a widow committed suttee, her family gained honor and respect and a shrine was built on the site where the ritual was enacted. Pilgrims circumambulating the town visiting the shrines generated a lot of income. That no longer works."

The room became quiet. An effect has a cause, Kumud thought. The cause may be irrational, unreasonable, or baseless, but its effect is real.

Chapter Seventeen
Terror in the Field

After breakfast the next morning, Kumud dressed in her lemon kurta, embroidered with pomegranate boughs, waited for Shyamli to draw her a map to the temple. Kumud was good with verbal instructions but Shyamli insisted upon her taking a shortcut and making certain she did not get lost. The walk through the streets was four miles; through the moong and barley fields was half that.

"As soon as you cross the fields, the Narayani Temple will be in front of you," Shyamli said, handing Kumud the map with icons of her home, the temple and the school.

Kumud thanked her and tucked the paper into a small shoulder bag hanging around her neck.

Shyamli saw the cloudy sky and said, "Hope it doesn't rain."

"I don't think it will. Besides, I like cloudy weather better," Kumud said. She bid her goodbye and left with great anticipation.

The temple was in the opposite direction of the

school, away from the zigzagging lanes she had walked the previous day. For the first half of her walk sunlight filtered through the cloudy sky. Turning right, she saw expansive barley and moong fields.

The far end of the fields was hidden behind the mist. At the edge of the fields grew *kikar* trees and around their trunks, red *rohira* flowers. A flock of crows perched on the upper branches of the trees was watching Kumud's every move. She headed toward the narrow path through two fields. The ground was uneven, and she was glad she wore sneakers instead of sandals, as Amrita had advised. A half mile in, the narrow path disappeared. She wrapped the chunni around her neck like a short scarf and with both hands separated the stalks laden with moong pods. Her arms stretched with each step, holding the stalks firmly apart. The clouds grew denser and darker, and soon she heard the pitter-patter of drizzle on the stalks.

The moisture intensified the scent of the moong crop. The farther she walked, the heavier the stalks became, and the more difficult it was to push through. The rough pods and leaves irritated her face, neck, and arms. Then rain thundered down. The space between the crowded stalks was airless, and she quickened her pace. Before long she hit a dead end and couldn't turn left or right. Willy-nilly, she ran through the stalks. When she stopped to breathe, something slithered across her sneakers. She screamed, turned abruptly, and ran. *I will never get out of this maze!* Panicked and panting, she tried pulling out the beanstalks as she went. That didn't work, so she continued pushing them down and crushing them with her feet. Suddenly, she found herself at the edge of the field. Not too far, the magnificent temple steeple peeked through the mist.

Able to breathe again, she sighed and gently pressed the bruises and cuts with a handkerchief. Not a soul was in sight.

She did not remember stepping inside this place before and even now had no desire to go in. But Guruji had a point. 'A Satimata devotee may know something about a possible suttee."

Why would someone disclose a secret to stranger? An outsider?

Her bruises throbbed as she ascended the stone steps and entered the enormous front gate of the temple. On the side walls of the covered passage leading to the main temple were placards with inlaid letters:

A Set of Thirteen Suttee Memorial Mounds: 1912
Narayani Temple Began: 1917 Completed: 1936
Propagating Suttee Ritual is Against the Law.

The third line, in red, seemed to have been recently added.

Outside the shoe room she unlaced her sneakers and handed them to an attendant. She trembled at the thought of an animal slithering over them. The marble cooled her soles as she walked. She stopped at a water spigot to wash the blood smeared on her forearms and the back of her hands. With cupped hands, she drank water to soothe her parched throat, then splashed it on her face and arms to cool the burning sensation.

The temple, Guruji had said last night, was the only major monument in Neela Nagar. Being a holy place made it even more important. The marble structure was five stories tall. Four courtyards surrounded the central building. On the ground floor against the eastern wall, were twelve canopied suttee shrines extending in a row. Beyond the edge of the western courtyard was lodging for the pilgrims.

Once a year, Neela Nagar was replete with pilgrims. It was their money that had financed the buildings and transformed Narayani Satimata's plain mound into a marble temple complex. The devotees who had made a minimum donation could find their names on the brick walks leading to the various buildings. But the names of the wealthy donors, with businesses in foreign countries, were etched into the marble slabs of the temple's assembly hall.

Somewhat steadied now, Kumud stepped inside the hall. The devotees sat facing the sanctum sanctorum, the purest and the innermost part of the sacred complex. Instead of an image inside the sanctum, a trident was enshrined, a sign of Narayani Satimata, the symbol of feminine power, *Shakti*. Devotees sat in lotus postures, either alone or in twos or threes, their hands folded in their laps or palms resting on their knees. Some had closed their eyes. The aroma of marigolds and incense sticks scented the space.

Oleographs of popular mythological scenes decorated the sidewalls. On the right center was an oleograph of Narayani Satimata engulfed in flames with her husband's head in her lap. From the sky peeked Mahadevi, the Great Goddess, with her right palm emitting rays of light that blessed the burning pyre. A print of the lord Shiva and the goddess Sati flanked the central image. On the opposite wall, twelve pen drawings delineated the events leading up to the death of Narayani Satimata's husband, her self-immolation, the guard building the mound over their ashes, and subsequently the construction of the present marble temple.

Kumud walked at a snail's pace towards the sanctum. Instead of feeling sanctified her muscles tightened, her skin tingled with suppressed rage. Was it an intrinsic reaction of her resistance towards the images and messages that surrounded her? Intellectually all this was familiar; she had studied and researched it. But emotionally she had not exposed herself to such surroundings before. The horrific memories slithering under the scab of her psychic wound had been triggered.

Looking around, she thought there is nothing new to see. No one to communicate with the sensations she was experiencing. She turned to leave when her attention shifted to a dignified middle-aged woman dressed in salwar-kameez. Her head was covered with a dupatta. She looked different from Neela Nagar women. Her facial features and skin complexion seemed to suggest that she was from northern India, possibly Punjab. The woman walked purposefully and stood facing the sanctum, her hands folded and her eyes closed. Kumud watched her pray.

After a few minutes, the woman bowed and opened her eyes. She glanced at Kumud, who was watching her. She smiled and turned to circumambulate the sanctum. Kumud followed as she circumambulated three times, as per ritual. The woman continued her walk toward the covered corridor where there was a gallery of twelve suttee shrines. She seemed to be following a set course taken by pilgrims.

The corridor was open to the courtyard and gardens. On the right were the heavily decorated silver doors of the twelve suttee shrines. Behind each door was visible the mound built over each suttee's buried ashes. The doors were kept open for the pilgrims to view the interior. These women who had become suttees were from Marwari families and exemplified Narayani Satimata's self-immolation.

Sitting against the pillars facing the suttee shrines, Kumud spotted several women wearing indigo clothing. A group of four were seated in a circle. They were of different ages. The elderly woman had her eyes closed in prayer. Another was absorbed in turning the beads of her rosary. Two more women, one young and other middle aged, were conversing softly. Kumud introduced herself as a writer and asked if she could sit with them. They welcomed her but said that they were about to leave for their respective homes. She said she had a few questions to ask. Would they mind answering them? They said they would be happy to answer whatever she wanted to know.

How was a widow's life different from a married woman's? What did they think about suttee? What purpose did the ritual serve? The youngest among them was first to answer. She said it was kind of an insurance that a wife would take good care of her husband's health, that she would not yield to the sexual advances of another man after his death, and thus disgrace her dead husband and his family.

Emboldened by what the young woman had said, the middle-aged woman added that men were possessive. Not only did their husbands want the wives to serve them when they were alive, but also to follow them in death.

"Obviously, you don't think men consciously think this way," Kumud said.

"If someone had courage to ask them, they would flatly deny it," said the young one. "The tradition is so internalized that it passes mindlessly through generations. Our community has such beliefs. This is our tradition. Outsiders just know about the tradition of suttee but people of Neela Nagar have experienced it recently. We honor it and keep the tradition alive."

"Most men love their wives. They don't talk about it. They rather not think about it." Another woman added. "If they would see their wives committing suttee such men may try to save them."

"The fact is no one has courage to do it. But who knows if we had become suttee we would have been at a better place." the senior most woman said, standing to leave.

"Perhaps unconscious thoughts color the whole community's thinking process," Kumud said. Finally, she asked, "Do you think these days if a woman becomes a widow she would commit suttee?"

"God forbid! No one deserves to live the life of a widow. On the other hand, who has courage to commit suttee? But why do you ask?"

"I may have heard wrong but is there a man in the town who is critically sick and may die?"

"We haven't heard anything." They said in unison looking at each other.

"One has to die someday why not die with dignity and honor and live happily in heaven." The one who had been quiet so far interjected. "What is there to live for?"

They seemed to agree. With their heads bent they stood to leave. Kumud thanked them for their time. She did not find a consensus this way or that way. They agreed about the fear of dying a painful death. They also doubted that by not committing suttee they might have forfeited their chance of a better life.

Kumud spotted the woman she had followed inside the temple. She was sitting in contemplation on a bench under a tree. Who was she? Kumud wondered. She carried herself as someone different, someone important. Kumud wanted to talk to her. Perhaps she had heard about the impending suttee. Should she ask her? What sort of question would she ask? Perhaps she could say she was doing research as she had told the widows, and ask her views about the temple, suttee, and the treatment of widows in Neela Nagar?

The woman stood to return to the main temple. She paced the corridor, unaware that Kumud was following her.

At the shoe stand, the woman slipped on her sandals while Kumud put on her sneakers.

Watching Kumud tie her laces, the woman asked, "What happened to your face and arms?"

Kumud explained how she had taken a shortcut through the fields to the temple.

"So, sorry to hear that! You must use turmeric ointment as soon as you reach home." She gently touched the smeared blood on her arm.

"You poor thing! You are hurt, and still you visited the temple, like an ardent believer."

"No, no, nothing like that," Kumud said without thinking. "But I'm glad I followed you. If I hadn't, I might have missed important sections of the temple."

"Oh, this is your first time to the temple. Are you new in town?"

"Yes. Visiting Guruji."

"Guruji and Shyamli. What a nice couple!" The woman smiled. Then she added, "I feel I've seen you somewhere."

"Really? I don't know where you could have seen me," said Kumud.

"You are Kumud Kuthiyala. Aren't you?" An expression of pleasure crossed the woman's face.

Kumud was shocked. "Yes, I am! How did you know?"

"I've been thinking about you for quite some time. And here you are!" she said enthusiastically. "I recently read your book. Your picture is on its back cover."

"Book? You mean the pamphlet?"

"Same thing. I loved it!"

"Oh, thank you!"

"An honor to have met you! I'm Nisha Umraodeo, the wife of one of the town Elders."

Kumud was stunned. She couldn't take her eyes off of Nisha Umraodeo's face. This was indeed a meaningful coincidence.

Chapter Eighteen
Guruji's Story

When Guruji was running his one-room school he had a mission. It was to transform the one-room school into an all-in-one government-certified primary, middle, and high school. If he was to fulfill his life's mission Shantilal Sharma knew that he needed an advanced degree and more teaching experience. He applied to several universities throughout the country, and after six months of restless waiting was admitted to a master's program at the University of Calcutta, West Bengal. He left Neela Nagar. Five years later, when he returned he not only had a master's degree in education but also a doctoral degree in Indian History. And a Bengali wife. He introduced her to his town, Neela Nagar and reacquainted himself with it.

Even as a young man, Shantilal was an idealist who dedicated his life to educating those who were forbidden to better themselves through learning. He had been tutored up to eighth grade by the only learned man in Neela Nagar. After that grade, there was no place in the town to study. His parents were too poor to send him

179

elsewhere. The only learned man suggested they send their son away to a city to study. That idea baffled his parents. No one in their family had left Neela Nagar for an education. They shook their heads in wonder at the teacher's suggestion.

Initially Shantilal's parents said no, for the suggestion was unusual and they had no money to support his education. But the child prodigy changed their mind. Shantilal said he would appear for a scholarship examination, being offered by the University of Madhya Shahar, to earn his tuition, lodging, and boarding. If he failed, he would return home. And if he succeeded he will stay back. His parents found the argument satisfactory, and he traveled to Madhya Shahar for the exam.

Shantilal not only earned the scholarship but also ranked first in the state. He graduated from Madhya Shahar high school and attended the University on scholarship. His only dream was to return to his town to reopen and expand his school so that it would become a beacon of education in Neela Nagar and Apna Gaon. Eventually he wanted to admit *all* children to his school, including girls and Dalits, the untouchables.

When he started a one-room school in his home; initially no child came to learn. But he did not give up. Gradually some boys joined his private tutorials. Then a girl named Kumud Kuthiyala began to attend. Her regular attendance encouraged Shantilal and helped him believe that he was on the right path.

The primary school worked well for many years, until Shantilal realized that if he hoped to extend to a middle and high school he needed a degree in education.

THE LAST SUTTEE

He joined the university in Calcutta.

He rented a room at a reasonable price from a kind old couple that included breakfast and dinner. The house was as quiet as a library, and he focused on his work undisturbed. He skipped lunch, curbing his hunger with tea the landlady provided.

He lived meagerly for two years, until he acquired his master's degree in education. Soon he was hired as a teaching assistant for two courses, Indian History and World Mythology. One class was held at noon and the other in the evening. In-between classes Shantilal studied. He also helped professors by tutoring students and correcting exams. The pay was minimal.

A young woman in his mythology course, Shyamli Sengupta, intrigued him. Like him, she was older than her classmates. She never missed a class and was always attentive. On the first test, she received the highest score, and the professor remarked on her paper, "most thoughtful."

On the last day of the class, Shyamli, who regularly attended his tutoring sessions, asked Shantilal if she could bring her five-year-old sister, Archana, to the class. She assured him that her sister would be quiet. On the day she came, Shantilal approached Shyamli and her sister and handed the girl a children's storybook and a drawing book with a box of crayons to keep her occupied while he taught. Shyamli was touched by Shantilal's thoughtfulness.

When the class was over, Shyamli thanked the teaching assistant for his generosity. Shantilala asked why their mother wasn't caring for the young girl, Shyamli hesitated. He waited, gazed honorably at her. Because of the sincerity of his question, she could no longer hide the truth. She confessed that the girl was not her sister, but her child. Usually her mother took care of the child, but she was sick and unable to look after her.

"Where do you and your husband live?" he asked.

"I am not married. I do not have a husband," she said haltingly.

"What!" he said, sitting back on the chair, "Why? How?"

"It is a long story."

"What happened? Tell me. . . . Why don't you take a seat?"

Shayamli sat at the edge of the chair keeping her arm around the girl. She said, "I was entangled in a bad relationship during my first year of college. I made a terrible mistake, and he called me impure and immoral. When I told him he was the father, he beat me and left me to fend for myself." Shyamli eyes welled, but she did not cry. "It took me six years to get back on my feet and return to college to complete my degree. I couldn't have done it without my mother's encouragement. With her support and love I could reclaim my life. My child thinks my mother is her mother."

Shantilal was dumbstruck.

"Thank you for sharing, Shyamli! I have noticed your dedication. You are at the top of your class and yet sit quietly by yourself. You have done well!"

Shyamli's mother brought her granddaughter, Archana, to watch Shyamli's graduation ceremony. Shyamli was awarded a BA in Indian Mythology. Meanwhile Shantilal had begun working for his doctoral degree. They began meeting outside the classroom.

When he met her mother, she liked him instantly. And when Shantilal received his doctorate in Education, the two were married.

Shyamli was familiar with Shantilal's mission, to remove darkness and ignorance in his town. She, too, valued education and promised to support him wholeheartedly. It was hard for her to leave her daughter and mother, but she truly loved Shantilal. Broken-hearted at the thought of leaving her daughter and mother and apprehensive about moving to an unfamiliar town, she did not know what to do. But at the same time she did not want to uproot the two women she loved. After much debate, they decided it would be best if Archana stayed with her grandmother, and visited Shyamli once a year.

Shyamli was inspired by Shantilal's belief that anything could be achieved if you devoted your heart and mind to it, and that big changes begin with small steps. His mission became her vision. They settled down in the house where Kumud had found them, and Shantilal worked hard to make his dream a reality.

Only after Shantilal had closed his one-room school and left for further study did some of the more progressive families of Neela Nagar pay attention to his efforts of educating their children. When he returned from Calcutta and reopened the school, many boys came to attend. Word of mouth soon brought many more. Shantilal came to be known as "Guruji." Years ago, his first and only girl student had been Kumud; with his second attempt, more girls wanted to attend.

Shantilal hired a second teacher from Madhya Shahar. His vision of the school included *all* children. He needed funds, so he wrote letters to the legislators, applied for loans from the state government, and invited politicians to raise money. But his effort bore little fruit. If he could persuade high caste families to send their sons and daughters to school, perhaps that might make rich landlords provide funds. Guruji was convinced that townspeople would eventually change their minds and he would be able to convince politicians and officials of the importance of education for all.

He travelled to Madhya Shahar to meet with influential people and members of the State School Board to acquire funds in hopes of expanding education to a high school. He carried his mission's goals to a few prominent landlords in Neela Nagar and ministers in Madhya Shahar. He asked hard questions and demanded their input. Where did they stand on the issue of Neela Nagar's progress? What steps were being taken to make basic education available in one of the remotest towns in the country? People from the town and village had paid enough taxes for chili farms and the leather factories. If they did not take actions and bring about some change, he intended to take his grievances to the capital city, New Delhi. When Shantilal finished speaking, he heard their snickers, but then one official cleared her throat and the room grew silent.

The crust of silence was broken by a gentle voice of Manorama Gupta. "You know, Dr. Sharma, I have heard about you. You have rich credentials and philanthropic ideals. A person like you deserves our support and respect," the woman said. "New Delhi will not solve your problems. Things move at a snail's pace there. But you make a valid point. So, this is what I say. If you promise to make a high school that is open to girls and boys of *all* castes from Neela Nagar and Apna Gaon, I'll make sure you get the necessary funds to construct your building."

Heads turned in surprise.

"Would you take responsibility for overseeing its construction, and once it is ready, be on its board?" she asked.

Shantilal Sharma had waited half his life for this opportunity. It did not take long for him to say yes.

"In that case, you have a lot of papers to sign," the woman said, tapping on a pile of paper on the table. She had already had the paperwork for him to sign. He was giddy with delight.

He knew the townspeople had a deep-rooted fear of western education, which they believed uprooted tradition and turned youth rebellious, and he worked hard to change their thinking. The landlords as well as shopkeepers and farmers wanted their sons to manage land, plough fields, mind the shops, and learn their family crafts. In fact, they thought western education to be the work of the devil.

While the Neela Nagar Middle School building was under construction, Shantilal tutored the children of Apna Gaon. He also went from door to door, talking to individual families about the benefits of education. He pointed out the difference between the successes of farmers who had completed their school certificate and those who had never stepped inside the school. Initially he advocated for a middle school, but once that goal was achieved, he talked about the benefits of a high school in friendly chats, discussions, and meetings. People loved him for his humility, his intellectual achievements, and his dedication. Even those who believed that modern education corrupted minds eventually agreed that his return to Neela Nagar somehow benefited the town. They admired his Bengali wife, who also was devoted to his mission.

When girls from Neela Nagar attended his school, he talked to them about Kumud. The girls' parents admired Guruji. Like Kumud, these girls wanted to learn and eventually persuaded their parents to look favorably on their education. With so many boys and girls, the school was moved from his home to a two-story structure with ten rooms.

But when Guruji suggested he open his school to the children of Apna Gaon, at first he received verbal and written threats from the town's older generation and three of the five Elders.

Guruji wanted his students to learn English, math, and sciences, then leave for high education in other towns or cities. He wanted his students to become self-confident adults and carry their own beacon of light.

Despite opposition from some parents, *all* the boys volunteered to do odd jobs for the school after school hours. On festival days such as Independence Day, Inspection Day or Graduation day, they cleaned the premises, especially the latrine tents, sprinkling lime in and around the tents and drains.

Some of his students who graduated from middle school established a foundation in Madhya Shahar to fight caste and gender discrimination. The state government also paved the roads and brought water and electricity to the town and village as a result of Guruji's alliances with politicians and local families who shared his vision.

By the time Guruji talked about his retirement, there were a dozen teachers at the elementary and middle school, and discussions were under way about the construction and management of the new high school.

Chapter Nineteen

Dreams

Finding Kumud at the door with scratched face and arms alarmed Shyamli. She gasped, "O Bhagwan! What happened? Who did this to you? I should not have let you go alone! Come in." She held Kumud's hand and closed the door behind her.

"Nobody did this to me."

"Here! Lie down, I will apply turmeric to them. We don't want them getting infected!"

"They look worse than they are, Shyamliji" Kumud said, touched by her concern.

"You should not have washed them; they will take longer to heal."

Kumud followed her to the kitchen. She sat on a chair while Shyamli blew air on the worst wounds around her wrists and the backs of her hands. She swabbed them with alcohol and sealed them with a turmeric and mustard oil salve.

"What happened?"

"I got confused while crossing the fields and panicked. I lost my way."

Kumud was hurt more than she realized. Her wounds throbbed. Shyamli gave her a pain pill and encouraged her to lie down and covered her with a white muslin sheet. Kumud was soon sound asleep.

She is standing outside the imposing gate of a mansion, looking up at the building. Gingerly she takes a few small steps, then courageously approaches the guard in a beige suit and red turban.

Instead of stopping her, he salutes and opens the iron gate for her. Ignoring him, she walks up the path to the home's main entrance. The door is open, and she enters a lavishly decorated room. A puny man is seated on a throne-like mahogany chair upholstered in green velvet. He is dressed in white shirt and churidaar and a red and yellow tie-dyed turban.

"Are you the Elder?"

"Yes, I am! Who are you?"

"I'm Kumud Kuthiyala!"

"What do you want?"

"You don't have anything you can give me. I simply want you to know that you are not the wise elder you think you are. You're a manifestation of Ravana, the demon of evil and destruction! In your presence blossoms shrivel! You turn healthy people into ashes! Aren't you ashamed of yourself? Don't you ever feel guilty?"

She watches as he grows ten heads and says, "You must be out of your mind! Otherwise you wouldn't dare speak to me this way! I am a Thakur! Everyone is expected to bow down to me in reverence. Gurkha! Escort this nobody outside the compound!" He stands as straight as a victory stone pillar, devoid of emotions, cold.

Gurkha enters and holds Kumud's arm. She jerks his hand away and says, "Not before I have my say. You allow female feticide, you let women burn—as if these were rites of passage. Under your watch, widows live with cattle! Where is your conscience? Are you blind? Do you see nothing?"

"You are right, Kumud Kuthiyala! I have ten heads but I can't see a thing."

"Are you alive or dead?"

"I am petrified in a time frame."

Kumud moves closer and waves her hand in front of the Elder's eyes. He doesn't blink. She touches his shoulder and watches his body, the throne, his footstool, everything turn to ash.

Kumud screamed and sat up.

Shyamli came running and gently patted her head, "A bad dream? What was so frightening?"

"Where am I?" Kumud said, coming out of the chimera. She looked at Shyamli and remembered where she was and why she had come.

"Would you like some water?"

Kumud felt out of it. She put her head back and said, "I'd like to lie down a little more, please." She closed her eyes. In no time, she was asleep.

With the last whistle, the train hisses and thunders, its wheels whirl and shunt. A girl holding a ceramic object shoves her hand through the window of the train compartment where Kumud is seated. She can't see the girl's face, but the object, a planter with a beautifully crafted miniature orange tree, glistens. The green leaves and orange spheres glow in the light.

"Please, Madam, cultivate this! Help it grow!" a female voice says, but the girl's lips are not moving. She is about to let go of the plant.

"But it is made out of clay and wax. How can I instill life into it?" Kumud says, grabbing the top of the tree lest it fall and break. The sharp edges of the leaves jab her fingers.

"You'll know how, you will!" the girl says and disappears

from the window.

Kumud finds herself holding the plant in her left palm and touching the smooth surface of an orange. The sensation spurs her to hold the fruit-laden plant with reverence. She catches a whiff of orange scent. The responsibility of cultivating a non-living thing feels heavy on her heart. How can she dig a stream in the desert?

She woke to a burning sensation on her wrists and forearms.

Shyamli was back with a bowl of fresh turmeric paste.

"I'm so sorry! This is not what you had come here for!"

"Shyamliji, my dreams feel so real. I wonder if they are trying to tell me something." She sat up.

"Vivid dreams reflect your anxieties, fears, future endeavors. Who knows what they mean!" Shyamli patted her head like her mother. Tenderly, she smoothed paste on her bruised skin as Kumud narrated her dreams.

Guruji returned home in a bad mood. He went straight to his room and changed into a khadi pajama and kurta. Settling on a woven bamboo chair in the drawing room, he watched his wife closely as she prepared the evening meal. Then he opened a newspaper. But before beginning to read, he placed the paper on his lap and asked his wife, "Where is Kumud? Did she have any success at the temple?"

"Did *you* find anything?"

"Did she?"

"She got lost in the fields and hurt herself."

"Injured herself? How?" Guruji was alarmed.

"She missed the trail that runs through the fields

and found herself in a tangled web of stalks—a fully ripened harvest can turn into a baffling maze."

"How bad are her cuts?" He sounded worried.

"A few are deep, but most are superficial. I applied turmeric salve. She should heal in a day or two. She is resting upstairs."

"Did she talk to someone? Get any information?" Guruji asked.

"You can ask her yourself at dinner. You had a long day too. Why don't you relax for a while?"

At dinner, Guruji gasped when Kumud appeared, shamefaced.

"Are you okay?" He asked

"I'm fine. Sorry about making a fool of myself."

"What happened to you?"

"I took a shortcut through the fields," she responded with a timid smile. "It was more frightful than injurious. My head was not in the right place, Guruji. And it all ended in nothing!" She sat next to him. "I did talk to some widows and met Umraodeo's wife, Nisha, who brought me home. She recognized me from the picture on the back cover of my pamphlet about suttee."

"Nisha is a smart woman, a person worth knowing. When we returned from Calcutta, she and her husband invited us for dinner a few times." Shyamli said.

"Was talking to the widows useful?" Guruji asked.

Kumud told them what she had learned from the women. "We only talked for a short while," she said, "they were in a hurry to return home. How was your day, Guruji? Did you find out anything?"

"The only thing I found out is that Kundan Singh, son of Jabbar Singh the Elder, is very sick. He is in the hospital. Village *vaid* has not been successful in treating him, so his father took him to the Seeker District Hospital. Singh's wife, Parvati, told me his prognosis is not good."

"Do you think I can talk to Parvati or any other family member?"

"Jabbar Singh would not want to talk to a woman from Ambayu. He considers it below his dignity to talk to women."

"That's unusual."

"Not in Neela Nagar. Because most of our women—from the wife of a Brahmin or that of an untouchable—regard themselves as subservient to men. So men treat them as such. They are imbued with the idea that they are born inferior. The men, on the other hand, feel superior and consider themselves masters of women. And a Brahmin man? He considers himself to be supreme."

"Have you been thinking about this the whole day?" Shyamli asked.

"As a matter of fact, yes! As I walked from one place to another, I pondered the status quo of female gender. I thought of *stridharma*, the role and responsibilities of mothers, sisters, wives, and daughters, how it is cultivated at a young age, how it gathers momentum during a lifetime of experiences. Because *stridharma* is neither modified nor controlled it floods minds. It needs to be dammed. But how do you stop a strong cultural flow that women do not find offensive? They continue to diligently perform their responsibilities, regardless of how men treat them. They never question their dharma.

THE LAST SUTTEE

"So true!" said Kumud. "Although my parents were not religious, I too was taught not to question tradition. From an early age, I was taught that a daughter is someone else's possession, that her husband's family is her real family. That she is a guest in her own parents' home. They treat her with tender and loving care because they know she does not belong to them. This teaching was so ingrained in my mind that when the time came, when all odds were against me, I had no courage to leave my husband. I believed that leaving would be against *stridharma*."

"Sorry to hear that Kumud. I must say, your Guruji saved me from all that humbug! If I married into an orthodox family, I would have been my husband's faithful devotee and an obedient daughter-in-law; my worth would have been based on how many sons I had! I would have believed that I must have committed a heinous crime in my previous life to become an unwed mother. Being his wife has freed me from the shackles of superstition and gender bias," Shyamli said, looking at her husband with admiration. "He is a remarkable man! We need more men like him."

Guruji gave his wife a quick smile. "We tend to forget we all are interdependent. But the net of rituals, customs, and behavior favor men. They are reinforced and kept alive by women's fasts, festivals, and feasts. What annoys me is when women themselves don't think about all this?" he said.

Guruji was right, Kumud thought. *Women ought to fight for their own cause. But each woman learns this the hard way. We are taught to speak softly, even if we seethe with anger. We are taught to move gently, even if we want to scream and run away. Such*

195

training makes us doubtful, indecisive.

As if reading Kumud's mind, Guruji said, "On rare occasions, when a woman makes a valiant effort to leave her husband and his family, to run away and taste freedom, they label her a prostitute, *bazari aurat.* Anyway ladies," he said changing the topic, "tomorrow Jabbar Singh will be at the hospital. Kumud, if you feel better by then, why don't you visit Parvati? If anyone asks, tell them you are writing a book about Narayani Satimata."

"I will do that. But Guruji, we still don't know who the mysterious man was who called me on your behalf."

Chapter Twenty
Parvati's Story

Parvati's father was one of the priests at the temple, admired and respected by the devotees of Narayani Satimata. He was married to a seamstress, a good woman. They were happy together except for the want of a child. For years they appealed to gods and goddesses in vain. Finally, they supplicated the goddess Satimata, visiting her temple every Sunday and offering her gifts and prayers on her festival days. Eventually, after ten years of marriage, they were blessed with a baby girl. In honor of the goddess, they named her Parvati, another name of the goddess Sati.

Parvati was an adorable baby and grew into a beautiful girl. Her parents pampered her as if she were the only child in the world. Parvati idolized her mother. She followed her everywhere, observing and imitating her every move. At breakfast, as the mother rolled *rotis* or fried *paranthas*, she handed small dough balls to Parvati to flatten with smaller rolling pin. She had also purchased a short broom for her daughter to sweep, and a small bucket and soap for her to wash clothes. Parvati even fetched water from the river in a plastic pot when they returned home as her mother balanced several earthenware pots filled with water, on her head. For Parvati, the drab household chores were fun things to do.

When she turned four, Parvati's father started to teach her alphabet. By six she was reading. At this time, the mother was pregnant again. Little Parvati asked why her tummy was hard and round. Her parents told her that a baby doll had made it her home and soon she would be ready to come out and play with Parvati.

"When can I play with the doll?" She would ask every night before falling asleep.

Her mother hugged her and said, soon, very soon as she tucked her under a sheet.

A few days before the baby's delivery as the mother tucked her into bed, Parvati began to cry.

"What is wrong my princess?" her mother said.

"Will your belly burst when the doll comes out? Will you die?" Parvati asked.

The mother consoled her. "Nothing like that is going to happen. The baby will come out and it will be strong and healthy, and I will feel so much better. Go to sleep now! Think of fairies, my princess." She wiped her eyes with her odni.

Between snivels Parvati said, "Will your tummy look the way it was before?"

Her mother nodded.

Touching her mother's face, Parvati said, "When do I get to play with the doll, mommy?"

"A day after she is born. But you have to be very gentle with her," the mother said, kissing her forehead and tucking her in.

THE LAST SUTTEE

When the contractions started, Parvati's father fetched a midwife. Parvati and her father sat outside their shack that was prepared for her delivery.

Parvati listened as her mother moaned and cried for hours.

The father brought something for the two of them to eat.

They drank brewed milk tea.

They strolled around and around their small home.

Time stretched.

They waited, and then waited some more.

Finally, the door opened. The midwife came out crying, "I'm so sorry. I couldn't help them. I could not save the baby. I could not save the mother."

Parvati's father burst into tears. Parvati could not make sense of what the midwife had said.

The midwife patted Parvati's father's head and said, "I'll let the neighbors know."

Her father cried like a child, repeatedly calling for his wife. He was still sobbing when neighbors came to mourn and console him.

Parvati ran to her mother's bedside. Dumbstruck by what she saw, she fell to the floor. She sat in a dark corner of the room, gazing at the women who cleaned and prepared her mother and the infant's body for cremation.

For almost a year, after the cremation and funerary rites, several neighbors cared of Parvati. When she returned home, it felt empty. She felt wretchedly alone, and her heart ached for her mother. Her sorrowful father seemed helpless. He tried managing the household chores, and she helped with the routines she had once loved doing with her mother.

The pain of loss lodged in Parvati's chest. She did not know how to get rid of the continual ache. Her father, dejected and dispirited, believed that Parvati, now eight years old, had handled his wife's death better than he had. He knew he could not love Parvati the way his wife had. He also realized that he was unable to do the things little girls needed. He decided to remarry.

Parvati's new mother, like the stepmother of folktales, was cruel. She treated her step-daughter as if she was a stranger in her own home. After all, she believed, Parvati's real home was her future husband's home. The stepmother treated her like a servant. Parvati did her chores with pleasure but her new mother didn't see that. More she abused her, the more she missed her mother. Slowly, a melancholic expression became permanently marked on Parvati's face.

One day Parvati's father said, "Would you like to visit Narayani Temple every Sunday, the way we used to with your mother?"

"I would." she said with a smile that he had not seen since his wife's death. "Would we do all the things we did with her?"

"Yes, we'll and we'll do whatever you want to do."

After being away for several years when they arrived at the temple, Parvati found herself gazing at the Narayani Satimata's Trident in the sanctum and the framed oleographs hanging on the wall. She found solace in those images. The place and images stirred cherished memories she had forgotten.

Their weekly visits to the temple slowly restored Parvati's mind. She looked forward to visiting the temple and silently gaze at the images depicting episodes of the goddess' life. She became devoted to the Trident enshrined in sanctum sanctorum. She listened to Satimata's myths and sang her devotional songs with such absorption that the sounds of other devotees singing with her disappeared in the background.

At home, Parvati read the pamphlets about the goddess that her father had collected. Although she had never stepped inside a classroom, her reading skills were higher than other girls her age because of her father's tutoring. She read the sacred stories over and over again, the way she looked at the temple images. As she read the stories the images came alive.

Parvati's stepmother gave birth to a baby girl when Parvati was eight; a boy was born when she was nine. Parvati helped her stepmother take care of the new babies, but she had little interest in them. The only solace she found was in her visits to the Narayani Satimata temple.

During their weekly visit to the temple, Parvati imagined herself standing alongside her mother watching the priest sprinkling water on the boulder behind the Trident and placing marigold over the bright red *odni* wrapped around it. She imagined herself sitting next to her mother as she offered gifts to the goddess, and tasted *prasada*, the blessed food. By now, in her mind, her mother and the goddess had become. The sorrow of her mother's death had been replaced by her increasing love for the goddess.

By the time she was ten, Parvati was captivated by the goddess. The sorrow at the core of her heart had slowly dispelled. At one of her weekly visits to the temple, as her parents offered rice, red bangles, scented sticks, and thirteen pieces of coconut to the goddess, she watched the senior priest apply thirteen black marks on the eyes and thirteen red marks on the Trident. Suddenly, Parvati saw the face of her mother in the Trident. *Here she is*, she thought, *my mother, my mentor, my goddess.* She sat silently praying, facing the Trident.

She was unaware of how much time had passed when her father said it was time to leave. Leaving her heart behind with the goddess, she reluctantly followed her parents.

"Does the goddess smile at you sometimes?" she asked her father on their way home.

"I'd feel blessed if she would smile at me, child. Does she smile at you?" he asked.

Parvati nodded.

"Why would the goddess smile at someone who ate her mother? Why waste her smile at ill omen and ill luck!" her stepmother interjected, then commanded them to walk faster.

He did not confront his wife or console his daughter. Since that day, Parvati protected herself from further jeering by not talking to her father about the goddess in front of her stepmother. But she continued to immerse herself in Satimata's heavenly and earthly depictions during each visit. At first, she imagined the goddess reciprocating with an attentive look or a smile or a blessing. But as Parvati's imagination became more vivid, the goddess became alive to her.

After returning home from a day of festivity at the temple, Parvati dreamed that Satimata sat at the edge of her bed. She smoothed her hair and tucked her in and before leaving, kissed her forehead. She watched the goddess float away through the window. One moment the goddess looked like her mother, the next time like Narayani Satimata. In her mind that experience confirmed the oneness of her mother and the goddess.

The following Sunday, after depositing their offerings, the family sat facing the sanctum of the goddess. Their eyes closed, they began to softly sing together, and Parvati's heart overflowed with a feeling of love that she had not felt since her mother's death. A sensation of maternal love spread from the top of her head to the soles of her feet. It was as if the goddess in the oleographs emitted rays of love towards her. After that day, Parvati never missed any of the goddess' auspicious events.

From then on, her absorption in the goddess was such that when she was in the temple, mythical space and time were real to her. Frequently, when seated in the inner hall, she had visions of Satimata emerging from the inner sanctum and the posters and framed pictures, or floating down from the sky to be in the same space she was in.

Parvati turned thirteen. Her parents began searching for a suitable boy for her to marry. Messages were sent in vain to various families in Neela Naga. She was beautiful but not coy, and she could read, and had opinions of her own. When she turned fourteen and began visiting the temple by herself, her parents became frantic. Her father grew anxious at not being able to find a match for his beloved daughter. But he did not lose hope. He kept his eyes and ears open and eventually heard that Jabbar Singh was searching for a suitable girl for his son, Kundan Singh. The Singh family was of a higher caste than the priest caste. Why would they agree to their son marrying a priest's daughter? But his daughter was a beauty, and she was smart, Parvati's father thought. There was no harm in letting the family know she was available.

To everyone's surprise, Jabbar Singh, the town's oldest Elder, and his wife accepted the offer. Some of the townspeople wondered, why Jabbar Singh would marry his son to the priest's daughter? Others praised the Elder for breaking the caste barrier and marrying into a lower caste and financially less fortunate family. Rumors abounded that Kundan Singh had married Parvati for her beauty and Jabbar Singh had agreed to the match because the priest was a good man. When did Jabbar Singh start caring about people, the townspeople whispered. Why did he commit to such an arrangement?

While townspeople busied themselves with gossip, Parvati turned her attention to the story of Narayani Satimata. She was fascinated with how the goddess, after her husband was murdered, asked the soldier to bury his ashes and weapons in the ground and cover them with dirt into the shape of a mound. The mound had lit itself into a blaze and attracted the attention of the people. She repeatedly read the chapter how Satimata committed suttee and how the funerary flames burned for thirteen days and thirteen nights. She mulled over how the fire of truth and faith—*sat*—burnt for centuries while Satimata and her husband, Tanamana Das were in heaven.

Parvati visited the temple on her mother's birthday to pay offerings to the goddess. Outside the temple, she deposited her shoes, washed her hands, and walked toward the main door. When she stepped over the threshold of the temple, she felt transported from the outer world to the sacred space of the assembly hall. Some devotees sat cross-legged on the floor, and others sat against the wall. Some were alone and others in groups of twos or threes. Their hands were folded in their laps, their palms resting on their knees. Some had their eyes closed while others were focused on the Trident facing them from the womb chamber.

Filled with piety, Parvati looked devoutly at an old oleograph before her, an iconographic image of Narayini Satimata. The goddess was seated on a rock in the half-lotus position; her right leg over her left knee and her left foot firmly on the ground. She was dressed in red and embellished with accoutrements of flowers, gold, and precious stones. One pair of her hands was in meditative gesture. Her second left hand held a white lotus flower, and her second right hand emitted rays of light. Turning her attention to her inner self, Parvati felt the presence of the goddess—the vessel of feminine, maternal, and magical powers.

The world outside faded from her mind. Only the sacred space inside was real—safer, more secure, and linked to the realm where eventually everything and everyone ended, the eternal abode where her mother had gone with her baby doll.

The setting was heavenly and serene. The goddess was seated under a tree, the *axis mundi*, the center of the universe. A stream of water flowed close by her foot, and small fish dotted the water. It was a perfect cloudless spring day. Holding on neither images nor sounds in her mind, Parvati let go of her desires and gently closed her eyes. She heard the gurgling of the stream and saw the fish move. The tree branches swayed in the wind. She saw the goddess put her right leg down, stand, and move towards her. Parvati was too afraid to open her eyes. The goddess took her hand in her own. Parvati was floating just above the ground. Feeling weightless and filled with grace, she was flying alongside the goddess. Or was it her mother?

Parvati opened her eyes and realized where she was. Euphoria continued to permeate her body. More devotees had come in, and the temple orchestra was preparing for devotional songs. The singer tuned his harmonium, the drummer prepared to keep beat on his *dolak* drums, while a young man readied his bells. The thought of listening to the music sent a thrill up her spine. Still feeling elated, Parvati joined the group as they sang. The goddess' sacred power, *Shakti*, which energized the musicians and made Parvati fly, transmuted back into the Trident and the framed oleograph. But the blissful joy continued to stimulate through music and her imagination.

With time, Parvati's visits to the temple strengthened her feelings of security and safety. Every part of the temple seemed filled with sacral energy and maternal love.

By the time, Parvati married Kundan Singh, Narayani Satimata had become her model, her mentor, her mother.

Chapter Twenty-One
The Girl Who Would Be Suttee

Kumud walked a half-hour through sandy lanes to reach Parvati's house. She rechecked the map that Guruji drew for her. From a distance, she spotted the blue house with its dark blue door and red fence, as Guruji had described it. A whiff of dung entered her nostrils as she approached the house. On the left, camels grazed under a group of neem trees. A crow sat on a dung heap. As she passed, it flew away. A rooster clucked, making a goat trot away.

An elderly man was seated on a charpai on the front porch puffing a hookah. Facing him a red lacquer swing hung from the ceiling at the opposite side of the porch. That must be Jabbar Singh the Elder, Parvati's father-in-law. *Why is he not at the hospital as Guruji had informed her?*

She approached the man, who had one leg folded over the other. He was dressed in white and wore a large red turban. His salt and pepper moustache curled above his lip; his beard divided in the middle. The fashionably set facial hair gave his deeply wrinkled face a look of authority. He gazed at her for several minutes with his fiery eyes. Then he turned his head and took a long puff.

Kumud hesitated to ascend the steps. At that moment, a young girl emerged from the front door, sat on the gently swaying swing, and waved to Kumud. Jabbar Singh removed the silver hookah pipe from his mouth and squinted, trying to recognize the visitor.

"Ram, Ram, Uncle! May I talk to you?" Kumud said.

"Who are you?" He narrowed his bushy brows and continued to smoke.

"I'm Prateek Poddar's daughter." She used the one name she remembered on the marble slab of the major contributors inside the Narayani Temple assembly hall. She was confident that he would not recognize her. So far no one had.

"From Singapore?"

"Yes."

"Far away. Why do you want to talk to me?"

"I have come to write a book."

"About what?"

About Narayani Satimata Temple. Guruji tells me your family is knowledgeable about the goddess."

"My daughter-in-law is a staunch devotee and knows a lot about her. Are you Guruji's relative?"

"No. But he was my teacher. He is like a father to me."

"He is a smart ass. Too smart for his own good."

"Is your daughter-in-law home?"

"She is not here at the moment."

"Can I talk to you?"

"I've nothing to talk about," he said abruptly.

Kumud did not know how to delay her departure. "May I have a drink of water?"

Jabbar Singh mumbled something to the little girl. She got up from the swing and asked Kumud to follow her.

Kumud ascended the steps, removed her sneakers, and entered the house. The girl handed her a glass of water. Kumud took a few sips and asked if she could use the bathroom. The girl led her through a dark corridor flanked by several rooms with doors closed. They crossed the courtyard and exited at the back of the house. Outside the outer wall were two outhouses, one for men and the other for women. Between the two was a water pump. Kumud asked the girl where the other members of the family were.

"At the chili fields."

Kumud pretended to use the women's outhouse. Once outside, the girl pumped water for her to wash her hands. Under the girl's steady gaze, she pulled out a handkerchief from her purse to wipe them. At the bottom of her purse she noticed candies she'd brought for the train ride. She pulled out several and held them in her open palm.

"Would you like a toffee?"

The girl stared at the colorful candies trying to choose one. Then she held out one palm for Kumud to give her one.

"Show me both hands." When the girl did, Kumud filled her cupped palms with candies.

The girl ran back. Kumud followed her inside the house. As they were walking through the corridor, Kumud said, "Would anyone else in the house like to have a toffee?"

"Bhabhi would." She slowed her pace near one of the closed doors, stopped, and said, "Bhabhi, do you want to eat toffee? This lady has so many in her bag."

They waited for an answer.

A partially hidden young woman peeked from behind the door. For a few moments, Kumud's eyes met hers. She abruptly closed the door.

The exchange triggered a memory in Kumud. The young woman's warm and tender eyes touched her heart. Many years ago, she had looked after a little girl named Parvati during one of the darker periods in her life. Little Parvati had temporarily warmed her broken heart. A latent, raw tenderness stirred, stimulating affection.

Kumud walked up to the door and whispered, "Parvati? I'm the lady with toffee. Would you please open the door? I want to ask you something about Satimata."

Parvati did not respond.

"I'd love to give you toffee."

The door creaked.

"Your father-in-law said you were not home."

"Don't talk to the foreigner!" Jabbar Singh cried from the front porch.

The door shut at once.

Kumud turned to leave, but instead came face-to-face with the old man. He had left his hookah at the porch and walked in.

"Didn't I tell you she isn't here? What are you poking around for? Listen to me, woman! I don't care if you are Prakteek Poddar's daughter. Get out!"

"I am leaving," Kumud said, hastening her pace.

THE LAST SUTTEE

She left the house and trotted quickly to Guruji's home in the intense afternoon heat.

"What did Parvati say? How did it go?" Shyamli asked when Kumud returned. She remained quiet as she unlaced her sneakers, leaving them near the door. She flopped down on the armchair and closed her eyes.

Shyamli promptly brought her a glass of cold water and waited for her to say something.

Kumud took a few gulps. "You won't believe who she is!"

"Who?"

"Parvati! She is the girl I cared for when I was married to Kumar. Her eyes, I can never forget them! Of course, she doesn't remember me. What I don't understand is why did Thakurs, the upper-class landlords, agree to marry the priest's daughter?"

"That has remained a puzzle. We believe that Kundan Singh's Casanova-like behavior made him notorious. It clashed with Jabbar Singh's ultra-conservative values. We think to reclaim his status, he made this drastic move. But we could be wrong; who knows what goes on inside Jabbar Singh's mind."

"There must be more to it than meets the eye."

"Anyway, did you get to talk to her? What did she say?"

"Nothing. She was shut behind the door to her room. She peeked for a moment. I might have been able to coax her to talk if Jabbar Singh had not popped in. He forbade me from talking to her."

"I am sorry it didn't work out the way you had hoped."

"I'm running out of time. It is not just sad but terrifying. I'm afraid that Parvati could end up like Sau Massi!" Kumud said, drinking the rest of the water.

"But then I was a helpless child; it is different now. I am going to try again tomorrow." She said resolutely, more to herself than Shyamli.

Chapter Twenty-Two
The First Meeting

Very early the next morning, Kumud took leave from Shyamli and Guruji and briskly walked to Parvati's home. She arrived just before sunrise and hid behind the outhouses and waited, her handkerchief on her nose. She hoped Parvati had not already used the latrine. After what seemed like a long wait, a young woman emerged from the back door, walked towards her, and disappeared into the women's outhouse.

When she exited and headed towards the water pump, Kumud stepped forward making her gasp in surprise.

"Don't be afraid, Parvati! I'm a friend from the past. You don't remember me. My name is Kumud," she said in one long breath. "I will explain why I am here while you wash your hands."

Parvati picked a piece of clay from a small mound, rubbed it on the front and back of her hands and between her fingers.

"I took care of you when you were five or six years old," Kumud said.

Parvati's head jerked toward Kumud. She took a good look at her, then continued to rinse her hands. She wiped them with a small towel that was tucked in the side of her long skirt.

"Those were happier days, which I didn't realize at the time. When I think of the time I spent with my neighbors now, I remember feeling not only pangs of sadness but also love from them, especially you. You bathed me, dressed me, and fed me—I remember it as a time of care and tenderness," Parvati said, tucking the towel back into her side. "After that my world turned upside down."

"After your father remarried?"

"Yes."

"How old were you?"

"Eight. You no longer live around here. Where do you live?"

"In Ambayu."

"A big city, I hear. Why did you leave Neela Nagar?"

"Because my husband died and I was afraid of what this town could do to me, a widow."

"Other widows live here," Parvati said nonchalantly.

"Yes, but their lives are filled with pain and self-doubt. But I am not here to talk about that."

"What are you here for?" Parvati said.

"I've come to talk about suttee."

"You missed an opportunity. As a suttee you are assured a place in heaven, next to your husband and the seven generations of your descendants would gone to heaven. Women are fortunate that way. Men don't get such an opportunity!" Parvati said with conviction.

"Who is there, *Bahu?*" a woman called from the house.

"I came to talk to you about something very important. Could we meet, Parvati, please? Can you come to Sau Massi . . . I mean Saubhagya Satimata's shrine? Please, Parvati, please!" Kumud begged.

"Bahu! Your *Sasurji* and I are going to be late for the hospital. Who is that woman?" the woman shouted standing outside the back door.

"Some lady from out of town. She is lost. She wants directions to the Narayani Temple."

Kumud pleaded, "Please, come soon. Will you come after they leave? I'll be at the shrine."

"Bahuuuu!" the woman called again.

Hearing her mother-in-law's ruffled voice, she said to Kumud, "I'll try my best. Although it might be better if you come here!" Then she hurried back inside.

Kumud walked to the place where Sau Massi's shrine was located, the site where she had committed suttee. Until that morning, an inner demon had kept Kumud away from the place. When the site came into view, her heartbeat quickened and her legs felt weak. Her pace slowed down. Like a traumatic scene in a movie, the memory of Sau Massi's self-immolation slowly moved in her mind. It felt raw, as if it happened yesterday. Palpitating under a thin veneer of healing, her heart wrenched. Again, she heard the cries of Sau Massi mingled with women wailing and singing, children crying, and men shouting *Victory to Satimata! Victory to Satimata! Victory to Satimata!* The acrid smell of burning flesh and wood came flooding back.

Like a tree trunk embedded into earth, she felt rooted to the ground. She closed her eyes and allowed herself to feel whatever she was feeling. The puss of remorse, pain and negativity still simmering in her heart for all these years drained to the ground and was absorbed by mother earth.

She stood firm. Stock-still. An unknown sensation seeped upward through the soles of her feet and into her body, all the way to the top of her head, transmuting her past feelings into a tranquility she had never sensed before.

When she opened her eyes, she became conscious of her whole body: her sensations, her feelings, her thoughts. She felt her own presence emanating into the surrounding space. She was determined she would not let memories paralyze her, delude her. She walked unwavering towards the *chabootra*, the two-foot-high concrete platform. Not too far from it, as a nine-year-old she had sat with her head in her mother's lap. She remembered how the area around the pyre was demarcated with lime. Another line ten feet from the pyre separated the people who came to watch.

Now, a *chabootra* was constructed on the space where suttee ritual took place. The sunrays heated the platform so that it radiated its own heat, as if it were still smoldering. No one had placed flowers on it. Instead cigarette and *bidi* butts and scraps of paper and plastic bags fluttered around the ground. Goat and chicken droppings polluted the space. Wild creepers covered the platform, burying the memory of Sau Massi. The areas not yet covered with vegetation had dominion of an army of black ants. An iron trident with two eyes, a nose ring and a bindi, all tied with a red chunni, stood firm at the center, screaming to be claimed as some female divinity. A discarded straw broom lay on the ground.

Kumud watched as a line of black ants emerged from one crack and disappear into another. From one crack a tiny bud also poked, eager to blossom into a flower. She tenderly touched it's one petal and whispered, "Sau Massi, it's me, Kumud!"

With her palms pressed against her chest, she bowed and resolved to make Sau Massi's self-immolation the last suttee.

Parvati did not come.

Kumud walked back to Parvati's home and knocked at the front door. Parvati opened it. She was alone.

"I am sorry. I did not have the courage to leave. But please, come in!" She led Kumud through the corridor to her room.

A bed was pushed against the longer wall, above which hung the familiar posters of the goddesses Sati, Parvati, and Narayani. Facing the bed was a sofa and an area in which to sit on the floor. Parvati invited Kumud to sit on the floor against the cushions.

Kumud rested her head against the wall. She was tired. But watching the serene youthful face of Parvati pouring water from a clay jug made her feel better. She drank the cool water.

"Who sent you here?" Parvati's gentle voice and narrow-set black eyes expressed sadness.

"Guruji. He said you would tell me why Satimata

inspires you?"

"What can I say. . . She does not just inspire, Narayani Satimata is like my own mother. I have been her devotee all my life. From early on my mother, and later my father, sang devotional songs to me and read her stories to me. We observed her fasts and celebrated her feasts and festivals. At times, when I am lost in my thoughts, I see Satimata smiling at me, blessing me from afar. When I told my father about it, he said that is goddess' grace."

"That indeed is, Parvati." Kumud said and then added, "You know Saubhagya Satimata committed suttee three decades ago?"

"Everyone knows that."

"She was like my mother. I called her Sau Massi. I loved her! She was perfectly healthy when she became suttee. She didn't want to do it."

"You are wrong! Why wouldn't she want to? She knew she would become a goddess and live with her husband forever. She was doing it for future generations on both sides of the family. She also knew the whole town would worship her."

"I know. Would you come with me to her sacred site? Please, Parvati?"

Parvati thought for a moment, then said, "I don't know. When?"

"Now."

"Now? Are you going back to her shrine?" She looked around the room then back at Kumud. "What if my father-in-law and mother-in-law return from the hospital when I'm not here?"

"That's a risk you have to take! Would you take

that risk for the sake of Saubhagya Satimata, whom you admire so much?"

Chapter Twenty-Three
Umraodeo the Elder

"If anyone knows about a critical situation in Neela Nagar, it would be Nisha, the wife of Umraodeo the Elder. If Parvati has decided to commit suttee, Nisha would know and have the wherewithal to stop it. Not by herself, but through her husband." Guruji told Kumud. Shyamli agreed.

At fifty-nine, Nisha's husband, Umraodeo Singh, was the youngest, wealthiest, and most articulate of the town Elders. Jabbar Singh, Kundan Singh's father, was the oldest at eighty-two.

Partly because of their popularity and partly because of their charisma, the five Elders made up *panchayat*—the elected leadership of Neela Nagar. Loved by some, detested by others, and feared by all they were descendants of the *Thakurs*—special envoys of the British government when royalty ruled in this part of India. They had become landlords and moneylenders. They upheld and defended local customs and kept tradition and rituals alive. These men were proud of their position in the town.

Umraodeo Singh was born into a prominent Thakur family. He continued living in his *haveli*, ancestral home, an expansive mansion built on a hill at the center of the town. It was one of the centuries-old residences scattered throughout the state. A wall enclosed the enclave, and people had to enter it through a massive wooden gate that was closed during nights. The mansion was surrounded by flowering trees and bushes that blossomed year-round. Only the tops of sycamore, amaltas, and gulmohar trees were visible from the bottom of the hill. A serpentine cobblestone path ascended from the main road to the gate.

Striding up the cobblestone path, Kumud was nervous. She summoned Durga, the invincible warrior goddess within, and gathered all her courage. She had come unannounced. Would they let her in? Even if they did, what would she say? How would she ask Nisha that if Kundan Singh died is Parvati to become suttee? How would Nisha react? Would Umraodeo become enraged? Kick her out?

She recalled the threatening image in her dream. Was that him? Surely, he wouldn't be like the blind man she dreamed about. Focusing on her thoughts and feelings helped calm her nerves. By the time she arrived at the gate, she was composed.

A small door in one of the gate panels was slightly ajar. No one stood guard. She pushed it open and stepped into the inner courtyard. She gazed at the sycamore, amaltas and gulmohar trees in their full glory against the bright blue sky. The white mansion glistened in the sunlight. Bluebells and a variety of marigolds in shades of yellow, lemon, and brown speckled with orange were arranged in a carpet-like design. Kumud inhaled their scents and walked to the main entrance and rang the doorbell.

Nisha greeted her warmly. "What a surprise to see you here! Please come in!"

Hesitatingly, Kumud said, "I'm sorry I came unannounced."

"I'm glad you came," Nisha said, leading her to the main sitting room and pointing toward an exquisite walnut chair with lavish velvet cushions.

"Come, sit! Make yourself comfortable."

Taking in the beauty of the interior, Kumud said, "I wanted to talk to you, and Guruji and Shyamliji said it would be okay if I just dropped in."

"Sure. Sure," Nisha said, sitting on a sofa. She patted the seat next to her and said, "Come sit."

Kumud sat opposite her on a less lavish lounger; she glanced admiringly at the furniture and the setting.

"How is your research coming? I told my husband about you. He couldn't recall your parents living here. He must have been away at college when your family left the town."

Just then Kumud heard a man clear his throat. "Here he is!" Nisha said loudly. "Listen! Come, see for yourself who has come to visit!"

The man entered, and Kumud felt his distinct presence. He had an intricate headgear, *pugdi*, tied neatly on his head. He had an aquiline nose, thick brows, and piercing eyes. His salt and pepper sideburns dominated his small ear lobes.

Kumud stood to greet him with folded palms.

"No need to get up," he said, and sat casually next

to his wife.

"My wife tells me you are from Ambayu and have come to write about Neela Nagar," he said, critically scrutinizing her. "What is it about this town that you want to write?"

"About the town's customs and traditions… and their effect on women."

Kumud had heard that Umraodeo could be overbearing. She expected to be intimidated; instead she was charmed.

He cleared his throat and said, "I suggest you write about the men of Neela Nagar, and from their accounts deduce the lives of women. After all, men lead full lives, though women do help them lead it. Besides, few women would be able to express themselves clearly and freely. Intelligent communication is not easy for the uneducated. Most women of the town are illiterate. What do they know about Hindu *parampara?*"

"Your wife is an efficient communicator," Kumud said, looking at Nisha, who smiled awkwardly.

"He does not include me in the 'women' category," Nisha said and looked briefly at her husband.

Before Kumud could continue, he interjected, "She is an exception. Don't you think so, Nisha?"

"Yet women are the ones who keep traditions and customs alive. Wouldn't they know about religious and social affairs more than men?" Nisha said.

Umraodeo turned a large diamond ring around on his left hand. He looked at her and asked, "Can you think of something in your life that has nothing to do with men, with me? Or your father or brother or. . . son?"

Nisha's face turned red; she shook her head and

stared at Kumud.

"You see she has nothing to say. It is a woman's nature not to think too deeply. They may be socially savvy, obedient daughters, faithful wives, and good mothers, but men are the beneficiaries of dharma. We know what women are all about. As I said, if you write about men, you will have written about women."

Umraodeo's initial charm quickly faded.

Kumud shifted her gaze from Umraodeo to Nisha and back. The silence was awkward.

"What about some tea?" Nisha suggested.

"No, thank you! I must leave. You've things to do."

"Stay!" Umraodeo blurted. "I'd like to continue our conversation."

Kumud had dealt with men like him, but she had a rare opportunity here, to sit with the most powerful man in town, someone who could help her in her mission. She must take advantage of it.

"Stay, Kumud. I'd like that!" Nisha insisted.

"Just one cup!" Kumud said.

"One cup," she said to Kumud. "Vardhan! *Chai lao!*" she shouted to the servant and settled back into her seat.

"What about independent women like Indira Gandhi? She reached the highest political office in the country," She said.

"She was corrupt, became a widow, and got assassinated. The only reason she led the country for a few years was because she was Nehru's daughter. Without his lifelong guidance, she was nothing."

"What about Narayani Satimata? She was a

woman."

"Now that kind of woman is rare. She sacrificed her life in honor of her husband. You see it is difficult to find a faithful woman like her in *Kali Yuga*, the present age. Women today could learn from her."

Kumud struggled not to react outwardly to Umraodeo's incendiary remarks. Then she asked, "Okay I've a question for you, why do you continue to propagate suttee?"

"A faithful, devoted wife deserves to have the freedom to be with her husband if he dies. If she wants to die with him, perform suttee, who are we to question her or stop her?" he said emphatically.

"But when she commits suttee, she is grieving, drugged, out of her senses. Isn't it our responsibility to save her from the clutches of the people who want her burned?" Kumud asked.

"I do not propagate the custom of suttee as you may think," the Elder thundered. "But I do honor the dedication and courage of a woman who chooses to be cremated with her husband."

"Do you believe that a vulnerable young woman, deep in sorrow, is in any condition to make such a decision? To choose between death and life—the most precious gift we are granted?"

"The most precious thing a woman is granted is her husband. Ask a woman who is unable to find one. A husband gives his wife the opportunity to serve and show her obedience, faithfulness, and devotion to him and his family, and thus to god. She accumulates *sat*, the power generated from being a good wife. In the absence of a husband, a woman does not have the opportunity to gather the power of *sat*. An unmarried woman does not get that chance, and a widow forfeits it! Unattached, she faces a brick wall, unable to put herself to any use. No path, no opportunity, no merit," Umraodeo said, and began twisting his pointed moustache upward.

What was Kumud to say to a man encased in such an outmoded worldview? She mustered courage and said, "Some townspeople think differently. They may not agree with you. Guruji is one such person."

"Yes, Guruji makes strange arguments. He asks why girls can't attend the same school as our boys? Why can't Dalits attend school? Why can't *all* young people attend college? I tell him go read *shastras*? Our ancient books explain why lower castes can't be in the same room as us, why they can't follow the same paths as the higher castes. They can in their subsequent births if they lead good lives. If they follow Hindu dharma, the rules and responsibilities of their present caste, they will be reborn again and again in better castes. Then they can sit on the same benches as our sons."

Kumud's breakfast churned in her stomach. She had come to talk to Nisha about Parvati; instead she ended up talking to her husband. Guruji and Shyamli had warned her about Umraodeo's views on women. But they had also said that the man was devoted to his wife and loved her immensely. Kumud desperately wanted some time alone with Nisha. How could this loving, handsome, educated family man sitting before her have such outmoded dark thoughts?

"I believe in the past and in the necessity of ancient traditions to secure the future of our community," he said, interrupting her thoughts.

"You mean the future of all people or only higher caste men?"

"Don't get upset, lady!" Umraodeo said. "Just think with a cool head about what I have said."

Kumud did not want to continue the conversation. She kept quiet and turned to Nisha. "Do you have any children?"

"We have one son, a computer engineer. He lives in Bangalore with his wife. They both work. They have a…"

Just then someone came through the front door.

"Jasso Rani, come here! Your grandma is talking about you," Umraodeo called affectionately.

A tall girl with two long braids hanging in front of her school uniform walked in. Not more than thirteen years old, she greeted everyone with a sweet smile. She turned to Kumud with folded hands.

"*Namaskar beti!*" Kumud responded.

Jasso Rani nodded and sat close to Umraodeo. He turned and kissed her on her head.

"Jasso, this is Kumud Kuthiyala." Nisha said.

"The lady who wrote a book about suttee?" Jasso said excitedly. "I recognized her from her picture. Are you our guest?"

Umraodeo restlessly shook his legs.

"Grandma gave your book to me." Jasso said to Kumud.

"That book is not meant for you!" Umraodeo said and stared hard at Nisha.

"I have already started reading it, Papu!" Jasso Rani said.

He flushed with frustration, got up and walked to

228

the window. He stood there with his back toward the women.

"Jasso graduated from Guruji's middle-school. She is excited about the new high school so she can continue to stay with us." Nisha said.

"Young women like you are Neela Nagar's hope for the future, Jasso." Kumud said. "It makes me proud when girls like you get excited about education." Kumud saw a glimmer of hope in Jasso, youth usher change, have power to transform a whole community. With young generation new possibilities arrive. She said, "What do you want to do when you grow up?"

"I want to be a doctor." Jasso said with such certainty that both Kumud and Nisha said, "A doctor?"

"Yes! In Bangalore, where mama and papa live, there are dispensaries and doctors in every neighborhood but here we have only vaids. They can't cure so many diseases. I want to be the first doctor in Neela Nagar." She said with her sweet smile.

"See how she thinks, Kumud! She amazes me." Nisha said.

"Young people of this town, like her, are our hope for the future." Kumud agreed.

"Your book has made me think, what if my husband dies. I don't want to burn with him. Suttee is unfair and heartless. I will not marry. I will live alone. No, Papu?" Jasso called out to her Papu.

He did not respond.

"Can I ask you a question?" Jasso said to Kumud. "Sure."

Umraodeo turned around from the window. He could not take it anymore. He walked to Jasso and extended his hand to her, "No more questions! Say good bye to Miss Kuthiyala. Let's get a snack. Aren't you hungry?"

Jasso held her grandfather's hand and said, "I am writing about how a woman doctor can help people and live by herself. Will you read it when I am done?"

"I'd be honored!" Kumud said.

"Where do you live? I can bring it to your home."

"Bring it to Guruji's home when it is ready."

"You make me proud Jasso Rani." Nisha said.

Umraodeo pulled Jasso toward the kitchen.

She bid goodbye to Kumud and they left.

That left Kumud alone with Nisha.

Seeing that Nisha was not in a hurry to leave, Kumud said, "The reason I came to visit you is because I want to know something."

"What do you want to know?"

"If Parvati becomes a widow, would she commit suttee?"

"Knowing her she would, I am pretty sure. This is of a great concern to me. If Kundan Singh dies she will definitely commit suttee. I don't know what to do. I feel so helpless. What can we do Kumud?"

"I don't know . . . yet."

When Kumud returned to Guruji home, he asked her about her day. She said she was disappointed by her conversation with Umraodeo, and briefly told them what had transpired between them at his home. For the rest of the evening she was contemplative.

Guruji was about to retire for the day, when Kumud asked Guruji, "How do you change someone's deep beliefs, Guruji?"

Guruji resettled on his seat and said, "Very slowly, if they change at all. People rethink things in spurts, but first there has to be a deep desire for change. People's thinking doesn't change unless something drastic happens to them—a traumatic experience, a fatal disease, death of a loved one. Such experience can make people rethink their lives. However, there have been times when a thinking individual without any obvious reason breaks through a crack in darkness and sees a glimmer of light."

Kumud nodded and bent her head.

"Don't lose hope! We'll find a way and stop the worst if it comes to that," he said.

"Be patient, Kumud, sleep over it. Tomorrow we'll be able to think with fresh minds," Shyamli encouraged.

Chapter Twenty-Four
Kumud's Candor

The noon sun was scorching hot as Kumud quietly led Parvati to Sau Massi's shrine, the site of her suttee. Their heads covered with odnis, they bowed before the *chabootra*, the concrete platform.

Parvati said she had visited the site once many years ego. Kumud pointed to the area where Saubhagya had performed her suttee and become Satimata. She directed her attention to the animal droppings, cigarette and *bidi* butts, and the fluttering paper and plastic bags. She pointed out the creepers covering the platform and the black ants.

"Someone should have replaced that tattered, faded odni," Parvati said pointing to the worn out wrapping around the iron trident. Their glances met, then Parvati turned her head.

They sat on two boulders facing the platform. Kumud turned to Parvati, and said, "Do you want to hear what happened the day an ordinary woman became a goddess?"

"I would consider it my privilege," Parvati said.

"Sau Massi was visiting her maiden family in Madhya Shahar where my mother and I also lived. She was about to return when summons came that she was needed immediately as her husband was not well. She returned to Neela Nagar at once.

"At the time Sau Massi visited us my mother had planned to visit her in Neela Nagar and stay for a couple of days."

"How old were you?" Parvati asked.

"I was nine."

Kumud looked at Parvati's innocent face, and the prospect of Parvati's tragic suttee cracked the damn of suppressed memories. Her gaze turned inward.

"The story I am about to tell you is from what I remember, things my mother and Sau Massi's in-laws told me, and what I read in newspapers and magazines. But it feels like I went through it all myself.

"We didn't stay. Circumstances forced us to return home the same day. Anyway, when Sau Massi entered the house, she heard her husband, Banarasi, howling with pain. He was tossing and turning, moaning and groaning. She stood helpless, her head hidden behind her muslin *odni,* and watched Banarasi's old mother seated at one edge of the bed and his older siblings on the other. She leaned silently against the doorframe and saw her husband die.

"The broad turban that Banarasi wore outdoors hung on a nail on the wall close to where Sau Massi stood. She touched it gently then brought her fingers to her eyes and heart, grinding her toes into the floor. Later she told my mother she felt more guilty than sad for leaving him alone for so many days."

THE LAST SUTTEE

Kumud's head was filled with images from the past. "My mother was very close to Sau Massi. They had grown up together. At age sixteen while my mother got married into a family in Madhya Shahar, Sau Massi was engaged to a widower from Neela Nagar, twenty-five years senior to her. His three sons were the same age as her."

"How ironic that her name was *Saubhagya*, the fortunate one?" Parvati observed.

"Imagine that! She was loving and giving, obedient and faithful to her husband and his sons, even his brothers. She eventually got along well with the women of the family. She fulfilled her responsibilities the way women in her own home had done. She modeled her life after the older women. She served all the men and women without complaint. 'You can complain all day and be miserable or just do your dharma,' she told my mother.

"The day we rode the bus from Madhya Shahar to Neela Nagar it was stifling hot. When we arrived at Sau Massi's home, she was not at the front door to greet us the way she usually did. Intuitively my mother felt something awful had happened. Men in groups of two or three huddled together talking. We spotted Sau Massi's stepson among then. Then Banarasi's brother whispered something to my mother. Her face turned white. She gasped and sunk to the front steps. Holding her arms tightly against her chest, she began to cry and rock herself. I moved closer to her, 'What is the matter, mother?' I asked. 'Nothing. Nothing,' she said.

"Sau Massi's stepson asked if we wanted to step inside to keep his mother company. He said Sau Massi was emotionally fragile. She may not let us into her room but we could sit in the back room with the other women mourners. I held my mother's hand as we walked inside. 'What did he say to you, Ma?' I asked. My mother's grip tightened and she said, 'He lied.' She pulled me closer as we crossed the porch and passed through a long corridor. We followed the sounds of lamentations mixed with singing to a crowded room. Standing at the door, we saw young and old women sitting on the floor. Some cried but most sang. When we entered, they moved closer to the wall, making space near the door for us to sit.

An old woman with a cracked voice led the others in song. She sang a refrain and the mourners repeated it.

> *I was a wife, a Pativrata,*
> *Now I am on my way to become Sativrata…. Don't cry…*

> *I was a bride and became a Pativrata,*
> *Now I am on my way to become Sativrata…. Don't cry…*
> *Soon I will be called Satimata… Don't cry…*

Women repeated the refrain, *Don't cry…*

> *The second time I will deck myself in my wedding chunari,*
> *to join my groom, my lord.*
> *I will become a Sativrata… Don't cry…*

"My mother quietly asked the woman sitting next to us, 'Where is Saubhagya?'

"'She is in her room. She has shut herself in and does not want to see anyone.'

"'We have come from Madhya Shahar to meet her.

THE LAST SUTTEE

We did not know about the death when we left home. We would like to see her,' my mother said.

"The woman nodded and asked a girl sitting next to her to take us to Saubhagya's room.

"Sau Massi opened the door when she heard my mother's voice. Her facial muscles relaxed when she saw us. The whites of her eyes and nose were red from crying. My mother held her in a tight embrace, and they both began to cry. But Sau Massi looked more determined than sad. She was not her boisterous self as she asked us to sit. Closing the door behind her, she stood solemnly with her palms folded.

"'I did not know Banarasi was so sick,' my mother said. Then, with her face crumpled, she asked, 'What is this I hear? Are you out of your mind?'

She separated Sau Massi's palms and held them in her hands. My mother cried silently. Tears flowed down her cheeks.

"'Don't cry, Geeta! All is for good!' Sau Massi said, patting my mother's head. On the side table, a lamp lit a framed photograph of her wedding day. Massi had removed her odni for the picture. Her slender neck and cheekbones were prominently visible. But her gaze seemed outside the picture. She and her groom, with crow's feet around his eyes, smiled separately. The camera had clearly captured her sensual youth and his middle age.

"'But why Sau? What has overcome you? You can take care of yourself. You can come and stay with me. You have grown sons.'

"'Banarasi was everything to me. Without him I am nothing.'

"'But you are! You are a whole world in yourself! You are the one who taught me about being a woman in my own right. When did you reach this decision? How can you even think about such a thing? What about the pain?'

"'His body will be burning too,' Saubhagya said as if in a daze.

"'But you are alive Sau; he is dead!' my mother exclaimed. She was standing in front of Sau Massi. She put her index finger under her chin and tilted her head slightly upward. 'Say, I am alive!'

"'But Sau Massi was not listening. Instead she said, 'If he is cremated and I am not, how will we unite in heaven? Don't you know what Narayani Satimata has said? Don't you believe in her valor and sacrifice? Haven't you visited the thirteen shrines of thirteen suttees? she said. Her speech was slow and slurred.'

"Like Sau Massi, Parvati, you believe in Satimata—in her songs, stories, legends." Kumud was trying to drill Sau Massi's story in Parvati's mind. "Like you, Sau Massi said to my mother, 'A widow's life is nothing. Geeta. Our *dharma* is written in the centuries-old *shastras*, still alive and thriving. In my husband's family, there were two Pativratas. Both had accumulated powerful *sat*, the power of a wife's faithfulness and devotion to her husband. When they sat on their husband's pyre, they self-combusted. Such courageous women become *Sativratas*! I am not a coward.'

"My mother ignored what Sau Massi said. 'Let anyone who calls you a coward go to hell! Don't do this, my sister Sau!' my mother pleaded. She helped Sau Massi sit on the sofa, and she sat next to her. Sau looked detached. She said, 'If I perform this sacred act, I will be a folk heroine and seven generations of our families will go to heaven because of my action.'

"I sat listening to their conversation. I think my mother forgot I was there. My nervous mother, bewildered by what she was hearing, kept babbling.

"'When did you start believing in all this stuff?' she asked. 'How did you become so different, Sau? We had similar dreams until we got married.'

"'There is a difference! I was always a Satimata devotee—you never were. When I moved to Neela Nagar, I came closer to her, and you became a city dweller.'

"'You didn't even want to marry Banarasi!' My mother cried.

"'But I learned to love him, grew to love him. He too was a devout follower. Together we observed Satimata fasts and festivals, celebrated the feasts, and listened to her myths. He memorized her prayers. When he sang them, people had tears in their eyes.'

"My mother was trying to convince Sau Massi that what she was doing was senseless. We heard wailing and singing outside her window. The mourners had moved from the back room to the front of the house. Saubhagya had asked for Banarasi's body to be brought to her bedroom. No one could refuse the command of a woman who had gained *oak*, the power of a woman ready to become suttee, and attained *sat*, so that she was worthy of suttee."

"*Oak?*" Parvati asked.

"Sau told my mother that *oak* is the belief that the fortunate widow who performs suttee attains the power of *oak*. She said, 'It runs through her blood. She accumulates the power by leading a life of purity, virtue, and truth. With her power, the widow can bestow boons or curses that will come true. At the suttee ritual, the *oak* empowers her body and transmutes into inner heat. So much so that when she sits on the pyre her inner heat combusts the wood, Geeta.'

"Are the powers of *sat* and *oak* the same thing?" Parvati asked.

"*Oak* is the same energy as *sat*, but is temporary and more intense. Its current passes through the body when a widow makes up her mind to commit suttee. Its energy combusts on the pyre. These are not scientific facts, you understand? These are what they believe."

"Then what happened?" Parvati was restless to hear more.

"Two young men brought Banarasi's bathed body on a bamboo bier and placed it on the floor of Sau Massi's room. She instructed them not to disturb her and closed the door.

"My mother and I watched as she prepared her husband's body for cremation. She massaged it with unguents, covered it with flowers and placed his turban next to his head. I watched with keen interest as she dressed herself in her bridal attire: full-length red *lehenga* skirt and a *kurti* blouse embroidered with floral motifs and birds embedded with mirrors. She adorned herself with her bridal jewelry, all twenty-four-carat gold: a gold chain in her parting so that its sun disk rested on her forehead, a large nose ring, sun disk earrings, five necklaces of various lengths, red glass bangles, rings, silver ankle bracelets, and toe-rings. Finally, she covered her head with a glittering red odni, her bridal veil.

"Bewitched by her beauty, I could not differentiate between goddess images I had seen at the temples and how Sau Massi looked then. I did not understand why my mother was so dumbstruck. I did not see any reason why Sau Massi should not dress and adorn herself like a deity.

"There was a knock at the door. My mother unlocked it and let an elderly woman in. She held a tall glass of white drink with green specks floating on its surface. 'Drink this! Time for the procession is almost here!' she said.

"'But I drank a glass before! Why do I need to drink again?' Sau Massi asked. She told my mother she was feeling tipsy.

"The woman said, 'This is an essential and integral part of the ritual! Just do it! You must consume all of it before I leave the room.' She stood watching until the drink was gone.

"Minutes after the woman left, Sau Massi said she wanted to give me something before they took her away. She selected a gold necklace from her jewelry box and put it around my neck, then turned me towards a mirror. I saw a sun disk pendant, similar to the one she had in her hair parting, set elegantly below my throat. I hugged Sau Massi's legs.

"I turned to my mother and asked for her approval, but she looked stunned. She kept saying Sau Massi was insane and helplessly wrung her hands. Why was my mother so upset? I wondered. She would stand up. Then sit down. Standing again to gaze through the window, she saw the women gathering. She chaotically paced the room.

241

"'I must inform the police,' my mother said. 'She can't do this. They can't do this to her.' She told me to wait and left the room. Sau Massi and I sat silently holding hands. I could hear loud lamentations coming through the window but they did not seem to disturb Sau Massi.

My mother returned. She said,

'Armed guards are everywhere. They have blockaded the town. No one can go out or come in!' She cried, 'Wake up, Sau! Wake up from your daze. Come back to me! Do you even know what is happening?'

"I was embarrassed for my mother because I felt Sau Massi in her finery was doing everything she was asked to do. But I could also feel that she was lost in a world of her own. Sitting close to her husband's dead body, she pressed her forehead to his, her nose to his, and her chin to his. Then she put her forehead on her husband's feet.

"I asked. 'What are you doing Sau Massi?'

"'Paying my respects before we begin our journey together. In a hundred years, Kumud, you, too, will be with us in heaven,' she said and sat with crossed legs near his feet. Turning to my mother, she said, 'Geeta, tell them I am ready!' My mother drained of energy, sat motionless. I opened the door. Two men stood waiting, a priest and an Elder.

"My mother looked at them with her eyes and mouth agape. They were bare chested. The priest wore sacred threads around his neck and torso and a dhoti that ran from waist to ankle.

"'Daughter, do you want to be cremated with your husband?' the priest asked Sau Massi.

THE LAST SUTTEE

'I want. . . virtuous and pious widows. . . have always done.'

'You are not being forced into it?' The Elder asked. Sau Massi shook her head.

"My mother interjected. 'She is dazed from a concoction they gave her to drink.' The men stared with deep hatred at my mother, their eyes flamed with blind belief. They ignored her and turned to Sau Massi, asking a few more questions to convince themselves that her act was consciously made and voluntary.

"By now more people had gathered outside the door. One of the senior priests who was also an Elder and another Elder declared that they were convinced that *Sativrata*—she was no longer Saubhagya Agarwal—was indeed worthy of committing suttee. The priest said if any member of the family thinks that Sau Massi was not the embodiment of truth—*sat*—they should say so now. If no one denied her *sat*, then from that moment on, no one would be allowed to prevent her from fulfilling her *stridharma*, her privilege as a woman, to commit suttee. The Elder said, 'This woman's resolve and courage in this Age of Kali is commendable. It is rare to find a widow who is so deeply committed to Narayani Satimata.'

"Four males came to the room to prepare Banarasi's body for the procession. Two wrapped the body with a white sheet and loosely tied it with two loops of white rope. They placed the corpse on a bamboo bier. The other two men joined them to carry it to the front of the house as they chanted mantras.

"The old woman who had led the singing brought a small glass with a thick concoction for Sau Massi to drink. She said she was not thirsty, but the woman insisted that the third and the final drink was the most essential part of the ritual.

"My mother cried out, 'Not again!' and held the old woman's wrinkled arm. She jerked it away and cried, 'Without her drinking this, the procession can't start.' Glaring eyes turned towards my mother. Trying to keep her anger under control, she watched helplessly as Sau Massi finished the drink.

"After the third drink, Sau Massi was unable to stand straight or keep her balance. She did not utter a word."

"I did not know a widow was drugged before committing suttee," Parvati blurted. "I always thought she was in such a devotional frenzy to her husband and the goddess that nothing else mattered."

"Oh, they are drugged, heavily drugged. Sau Massi was helped outside the house and made to stand facing the front wall. They rubbed ash brought from the cremation ground onto her cheeks. A woman applied vermillion to Sau Massi's palms while another woman held a bowl of the red liquid. They asked her to make handprints on a raised mud square that had been prepared several days earlier. The women helped her make thirteen imprints of her palms. The palm prints would be visible for posterity to see and know that a woman from this household was a Sativratta—a lavish blessing for seven generations of the family and the town.

"Two young women, one in purple and the other in orange, helped her walk. They strode with confidence behind Banarasi's litter while Sau Massi wasn't able to keep her head erect. Alongside them came the Elders, the priest, and the other men of the family. The procession headed towards this *chabootra.*" Parvati pointed to the brick and concrete platform that was then newly constructed for the ritual.

"We may have walked for fifteen minutes when I heard a painful cry from an old woman wearing indigo. She said to another woman walking next to her, 'It should have been me! Saubhagya still has many years ahead of her.'

"My mother and I quickened our pace. We fell in line with Sau Massi. One of the two hairpins that held her red veil had slipped and fallen. Even in her stupor, she tried to pull it down, but smeared her face with the vermillion paste on her hands. Her hair was disheveled, her face lifeless, and her skin streaked with red; she looked like a ghost. With a pang in my heart, I saw her unsteady steps. I looked up at her; tears rolled from my eyes.

"'Don't. . . Kumud. . . I. . . suttee. . . honor. . . ' she slurred. My mother caught her back. For the first time, I realized why my mother did not want her dear sister/friend to get snared into the dreadfulness that was to come.

"'Please hurry!' an Elder shouted. 'The sun is about to set.' The women continued to sing in high and low tones, *I'm a Pativrata now, and soon I'll become Sativrata. . . Don't cry.*

"We wove our way through narrow lanes with blue houses on the both sides. The procession reached the wider road of the market lane. The shops had been shut down for the day. Finally, we arrived at the southern end of the town. From there the procession of men, women, and children moved slowly until the suttee site became visible, this very ground marked with *kikar* and *neem* trees. Wild vegetation grew around the edges. We saw several *chabootras* constructed over the sacred suttee site where women had performed the ritual through the centuries," Kumud pointed to the eastern edge of the place where platforms were still visible.

"About fifty feet away from where we stood we could see on the *chabootra* the three-feet high and six-feet square pyre that had been arranged for Banarasi's cremation. A man appeared suddenly from nowhere and stood before Sau Massi, forcing her to stop. He screamed, 'Who can assure me that this woman is pious enough to become a suttee? How do we know she is worthy? If she has not followed stridharma throughout her life, she must be stopped! And if you are uncertain of her purity and say nothing, you would be committing crime against Narayani Satimata.'

"By now, the procession had increased in size. More people had joined as it had passed through the lanes and the market. Many more were waiting at the site. The crowd was frenzied with a fervor of human sacrifice, one sanctioned by local authorities. Like addicted fiends, they were desperate for it to begin. To drown out the intruder's words, women raised their voices in song.

"'Who are you, young man, to stop us?' asked the priest who had approved the suttee. 'You must know what the *Shastras* say; it is written in sacred books that whoever prevents a *pativrata* from becoming *suttee* will be cursed along with many of his future generations. Besides, she has been a pativratta—the whole village knows, and we questioned her. Her motives are pure and true.'

'I. . . cur. . . sssse you. . . my. . . pow. . . er. . . of *oak*, I can. . . c. . . ur. . . sse you. . . oak!' Sau Massi slurred.

"Several people nodded in agreement with the intruder, and he shouted louder. Women tightened their grip on their children's hands. Then a distant aunt matched pace with Sau Massi and grasped her arm where a dozen red glass bangles adorned her wrist. The aunt's blue veined hand trembled as she put her wrinkly index finger under several of bangles and yanked them. They shattered, cutting Sau Massi's hand.

"'Why. . . w. . . hy did y. . . ou. . .?' Sau Massi asked, looking at the oozing blood.

"'A widow can't wear red bangles!' grunted the woman.

"'But I. . . wil. . .l bb. . . e with him. . . ' Sau Massi pushed the aunt away and then wiped her blood on her skirt.

"The Brahmin who was watching what happened said that if Sau Massi's bleeding stopped immediately, it would be a sign that she was an incarnation of Narayani Satimata. The singing stopped. Eyes turned towards Sau Massi, and the intruder became quiet. A freeze passed through the townspeople as the Brahmin checked Sau Massi's wrist.

"'There is no blood! She is indeed blessed!' he cried.

"I said to my mother, 'Did you hear? Sau Massi's bleeding stopped by itself! She did not even cry?' My mother did not respond. She looked dazed, dejected, and confused.

"By now any opposition to the ritual had collapsed.

The mourners surged forth with songs of praise in honor of *suttee*. The two women were no longer able to carry the wobbling Sau Massi's weight. Two young men took their place at her side. Her head bobbed as the men dragged her along. Only her toes were touching the ground.

"I had no idea what we were about to see. My mother must not have wanted me to witness the horror. But now, when I think about it, what could she do about it. Did she hope to protect me? How should she keep her daughter innocent? We could not leave because men were guarding the precinct. Saying nothing, she held me tight while I pestered her to remain close to Sau Massi.

"As I recall now, no police or government official was there. The last-minute preparations had been completed without a hitch. People sat watching on water tanks and tree trunks and from the terraces of their home. The procession had swelled five times by the time we arrived. Every resident of Neela Nagar was there.

"Up until this point, I did not find anything bizarre. The women's sobs and lamentations were expected because a loved one had died. My mother's behavior embarrassed me, but I thought she acted this way because of Sau Massi's loss and her drunken behavior. I found nothing wrong with Sau Massi's desire to meet her husband in heaven. What I did not know was how she was going to make that possible. I was curious.

"The sacrifice was ingrained in Sau Massi, in contrast to my mother, whose attempts to convince her of the meaninglessness of the sacrifice were thwarted. She had been unable to persuade her that the life of a widow was worth living. But Sau Massi's unconditional and unquestionable belief was prevailing. The family and community, inebriated with superstitions and blind faith, watched in blinded passion.

"A thick white line with lime was drawn around the pyre on chabootra to separate the people who were seated or standing on the sacred ground. A sea of scarlet and yellow turbans and black veils vied for a clear view. No one was allowed inside the demarcating. The four men carrying the corpse placed the bier on the top of the pyre. The priest made Sau Massi walk seven times around her husband's pyre, the way she had followed him around their wedding fire. Then he asked two young men holding Sau Massi to help her sit on the pyre next to the dead body. Another priest and two young men holding long swords stood guard. One of the men wiped the red mark on Sau Massi's forehead that she had so carefully applied. Then he commanded she sit cross-legged. Her head swayed as the guard placed the head of her husband in her lap. The priest and the Elders circumambulated the pyre, as the two men wielding swords stood firmly beside the recent widow.

"It was at this moment that an inkling of what was happening hit me," Kumud said, breathing heavily. Her eyes were wide and wet with fear, and she began to pant. Tears rolled down her cheeks. Her suppressed memory came alive.

"Kumud Didi, you don't look good." Parvati said. "Why do you have to tell me this with such detail? Why do you have to talk about the past?"

"I must! I have to! I have been carrying this demon child in me. I have to let it out!" Kumud's body shook.

"Please stop! Tell me tomorrow! Not now," Parvati said, standing to leave.

"No, sit down and listen! You must listen to the whole story! I am expelling venom from my womb that has been dead in me for years. It has come alive. You have induced the pain, so sit and listen," Kumud commanded and pulled Parvati back to the rock.

Parvati sat down slowly, fearful of Kumud's wrath.

"The priest urged Banarasi's father to begin the rite lest the sun should set behind the horizon. Tradition demanded the ritual to be completed before sunset. Sau Massi's head was bent under her long drawn odni. She was in no condition to watch as the priest poured generous amounts of ghee on the dead body and around it. Then he lit the fire. A man with a bucket paced around the bier throwing handfuls of vermillion powder every few paces.

"Gusts of the powder obscured our view. Banarasi's brother lit the pyre at all four corners, making sure it was ablaze. At that moment, my mother commanded that I face her away from the bier. She tried to put my head in her lap. But before she could force me onto her lap, I saw Sau Massi struggling to get out. The men held her down with their swords. The last thing I remember seeing was plumes of smoke and blazing flames behind a cloud of red dust. And Sau Massi's screams. My eyes were closed, but I smelled the wood burning and heard the lamentations and cries; I caught whiff of burning flesh, and my heart bled. That wound has not healed yet, Parvati." Kumud cleared her throat to hide her sob.

Parvati sat silently on the rock, waiting for Kumud to continue.

"My mother could keep me from watching, but

she could not block out the sounds and the smells. I heard the deafening drums and frenzied shouting of *Jai ho Sati Mata! Jai ho Sati Mata!* Victory to mother Sati! Victory to mother Sati!

The scene turned macabre.

'Did Sau Massi come out of the pyre?' I screamed at my mother, pushing her chin up. 'Why aren't you helping her get out?' She didn't respond, and I freed myself from her hold and ran towards the pyre. Before I could cross the white line, a man stopped me, picked me up, and held me tight. The more I struggled, the tighter he held me. Then Sau Massi's screaming ceased, and he let me go. I saw her slumped body, no longer decked in bridal attire.

"Yet I kept screaming, 'Somebody help! Help Sau Massi! Ma, tell them to stop! Mother! Help Sau Massi!' My screams were drowned out in the beating of the drums and the shouts of *Jai ho Sati Mata!* The man handed me over to my mother, who was still seated on the ground. She held me tight against her bosom. Sau Massi was no more. Suttee was over.

"When my mother let go of me, I kicked her with formidable force. I used my fists wherever I could—on her chest, her head, and her shoulders. She tried to calm me, but I screamed, 'How could you let something like this happen? Why didn't you help her? I'll never let something like this happen! Never! I'll call the police! I'll pour water! I'll throw sand!' I said whatever came to my mind. She let me scream and hit her. I was doing to her what she wanted to do to herself. I wanted to do to the whole world what it had done to my Sau Massi. 'What kind of mother are you?' I screamed.

"Blood dripped from her nose, and I wiped it with my hands and my best dress, which I had worn to visit Sau Massi.

"Someone gave my mother a glass of water, and she thanked him. She gave me a sip and then drank some more. She dipped the end of her handkerchief in the remaining water and cleaned her nose and face.

"Seeing her quietly clean herself, I somehow knew that she was hurting as much as I was. She was the only person in the whole town who wanted to stop this tragedy.

"I looked around and saw that almost everyone had dispersed except the two men guarding the smoldering pyre. The ground on which earlier that morning peacocks and peahens danced had turned gruesome.

"Our energy seemed drained, our legs frozen. We struggled to get up. Finally, we stood and began walking towards the bus stop when my mother turned towards the men and asked, 'Why are you guarding the ashes?'

"'Not the ashes, Mother! This is no longer an ordinary ground. A suttee has been performed here. This is a potent site now, imbued with tremendous power.'

"'So why guard it with weapons?'

"'It must be guarded against *jadu-tona*, malicious witchcraft.'

"'By whom?'

"'People from other villages who are jealous of our fortunes,' said the man who had given us the water. 'An immense opportunity has burst open. Now, pilgrims will come to pay their homage to this sacred site. They will buy offerings of coconut, red odni, red glass bangles, and red *sindoor*. They will buy food. They may need a place to stay—In a few years we'll earn enough to build a shrine for *Satimata* Saubhagya.'"

"And you witnessed all this?" Parvati said.

"Upon hearing what the man said, my mother's lips stretched in a sad smile. Her eyes welled, and two tears trickled down her cheeks. Turning her back on the men, we walked briskly towards the bus stop. Sau Massi, the Fortunate One, was worth more dead than when she was alive."

Kumud took a deep breath and cried out, "Look at this, Parvati! Look at the Saubhagya Satimata's shrine!"

The light of the evening sun reflected on the two women. Kumud stood and looked hard into Parvati's eyes. "And I witnessed all that!"

"And you witnessed all that," Parvati whispered in reply, bowing her head in silence.

Chapter Twenty-Five
Flight to Ambayu

Following her talk with Parvati, Kumud's frustration peaked and her fears intensified. It seemed to her that everyone in Neela Nagar except Guruji and Shyamli was fanatical about suttee. Parvati's husband, Kundan Singh, was still alive, but townspeople spoke in hushed tones about his impending death. The market street stores had stopped playing music on the radio. It was as if they were passively waiting for something to happen. A quiet hush fell over the town.

Was she crazy to have come all the way from Ambayu in an attempt to help Parvati? What should she do? It had been four days since she had arrived, and she had achieved nothing. Should she continue to wait as an uninvited guest in Guruji and Shyamli's home? The crescendo of the suttee ritual would last only for a few hours, and then the townspeople would go about their routines. No change. No transformation. No redemption. Whom was she helping? Did anyone need to be helped? She felt hopeless.

She needed fresh air, and a place where she could

think freely. She remembered the Chamunda temple on the hill.

"I'd like to be alone for a while, Shyamliji," she said to her hostess. "Perhaps take a long walk or climb to the temple on the hill."

"Good idea! Go now, before it is too late!" Shyamli said.

Dev had said something similar to her many years ago; 'Leave now before it is too late!' Kumud thought of him as she left for the temple. He had returned unannounced to Kumar's home in his police uniform. Seeing him there had confused her.

"Leave now before it is too late!" he had whispered to her. "I read your journal. Just leave!" he repeated. "They can't coerce you into committing suttee!"

"Why do you care now?" She whispered.

"Who is it?" her mother-in-law had called from the kitchen.

"It's Dev! He has come to deliver a parcel from my . . . ."

"Again! Only a few days ago she sent a box of your favorite *ghewar-mawa*," her mother-in-law interjected.

Dev walked in and told Kumar's mother that he was in Madhya Shahar on work-related business and had again visited Kumud's mother. This time she had sent a basket of fruit from Jaipur Fruit Market.

"Jaipur Market? Nice of her! Can I get you a cup of tea?" She asked.

He politely refused, said he was in a hurry. He mouthed the word, *Leave!*

Kumud carried the basket to the kitchen and

returned.

"Where to?" she whispered nervously.

"Come to the front window."

Dev bid goodbye to Kumar's mother and left. Kumud went to her room. Standing outside her bedroom window, he said, "Listen, Kumud, I could hardly have imagined your fate would take this turn."

She sighed. Drained of spirit, she simply looked into his kind, honest eyes.

"Run away! One of the reasons this family welcomed you with open arms is because of your connections with Sau Massi. They expect you to follow her lead," he said with deep anguish.

"What do you suggest I do? Where can I go? How? How can I leave Kumar when he is so sick?"

Kumud noticed Dev's frustrated expression before he left.

That night, having fed Kumar, Kumud was seated next to his bedside while he slept. A tap at the window alarmed her. Who could it be at this hour? Recognizing Dev's face against the windowpane, she opened the window.

"Listen carefully!" he murmured and slipped an envelope through the window. "Tomorrow morning the weekly bus picks up pilgrims from the temple for a ride to Madhya Shahar. Take that bus. From Madhya Shahar, catch the first train to Ambayu. When you get there, hire a taxi to Save Girls' Souls Orphanage center. Ask to meet the director, and tell her my name. I have written her a letter explaining everything," he said pointing to the envelope.

Kumar moaned and turned in his bed.

She kept her finger to her lips. They remained quiet for a few moments.

He said hurriedly, "All the details are in this envelope. Leave! Kumud, leave as soon as you can." Then he disappeared as quickly as he had come.

She had four hours before Kumar's family would arise to begin the day. In the dark room, she managed to put a few personal items, clothes, and shoes into a handbag. Prepared for the journey, she waited near the window for the right time to leave. She opened the envelope and found a bus ticket, a train ticket, one thousand rupees, and the name and address of the person she was to meet. *Who was Yuna Li? How did Dev know him? Or was it her? How was Dev so sure that he would help me?*

The house was silent. She held her breath. Her heart raced as she gently closed the front door behind her. She covered her head with the pallu of her sari. Looking around, she saw no one. Her pace quickened. What if someone saw her and asked where she was going? What would she say? She could say she was going to Madhya Shahar. Leaving her sick husband behind? She could say she was going to buy medicine available only at a pharmacy there.

Dawn was breaking when she reached the bus station. She handed over her ticket to the driver, who was groggy with sleep. Her head and face were covered; no one questioned her. A handful of sleepy pilgrims were scattered around the seats. She sat behind the driver, and they rode in silence.

She had been to the Central Railway Station in Madhya Shahar with her mother when they picked up visiting guests. But today, she had to reach the railway station, catch the overnight train to Ambayu, and then hire a taxi to the orphanage. The three segments of her journey panicked her. What if she missed a connection? What if she never reaches the orphanage?

Dev had reserved a sleeping berth, but she couldn't lay down. She sat the whole night with arms wrapped tightly around the travel bag she balanced on her legs. By the time she reached Ambayu, her bottom was sore and her back aching. The pain was forgotten when the train reached Ambayu Station. The multitudes rushed to disembark. She smiled faintly. She was in Ambayu. Phew! What a relief!

A river of people passed her as she walked towards the exit. For a few minutes, she forgot her fears, her pain, even the reason she was there. She looked at the high central dome, the octagonal ribbed structure that crowned the structure. At the center, a colossal female figure stood holding a flaming torch in her right hand and a wheel with spokes in the left. The caption below it read, "Progress."

She had seen photographs of large buildings like the Ambayu train station. But the high ceilings and decorative columns and arches overwhelmed her. Like an ancient monument, it looked like a combination of Indian and English architecture. She touched the wall, dirtied by years of weathering. She could not discern out if it was limestone or sandstone. The floor of the platform, though worn off, was made of marble.

She turned left onto a side wing. It was the eighteenth and last platform that led to an open courtyard that faced the main street. A row of rickshawallas and taxiwallas were silhouetted against the sky. In the distance, she saw rows of strikingly arched windows of the station. To attract the attention of newly arrived passengers, the drivers shouted over each other at once. Kumud awoke from her stupefaction and spotted a taxiwalla who seemed the least frightening. She read the address, and he nodded and asked her to follow him to the taxi stand.

The ride was a blur. Instead of watching the passing scenery Kumud was lost in the thoughts about what she had left behind and the unknown she had yet to face. It was taking long to reach the orphanage. She was restless.

The taxiwalla stopped in front of a building.

"Is this the right place? Are you sure?" Kumud asked anxiously.

He assured her she was at the right address. She exited the taxi and asked him to wait.

"What for?"

"I want to make certain this is the right place."

"Lady, I told you this is the right place!" he said irritably.

Kumud ignored him and walked into the building. The atmosphere was humid, different from the dry air in Neela Nagar. It smelled of salt. Christine, the receptionist assured her that she was where she was supposed to be. Kumud returned and thanked the taxiwalla for his patience, and paid him a little more than he had asked.

"May I see the director?" she said, returning to the receptionist.

"Please wait here!"

Kumud sat on a bench and reread Dev's note to read the director's name, Yuna Li.

THE LAST SUTTEE

The building was old. Its interior beautiful, with its cream-colored walls and touches of gold that had tarnished with time.

The receptionist returned and asked Kumud to follow her.

They walked into the director's office. Kumud greeted her with folded hands and nervously introduced herself as Dev's friend.

"Who?" Yuna Li eyes narrowed.

Kumud's mouth felt dry. She said Dev was the police inspector from Neela Nagar.

"Neela Nagar! Yes, yes, I remember now. A few years ago, there was a runaway girl from that town. She wanted to try her luck as a Bollywood actress but ended up on the streets. After a year of desperation, she was brought to our orphanage. Inspector Dev came to escort her back to her family. I remember Dev, because he worried whether her family would take her back."

"That sounds like him," Kumud said.

"What can I do for you?"

"Please hire me! Give me a job! I'm a certified teacher. I can tutor children," Kumud said, looking into the director's black eyes. She was listening. And Kumud was thankful. She continued. "I can tutor in history, English, or any other subject the children need help with. I am prepared to do any work as long as I have a room to stay and food to eat." She handed Yuna Li the letter that Dev had included in the envelope.

The director attentively scanned the letter. She said, "I'm so sorry to hear this. Are you and Dev sure about suttee happenings in Neela Nagar? Why did you marry into this family?" she said, motioning for her to take a seat across the table from her.

Kumud told her how she ended up in a town that she vowed she would never return to, how she had been cheated out of her marriage, how her husband was dying of an unknown disease, and how she was afraid of being forced to commit suttee.

"I can't believe that this barbaric custom is still followed in certain parts of the country!"

The only thought in Kumud's mind was how she was going to convince Yuna Li to give her work to do and a room to live in. She fidgeted on her chair. How was she going to convince the director that the story she was telling was true?

Trying to keep up her courage, Kumud, candidly but succinctly, narrated those parts of her life that Dev had not written about in his letter: her witnessing suttee at age nine and losing her father to cancer, her unrequited love and being married to a homosexual, her husband's impending death, and, worst of all, her fear of living a widow's hell or being burned alive.

Yuna Li was aware of the heart-wrenching stories of girls who she had admitted to the orphanage. But none of their stories were as bizarre as Kumud's. As she told her story, Kumud appeared to be a woman who controlled her passion, someone who said only what needed to be said. A cauldron of emotions seemed to boil in her heart, but somehow she was keeping it under control.

"Let me call Dev," the director said.

"Certainly!"

Yuna Li asked her to fill in an employment application. She wanted to make a few phone calls before making her decision.

As she filled in the questionnaire, she realized that for the first time since her wedding night until that moment, she could breathe easier.

She completed the form and handed it to the director. Looking through it, Yuna Li said, "Let's give it a try for a little while. I cannot promise anything on a permanent basis."

Kumud told the director that she would not regret her decision.

Remembering her flight to Ambayu as she walked, Kumud found herself at the bottom of the hill of Chamunda Devi Temple.

Chapter Twenty-Six
The Vision

The Chamunda Devi temple peak, gleaming under the light of the setting sun, beckoned Kumud. She climbed vigorously halfway up, then rested on a flat rock. From there she had a breathtaking view of Neela Nagar, Apna Gaon and Tapasya River. She circumambulated the first spiral around the hill to a boulder, which indicated the beginning of the second spiral. She breathed long and deep and continued her ascent. There were four more spires to climb, the last one ending at the peak. At the top, she would have a birds-eye view of the world below.

The Tapasya River ran through the two habitats, the blue dwellings of Neela Nagar towards the north and the white huts of Apna Gaon towards the south. Depending on one's perspective, Tapasya River either divided or joined the town and the village. The river flowed from west to east, bending around the Chamunda foothills and eventually streaming southward. The old school building was visible to the east, and behind it she could see the new high school. Umraodeo Singh's mansion, on the top of the second highest hill, overlooked the homes of the town and the distant village. The gold-painted domes, columns, and spires of the Narayani Satimata Temple shimmered in the last glimmer before the sunset.

A town of blue houses was dotted by green fields and surrounded by the wilderness of the desert. The landscape was dreamlike, even fragile, despite of the dark, threatening mindset of its people. She wondered what went on inside the houses of the town and the village huts.

She was circling the third spiral when she slipped and fell, hitting her head hard against a rock. She saw stars, and when she regained her wit, she felt vibrations beneath her. When the ground settled she got up. The vibrations returned, this time with higher frequency. As she was gathering her bearings, she saw an open doorway in the face of a huge rock.

Enticed by the darkness behind the door, she staggered towards it, then through it. A dark passageway seemed to widen into a chamber. She could not see anything, yet she felt as though she were being guided. She blindly crossed the chamber. At the other end, the ground sloped down into a narrow staircase. She took off her sandals, left them there and stepped down. The soles of her feet felt cool on the smooth stone. A chill passed through her body.

Where was she? What was this? What was happening? She gasped for air. Her tongue felt parched, her throat dry. Suddenly a second chamber opened up. She touched the wall and groped for the exit. But retracing her steps back to the doorway seemed impossible. She continued moving forward.

THE LAST SUTTEE

Suddenly she found herself facing some kind of innermost sanctum of a shrine. It was the most exquisite shrine she had ever seen, shimmering mica and opaque marble. It enshrined a statuesque image, a central figure flanked by two other carvings. Mesmerized by its beauty, she was filled with deep reverence.

Did she imagine the image move? A gasp lodged at the back of her throat. A rod of lightning momentarily illuminated the image. Then a few more seconds of light. The image was draped in a sari and embellished with gem-studded ornaments. One moment the image was an awesome goddess, and the next moment it was the face of Sau Massi engulfed in flames, begging Kumud to help her. Then hundreds of Sau Massies reflected on the shimmering mica walls whispering the words, "Kumud, help me! Kumud, help me! Kumud, help me!"

But there was no sound.

Kumud turned back to leave, hundreds of Sau Massies became one and then the one was transformed into an awesome wrathful goddess. Her three eyes glittered like sun, moon, and fire. She held a sword of knowledge that severs ignorance.

"I don't know what to do! Tell me! What should I do?" Kumud cried out. She heard her own echo. She turned to run but hit a wall and fell face down on the wet floor. When she sat up she was soaked. She spread her arms upward and wailed.

In the utter silence of the caverns she heard her own breath.

Kumud! She heard a sweet feminine voice calling her name. Momentarily, she held her breath, waiting for the caller to appear. No one came.

Again, she heard her name. *"Kumud!"* It sounded like the song of blossoming flowers, but she couldn't see anyone.

"Who is there?" she called. "Anyone?"

"It's me!"

"Who are you?"

"It is I. Me in you."

"You in me? I can hear you, but I can't see you."

"I am within you and without you. Wherever you go, there I am. I am your companion and your mentor. I desire only what is best for you."

"Why don't I see you?

"Because you *are* my form. I am your essence. You are my form. Why are you afraid? Why are you confused?

"I am no longer afraid. Please show yourself to me! If you are real, face me!"

"You can hear me, can't you? I am the silent voice within you. Trust me! Try to listen to what I have to say. You will understand who I really am," the exquisite-sounding voice went on.

"Trust you? I don't even know who you are."

"I am your higher self, your true self. I know everything about you."

"You do? What do you know about me?" Kumud said defensively.

"Until now, you have made the choice of not listening to me. Your anger, doubt, and hatred keep you from experiencing me. But if you look deep in your heart, you will find me. People worship me. They look for me in clay images, but that is not who I am. My essence is in everyone. I'm the one who one truly is, stripped of the past emotional wounds."

THE LAST SUTTEE

"Are you the ghost of Narayani Satimata?" Kumud said in frustration. When there was no answer, she continued. "Are you Chamunda Kali, the goddess of this hill?"

"I am neither Satimata nor Chamunda Kali. I am not a thing or a place or a person. I am your essence."

"I do not believe in visions! What a day for you to appear! Please go back to wherever you came from! Don't you have female infants to kill, brides to burn, widows to immolate? Go to your temples and *pithas* so your blind faithful followers can glorify your name! Why waste time with a woman like me?"

"Know me as the will that brought you to Neela Nagar, to this hill! Know me as the love you have for Shekhar! Know me as the love you have for your girls and all the people you have ever loved in your life, the love you are capable of giving, the unbound love you had for Sau Massi. The love you have for yourself. That is your power; that is the energy with which you can empower the world. That is me. I am around and within you. Sense me, know me, feel me!"

"Then, what?"

"Then you will know that I am neither in myths nor legends nor images. Those you call faithful may create images for their own glory, or to overcome their fears and guilt. But until someone with the integrity and sincerity of an open heart awakens me, I will not show myself. The flattery and adulations of false worshippers who hold tightly to their customs and rituals do so for earthly power. That has nothing to do with the attainment of inner power and wisdom."

"Why don't you stop them? Are you blind to the

brutal values and beliefs your worshippers and devotees hold?"

Kumud felt as though she was conversing with a wise old woman. The sweet sound of her commanding voice and presence kept Kumud spellbound.

"The people who believe in them are oblivious to the things you abhor. It is unguided faith, not religion. The trauma you experienced as a girl allowed you to find another way, but you have bent too much in the other direction. In doing so, you've dislodged the yoke that connects you to the cosmic spiritual flow. If you go deep within, you will find it gushing forth within you. You have buried me deep inside your core. If you had linked to me, I would have guided you at life's crossroads. Let me dwell in your heart, Kumud. Know that I am you, and you are me."

Kumud woke up on the side of the hill, expecting the stone entrance before her. She pinched herself hard to determine what was real and what was imagined. But there seemed to be no the difference. She had slipped and fallen unconscious. Turning her head, she saw nothing but a wall of rock.

Yet the Presence she had experienced felt real.

The evening light steered her towards the walkway of the third spiral. She scurried down the hill and back to Guruji's home.

"Where were you? We started to worry," Shyamli said when Kumud returned from her tryst with the goddess on the sacrosanct hill. "Did you climb all the way to the temple?"

"No, only halfway. It was getting dark, so I decided to return." She could not meet Shyamli's eyes.

"Good! Go wash up for dinner," Shyamli said and went to the kitchen.

Throughout her walk back from the Chamunda Hill, Kumud mulled over her experience. The transmuting image of the goddess and Sau Massi, the goddess' teachings, and her newfound understanding of her feelings about the sacred. Was it her own wiser self who had spoken to her on the hill? Would she hear that silent sound again? The goddess had said 'she was her.' Was she? Goose bumps prickled Kumud's skin.

Chapter Twenty-Seven
The Third Meeting

"It's you again, the woman from the big city with no husband! Why are you here at this time of the day?" Jabbar Singh yelled even before Kumud reached the front porch. He was sitting on his cane chair, smoking hookah, as always. "If you were not Guruji's guest, I would not even talk to you."

"*Namaskar,* Chacha! I'm sorry that I am not welcomed here."

"That's for sure."

"Chacha, I'll be greatly obliged if you allow me to talk to your daughter-in-law."

"Stop badgering her! What do you want from her that is so important?" Like a malevolent guard at the entrance to a Buddhist temple, he kept watch over his dominion.

"As I said the last time, I know your daughter-in-law is very knowledgeable about Narayani Satimata. I'd like to learn from her. May I see her, please?"

Jabbar Singh did not respond.

273

"Chacha, please ask her. Please! If she says no, I'll leave."

Jabbar Singh didn't budge. He took a long puff from his hookah pipe, creepily blowing the smoke in her direction. His eyebrows narrowed as he stared at her. He inhaled several short puffs, coughed, and said, "No!"

Kumud saw a woman appear from the front door to the house, with her head and face covered with odni. It had to be Parvati.

"There she is!" Kumud said. "How are you, Parvati?"

Jabbar Singh remained uncharacteristically quiet, and Kumud walked right past him and followed Parvati indoors. Once they were in her bedroom, she said to Kumud, "I asked Saubhagya Satimata for a boon."

Hearing Parvati invoke Saubhagya Satimata's name made Kumud's heart spasm. She stifled the pain and asked, "When? What sort of boon?" She searched for the right words to save the young woman from herself.

"When I returned from her site, I asked her to help my husband regain his health."

"Has it come true?"

"No, he is getting worse. The new goddess does not yet have the power to heal. Doctor says it's only a matter of days."

"God forbid, if he dies. Couldn't you go back to your parents' home?"

"My home is my husband's home. I am his possession now, no longer my parents' responsibility. They have two more daughters to marry."

"You're young. You could go to college, get a degree, be on your own instead of depending on your parents or in-laws."

"That won't happen. I will go with my husband, and we will live healthier and happier lives together in heaven. My *suttee* will bless seven generations of our families. His family will gain spiritual clout; even the town will benefit economically. The townspeople will build a shrine in Parvati Satimata's honor."

Like the one they built in honor of Sau Massi! Kumud wanted to interject, but Parvati was in the grip of passion.

"Pilgrims from far-off places will visit on my annual feast day."

"Who told you all this?"

"I overheard my father-in-law discussing it with the Elders. He said that as a widow, I would be better dead than alive."

"I'm a widow, Parvati. I chose to live. I am living a meaningful life--helping other young women lead productive lives."

"Did you come to see me because my husband is dying?"

"No, I have come because you have decided to become suttee," Kumud blurted. She looked hard at Parvati. *Is she Sau Massi reborn? Does she understand her own words?*

"And write about it?" Parvati sounded sarcastic.

"Yes, write about it," then Kumud changed the subject, "Do you feel responsible for your husband's sickness?"

"No. He was sick before we were even married." Unaware of how unsettling this information was to Kumud, Parvati chattered on. "If my family had known about his terminal sickness, they would not have agreed to this marriage."

"Kundan's family knew he was terminally ill *before* you got married? And your parents did not?"

"That is right. When my father-in-law sent a middleman to our home, my stepmother said, 'How can Thakur marry the daughter of a priest? Something is not right here.' She said that, not doubting the match but out of her jealousy for me. People admired Jabbar Singh for such an unconventional decision. It was not like him. They convinced themselves by saying that he knew how much I had suffered living with my stepmother and stepsisters."

Kumud gulped down the bitter taste in her mouth. "Hmmm! No use talking about that now. Tell me, will you blame yourself if Kundan Singh dies?"

Parvati grew thoughtful. She looked deep into Kumud's eyes and said, "During some sleepless nights, when I am alone, I ask myself what mistake did I make and what misdeed did I do to cause this calamity to befall me. I ask myself what can I do to stop this from happening to me? I cry and try putting myself back to sleep."

"Then you do blame yourself for his sickness."

"At times. . . I don't know why, but at times, I suspect that the devotion I feel in my heart is not for my husband."

"Then you're not a *Pativrata*, a faithful and devoted wife. Are you?"

"I don't know."

"You seem to doubt your *sat*. If you're not a *pativrata*, what makes you think you will become *Sativrata*, the virtuous one, after self-immolation?"

THE LAST SUTTEE

"I don't know. I am confused."

"Do you know suttee is less a matter of purity and truth and more about making money? It is a business." Kumud suddenly felt as though she may win over the girl.

"Business? Why do you think the Elders would mix something so pure with something so selfish? You are wrong!" Parvati said.

Kumud was thinking how to answer her question. Then she said,

"Remember Sau Massi's shrine? That is how much the Elders care about her or you."

Parvati paused. Then ignoring what Kumud had said, she said, "I thought you were interested in Narayani Satimata's story, her *sat*, and the sacrifice she made for her husband."

Kumud had thought that their conversation at Sau Massi's shrine was slowly turning Parvati her way. But now she realized she had not made any inroads to changing her beliefs.

"*Sat* is powerful. Remember, you told me about the power of *oak*, so powerful that it self-combusts," Parvati continued with zest.

"How do you know? Have you seen a pyre igniting itself?" Kumud blurted.

Parvati was no longer listening. She went on, "When a suttee mounts her husband's pyre, the bond they established at their wedding fire is completed as their souls merge for eternity."

Kumud realized she could not change Parvati's confused mind in a day or two. The young woman was conflicted between self-preservation and dishonoring her families. The female role models she admired were either queens who performed jauhar or the mythological figures who glorified suttee. She was trying to live the values and convictions that she had learned from her childhood. She clung to the notion of uplifting her mundane life to that of a divinity. And she was given an opportunity to do so.

"What do the other women of Neela Nagar think about suttee?" Kumud wanted to extend her talk with Parvati as long as she could.

"They believe only a courageous woman can go through it. They praise and pray for the fortitude she represents. Suttee may be banned by our government, but no one can ban Narayani Satimata's teaching that this paramount sacrifice has transformative power."

Kumud listened patiently, keeping in mind what Guruji had advised: If you believe your way leads to the truth, you must first understand the belief of the people who vehemently oppose you.

"I must leave you now, Parvati! From the bottom of my heart, I hope and wish your husband gets better."

"The doctors at the city hospital say the disease has spread beyond cure."

"Why didn't you stay with him in the hospital?"

"My father-in-law asked me to stay home. I am afraid my husband will die in the hospital. When I saw him last, I told him we would meet in *svarg*, in heaven."

Parvati's life story paralleled Sau Massi's.

Kumud tried to make sense of what Parvati told her. She talked about who and what she knew about Narayani Satimata's exemplary life, but her knowledge was abstract. What she spoke came from her head not, even once, from her heart.

THE LAST SUTTEE

It was happening all over again.

Chapter Twenty-Eight
A Good Plan?

"What did Parvati say?" Shyamli asked when Kumud returned home.

"She said what a girl raised in a traditional family in Neela Nagar would say. She is a believer." The day's experience drained Kumud of conversation. She wasn't in mood to talk, so she said, "She remembers me, and she remembers being cared for by others when her mother died."

"That's it?" Guruji said. He seemed troubled. "You spent the whole day with the girl yet she is fixated on doing suttee? What did you talk about?"

"One thing Parvati mentioned that I can't get rid of is that Jabbar Singh and his wife never told Parvati's parents that Kundan Singh was terminally ill when they agreed to the marriage. Can you believe that? Parvati seems undisturbed by their misdeed. I'm so frustrated; I don't know what to do."

"Oh Kumud! Now it makes sense why Jabbar Singh married into a family below his caste—his son was sick and Parvati is so pretty. What a shame!"

"The mind of that malicious man is worse than his savage disposition!" Guruji said in vexation.

"She needs to reconnect with whom she really is. It feels as if she has a sheath wrapped around her real self. She is doing what she thinks she is expected to do, what she believes is the behavior of an ideal woman. It's what she learned from reading pamphlets published by the temple and listening to the female relatives she admires. She must listen to herself!" Kumud blurted with such intensity she surprised herself.

"Rarely anyone does!" Guruji agreed. The room became quiet. The three of them were lost in their individual thoughts.

Kumud realized she was facing a wall. There was no solution, no plan of action. Her earnest effort resulted in nothing. A silly idea floated in her head, and she softly said, "I think I have a plan."

"A plan?" Shyamli said.

"Tell us?" Guruji looked up expectantly.

"I was thinking of gathering the town widows and brainstorming my idea with them."

"Most are uneducated," Shyamli said. "How are you going to know who is for *suttee* and who is against it? You may disrespect their beliefs."

"They may be illiterate, but stupid they are not," Guruji said. "What do you have in mind, Kumud?"

"From the few widows I've talked to, I have learned that there are twenty widows in town, and more than half are against suttee. And the ones who are for it, did not commit it for one reason or another. I feel certain I can convince them to turn against this ritual. Almost all of them work for landlords—grinding chilies into powder." She stole a glance at her host and the hostess. "You may find my idea silly or bizarre. You still want to hear it?"

"Go on, Kumud," Shyamli said.

"On my way back, I remembered that at the end of Sau Massi's suttee, the pyre needed more ghee. The flames were not high enough, not blazing sufficiently to consume the pyre. The guard screamed to the widows, 'Bring as much ghee as you can from your homes!' You know only widows can approach the cremation pyre.

"What if the widows stand with buckets at the site of suttee even before the ritual starts? If the Elders ask what they are doing, they could say they remembered there had not been enough ghee for a blazing fire at the last suttee. This time they came prepared. But instead of ghee, they would carry chili powder in their buckets," she said sheepishly.

"For what purpose? What if someone peeks into a bucket?" Guruji asked.

"We can have them sit around the pyre with cloth covered buckets in front of them—there is no rule against that. And when the pyre is about to be lit, the priests and the guards will say to them, 'Oye, you widows come and pour your offerings.'

"They would say, 'Come and get it if you are so eager to burn a woman.' And if the men came closer, the widows would dip their brooms in the red-hot powder and, like witches from hell, cackle as they sprinkle the powder as liberally as the red vermillion. The men would sneeze and cough unbearably. Running helter-skelter, they would fall to the ground in pain. Then they could create more chaos by sprinkling the powder everywhere.

The spectators would not know what made their eyes itch and their noses run and wrinkled. The warrior widows would continue to wield their powerful weapon until people ran and the ground were empty."

"Then what? They have to return home to their families," Guruji said.

"By the time things settle down, the auspicious time of performing the ritual would have passed. They can't restart the ritual— that would be sacrilegious and unprecedented," Kumud said.

"Future generations will remember how the suttee ritual was defeated by widows using red chilie powder," Guruji laughed, amused by the thought.

"In the meantime, you or someone else would bring a regiment of police constables to arrest those who illegally sanctioned the ritual—the Elders, the head priest, especially Jabbar Singh, and whoever else is involved," Shyamli said smiling.

"No widow would actually do this! After all, they have to live here after you leave," Guruji said.

"When whatever happens reaches the U.S. media, they will call it "The Chili Gate!" Shyamli joked.

The two women giggled.

Guruji became thoughtful for a few seconds and then let out a big laugh.

Chapter Twenty-Nine
The Minister is Coming!

Festivities for opening the new high school were to take place the next day. Guruji had invited the minister of education to dedicate the building several months earlier. A high-level official's remarks seemed essential in establishing the significance of the new school. They would be remembered for a long time.

Everyone was excited about the celebration, whether they agreed or disagreed with the opening of the high school. They reminded each other, "The minister is coming!" In Neela Nagar, the Elders, landlords, police, and priests babbled on about his being there; in Apna Gaon, the peasants, potters, barbers, dyers, and leather workers chirped, "The minister is coming!"

The minister's effort at the state capital had resulted in Neela Nagar and Apna Gaon getting an adequate supply of electricity and clean water. The town and village people could stay up after sunset, and women could begin their day long before sunrise. No more earthenware oil lamps or kerosene lanterns. Children did their homework under bright electric lights. Late into the evening, mothers embroidered clothing with brilliantly colored threads while fathers smoked hookah and chatted. And the women and girls no longer had to carry water from the river. People bathed at home instead of at the riverbank. Water and electricity was in abundance.

When the people needed water and electricity, their voices joined with Guruji's. But on the high school issue, they were divided. Most were against an integrated school. What kind of school would educate girls, boys, and Dalits together? Westernization was creeping into the blue town, and the inhabitants were not yet sure about the change. Many of them wanted to know the minister's opinions on the matter.

Those against integration knew that even if the minister spoke in favor of it, they would defy him. But if he spoke against it, they would welcome his decision. After all, the ministry of education had provided the funds for its construction. They abhorred the idea of co-education and integrating castes. For them, the school was the center of a yet-unclear woe and vexation. Educational institutions had westernized the way of living in the rest of the country and corrupted young minds with all that was impure and taboo. The demonic age of delusion and darkness—Kali Yuga—infiltrated such places. Although they admired Guruji as a person, they abhorred his idea of "higher co-education."

There were also townspeople who were open to integration and restlessly awaited the minister's speech. With the new high school, their young ones would no longer have to go to another town. These people admired such reformists as Guruji, his wife, and families with similar beliefs as theirs. The village dwellers twittered in hushed tones about their children's right to an education and for their dreams to become a reality. They remembered how Guruji, against all odds, started the elementary school in his shack and grew that into a middle school. With the new high school, the ball was rolling. They must fight alongside him for the integrated high school.

At eight on the morning of the inauguration, Kumud heard a knock on Guruji's front door. She opened it and was greeted by three middle school graduates—soon-to-be ninth-graders—all neatly dressed in white shirts, khaki shorts, white socks, and black shoes. They smiled with pride—three heads of black hair, oiled and combed, their eyes twinkling with anticipation.

"Come in!" Kumud said, moving aside. "You have guests, Guruji!" she called, and led them to the drawing room where Guruji was sorting through papers.

One by one the boys greeted him by touching his feet in supplication, and he blessed them by placing his hand on their heads. "Come, children, sit down!"

They sat close to one another on the sofa, leaving space for Kumud. She sat and gently stroked the back of the boy sitting next to her.

"Guruji, we came here first to thank you for all you have done for the advancement of education in this town," one said. "A high school would not have been possible without your effort and presence."

"I am very proud of you!" Guruji said, looking at each of them, one by one. "By going to school and studying hard, you will bring changes to your town and village that you are not yet aware of. The destiny of this place lies in your hands." He thought for a moment and then asked, "Where are the girls?"

"They are not coming," a boy with dimples said.

"Why not?" Guruji raised an eyebrow.

"Is there a problem?" Shyamli, who had now joined them, asked.

"My sister wanted to, but my father did not let her. He would not give money for her school uniform. He said, imitating his father, 'No daughter of mine will attend a school with boys and the village scum.'"

"My father also said something like that, and my mother agreed," the third boy said.

"Where were they all this time? Sleeping?" Shyamli said in frustration. "Why did they not tell Guruji earlier? Do your fathers know that the government will stop funds if the townspeople refuse to send their daughters to the school? We can't limit admission to boys. We have to accept girls and boys from other castes."

"Don't ask them, Shyamli. They don't know!" said Guruji.

The dimpled boy shrugged his shoulders.

"My mother said eighth-grade girls are of marriageable age. They have studied enough. They should be at home or with their husbands, not in school with other boys," the third boy blurted, causing the other two to giggle.

"Are your parents and siblings coming to the opening ceremony?"

The boys didn't know.

"Eighth graders are working hard to prepare for the day," Shyamli said.

"People from other towns and villages are talking

about the new school, wondering why Neela Nagar is moving forward while their towns are still bent on dousing the intelligence and enthusiasm of their children," Guruji said.

"We know the people who are adamant about keeping things the way they are," Shyamli said to her husband. "How is the minister's coming going to change their attitudes?"

"It may take centuries, as much time as it has taken for the old ways to take hold," Guruji said thoughtfully. "The minister's speech, however, may put some sense into their heads."

"Don't you think she is coming for political motives?" Shyamli said. "Politicians don't do things out of the goodness of their heart."

"I didn't realize the minister was a woman." Kumud said

Guruji stood. "Wait until you hear her. I have asked her to talk about education and tradition, specifically about girls and the caste system." Picking up his Nehru jacket, he said. "It's time for us to leave. The ceremony starts at ten. Let's go!"

Vehicles carrying the dignitaries were parked in front of the old school. People had lined both sides of the entrance. Several men and women descended from the cars and vans, and the people cheered, "Manorama Gupta Zindabad! Long live Manorama Gupta!"

The crowd eventually settled, and people took their seats. A man with several aides appeared onstage, but Manorama Gupta was nowhere to be seen. The man approached the podium and said, "I apologize on behalf of Madam Manorama Gupta. She is unable to attend this ceremony due to an unavoidable circumstance."

The announcement had the effect of a sharp pinprick on a fully extended balloon. No one listened as the man spoke about Mrs. Gupta's work and accomplishments. "A tireless worker, she does not let any obstacle, large or small, stand in her way, even when she has pressing engagements. When she starts a project or a program, she stays with it until it is done...." On and on he went.

The audience grew restless. Guruji was frantic. Looking around, he saw the people whispering. Seeing her husband's anxiety, Shyamli was concerned.

". . . the slow-moving government machinery frustrates Manoramaji," the official droned on. "She was exposed to its ways from her first moment of consciousness. Her father was the chief minister of the state, her mother the minister of welfare. As minister of education, she has received many letters of solicitation, including one from Guruji. He wrote how Neela Nagar was isolated and needed clean water and electricity. He wrote about how removed from civilization you felt. Manoramaji went to work immediately because she understood Guruji's plight. His letters impressed upon her the urgency of your appeals. So, this morning, as I stand behind this lectern, I am proud to tell you her story...."

"We have not come to hear you!" someone from the crowd shouted.

"We want Manorama Devi!" another voice added.

There was commotion in the crowd. "Where is she?"

"Kumud, why don't you speak to the crowd!

290

Guruji will introduce you! Please, think of something that will inspire them, tilt their thinking a bit," Shyamli pleaded.

Guruji looked expectantly at her.

Kumud would do anything for the teacher she admired and respected. But what should she say to a crowd whose thoughts and beliefs were so different from her own? Her hands were sweating. She turned to look at the assembly: townspeople, mostly men, seated in the front rows, a scattering of men and women from the village sitting self-consciously in the back rows, and some standing in the aisles. She felt as she had at Veena's wedding.

"Kumud, this is the chance of a lifetime," Shyamli whispered in her ear. "You can win them over, make them trust you. Just be yourself."

Kumud's eyes were on the children, and she nodded slowly to Guruji. He walked to the podium and introduced her as the daughter of Neela Nagar, an educator, the director of an orphanage, and a social worker.

Kumud stepped onto the stage and stood behind the lectern. She adjusted the microphone and again looked at the children of various ages seated cross-legged on a *durri* spread over the ground. The three soon-to-be ninth-graders she had just met that morning cheered for her. Suddenly her nervousness melted away.

She waved at them, and they waved back.

Kumud thanked Guruji and his wife, Shyamli, for hosting an uninvited guest; she thanked Umraodeo Singh the Elder and his wife, Nisha, whom she had followed at the Narayani Temple on the day she arrived. Then she moved the topic to the inauguration of the school. She emphasized the significance of the occasion because it celebrated the light of knowledge and wisdom in young people's lives. She thanked the teachers for making the children's dream of getting an education possible. The Neela Nagar High School was the beginning of a new era when boys and girls could obtain their school certificate without leaving their town or village.

This brought cheers from all the children and some parents.

"Stop trying to be the next Indira Gandhi!" someone shouted from the crowd accompanied by some jeers, and a few laughs.

Kumud ignored them and continued. "Last October, on the day of Deepavali, I lit the first lamp with a match, and then lit a hundred other lamps with the first lamp. At that moment, I felt how Guruji was the first lamp to be enlightened by education. Since then he has lit the minds of hundreds of boys and dozens of girls, helping them to become educated and independent. A handful of his students have tried bringing light into their own homes. Education is the flame that can enlighten a whole town if its inhabitants allow it. When I meet a college graduate from Neela Nagar who has studied at Madhya Shahar University, I feel as an astronomer might feel when he discovers a new star."

Some turned towards Guruji and the other teachers and cheered. Kumud joined them, then continued. "But we must not let our enlightenment end with the construction of the high school. For a minute think about the things in our community that need to be changed or improved. Or even replaced with better things? Let us work together to bring the town and the village into the twenty-first century." The children clapped, although most of the adults remained silent.

"Some of you may wonder why girls should attend school after the sixth or eighth grade, and some may wonder why at all. Why do children need an education? Who ever heard of sweepers, potters, and dyers reading or learning math? For what reason? You learn trades from your fathers, so why go to school if you are going to tan leather or farm?" She sipped water from a glass on the podium. How was she to tell them that perhaps some higher caste members would be better fit for cleaning latrines while lower castes ones oversee the land, teach, or manage a factory or a pharmacy? She controlled that thought. If she offended them, they would leave.

"Education is the key to self-awakening and healthier lives. I am standing here today because my parents understood the value of an education. I went to college and worked hard. Now I help orphans become self-reliant. I do not see myself as a member of the weaker gender. If you want an enlightened community, do what other great towns do, educate your daughters as well as your sons."

Jabbar Singh stood and shouted, "Progress? My foot! We don't need change! Go back to Ambayu, or wherever you came from. Bring as many changes as you want there! We don't want you here!"

Jabbar Singh's influence was strong. People sitting around him stood and roared against her. One said, "No girls in school! No low caste in school! Go back! Leave our girls and women alone!"

Kumud wasn't taken aback by the Elder's action.

She remained calm. Guruji stood and said, "Calm down, people! Please, sit! Are we wild creatures? We are supposed to be civilized."

Guruji's words had a calming effect on some of those present. Half stood and left, but Kumud was not insulted or dissuaded. When the assembly quieted, she resumed her speech.

"As I was saying, one flame lights many lamps. Education lights many minds. It is like a chemical reaction, but unfortunately many children never get to strike the match. Mrs. Manorama Gupta was unable to attend our celebration, and that is unfortunate. Do you know she was born not too far from here? If she had been killed before she was born like hundreds of other unborn females, if she didn't have an education, or if she had immolated herself when her husband died, she would not be a minister. And if it wasn't for her, our town wouldn't have electricity and water, nor a high school. Girls and boys, you're in good hands with Guruji and your teachers. Work hard towards graduating and receiving your certificate. Go out into the world and bring back knowledge for making our chili and leather businesses stronger. Contribute to making your town prosperous! Light a fire against antiquated beliefs and outmoded traditions. Eliminate darkness. *Namaste!*"

The remaining people cheered, "*Jai Hind! Namaste!*"

Kumud felt spent as she walked down the podium. She walked silently home with Guruji and Shyamli.

"What is the matter, Kumud?" Shyamli said. ""Why so glum? You should be proud!"

"You saved the ceremony," Guruji remarked. Both

looked pleased.

"That's not why I came here, Guruji."

"This was the first step," he said.

"You were better than Manorama," Shyamli added. "Your passion was selfless, and it showed. Our dream is progress. Manorama's dream is to be the next Chief Minister. Everything she would have said would have furthered her selfish goal. But not you." Shyamli added.

Chapter Thirty
Would Kundan Singh Die?

A mere phone call had propelled Kumud to leave Ambayu and journey all the way to Neela Nagar. She thought the caller had been Guruji, but it wasn't. Then who was it? And why was the caller so sure of Kundan Singh's death? Why did she believe him? She sat in Shyamli's living room wondering about that phone call. And how she could change Parvati and the townspeople's mindset if Kundan died. She got up to leave for Parvati's home.

As Kumud was locking the door behind her, she saw a man sprinting towards her. Breathless, he asked, "Is Guruji in?"

"No."

"Is Shyamliji in?"

"No one is home. They left early this morning. What is the matter?"

"Would you let them know that Jabbar Singh's son, Kundan Singh, died in the hospital. They are bringing him home."

"Died? Are you sure? I mean, I don't know if I can

reach them. They have gone to Somnath Pandey's home for his son's *Upanayana*."

Although she had been expecting the news, it still shocked her. This was the moment she feared. What now?

"Are you sure Kundan Singh passed away?" The stupidity of the question alerted her to the fact that she was not prepared to handle the reality. She didn't want him to die, and she didn't want Parvati to die with him. She felt the emotional intensity in her heart, in her mind, and in every pore of her body.

Kumud answered her own question, "Of course you are!"

"Who are you?" he asked.

"I'm a friend of the family."

"Are you Kumud?"

"Yes! Why?"

His tone changed. "Parvati wants to see you right away."

"What is your name? Are you related to Parvati?"

"My name is Umeed. She is like a sister to me. We must save her! I heard you speak at the school opening. I told her about it, and she said she knows you. I think only you can change her mind. We have to save her, Didi!" he said with tears in his eyes.

"What are we going to do?"

"I don't know. She is a true believer. She will do whatever she is determined to do. But we must try. You must try."

"I certainly must do something! We must not remain silent any longer. We must not let other people control her life," said Kumud. Looking at Umeed, she added "You are a young man; for god's sake, help me think of something!"

"Like what? This is an ancient tradition; she believes in it. What can I do? Tell me what to do and I'll do it."

They both felt panicky.

"We can make an uproar," said Kumud. "People need to hear your voice. Let all the men who think like you come together. Create a tumult so loud that it reaches the Elders."

"What do you have in mind?"

"I am not sure but something must be done, Umeed! But first I must see Parvati."

"Follow me; I know a shortcut." He turned, and began walking fast. Kumud hastened to keep up.

Outside Jabbar Singh's house, Kumud could hear the cries of women in mourning. Painful memories of Sau Massi's suttee flared, and Kumud's muscles constricted at the thought. Turbaned men smoking *bidis* and exchanging words crowded on the porch, around the front of the house, and in the side alleys.

Umeed left Kumud, and she walked inside Parvati's home.

Parvati was seated cross-legged on the bare floor as the tradition demanded. She stood when Kumud entered the room. Her face was pale and her eyes shrouded in fear. They hugged. Parvati rested her head on Kumud's shoulder and stayed there for a few moments. Kumud helped her sit on the bed. Parvati sat erect. It seemed she had something to say, something momentous.

"As soon as Umeed gave me your message, I came. How are you doing, Parvati?"

"I'm afraid, Kumud Didi," she said. "And very sad."

"Of course, you are?" Kumud rubbed her back. "Your husband has passed away."

"It's not only that," Parvati said, as she wiped her tears.

"What is it then?" Kumud said, tucking a loose bang behind Parvati's ear.

For a few moments, the room was quiet. They could hear men talking and women mourning. The pause comforted Parvati and gave her courage.

She said, "My husband is gone. And today I die with him. A widow has a better life in heaven than on earth. I don't want to live a widow's life. I have seen them. So why am I not ready to die?" Parvati moved closer to Kumud and held her hand. "Why am I so afraid?" she whispered. Her hands were sweating.

"You have a long life to live. No one wants you to sacrifice the beautiful life that awaits you. You have so much to live for."

Parvati remained quiet.

Kumud wondered what was going on in Parvati's mind. She quietly rubbed her back.

"I can't get Sau Massi's shrine, and the scene your described about her suttee, out of my mind. The thought of my body burning . . . ." Tears flowed, wetting her lashes and cheeks.

"Didn't you think of this before?"

"No, I wanted to be just like Narayani Satimata. But this morning as I was pouring ghee from a stewing pot into a lamp, my hand shook and the boiling ghee fell on my hand. It was painful." She extended her hand to show Kumud her burnt fingers. "I thought of Sau Massi seated on the lit pyre. That's when I realized how I would feel when they pour ghee on my body and lit the pyre. Suddenly, I thought of what you said the other day."

"Oh, my sweet Parvati! Sweet innocent Parvati. You are not a goddess, my dear. You are only human! You don't have to be like Satimata."

"But a *sativrata* accompanies her husband to heaven, doesn't she? What would people say? Won't it be shameful? I can't change my mind now; can I?"

"Your life belongs to you. No one else has any right over it, or any right to treat it in a way you don't want."

"Your talk is strange. I do not know anyone who talks the way you do."

"By *not* committing suttee," Kumud said, "you will be changing so many lives. You will open people's eyes, start a revolution in Neela Nagar. You will become a role model like Narayani Satimata—only different."

"But I will not be a *sativrata*, but the opposite of what I believe in." Parvati moved uncomfortably and pulled the edge of her odni over her eyes. It had slipped back, showing her beautiful thick, shiny black hair.

"The words you spoke initially had meaning; what you are saying now is an empty belief," said Kumud. "Future generations will know you as Parvati who-transformed-*pratha*, the ancient tradition of Neela Nagar. Your name will overshadow that of Satimata. What Narayani Satimata did five hundred years ago may have been right for the times, but at the dawn of the twenty-first century, Parvati, you have an opportunity to change things and make an exemplar of your life. It does not behoove a woman like you to waste an opportunity like this. You will be setting a new path for girls and young women who will be watching your every move."

Parvati's head tilted and she gazed on Kumud's face. "But where would I go, what would I do? No widow has charted a useful or gratifying life for herself after her husband's death without the help of an outsider."

"You'll be taking the first step on an uncharted path. That is scary, but also wonderful."

"How can you say that?"

"Many years ago, Parvati, I also found myself in a similar predicament. Someone helped me flee Neela Nagar, and I found a new life far away from here. You can too, Parvati. How many women are courageous enough to take that first step into wilderness? You certainly will need time to think through all this. You may live with your parents for some time, or you may decide to go back to school or work outside the home. Slowly answers will come to you, Parvati."

"My parents don't want me. I won't be welcomed into their home."

"What kind of parent wouldn't want their daughter back home? Have you asked them?" Parvati shook her head. Kumud continued, "They hesitate because they also are afraid. Society tells them their married daughter belongs to her husband's home, married or widowed. Ask them!

"Imagine what a year this would be! The year when the first high school was inaugurated; the year a young widow chose not to commit suttee; the year a widow went to college. People would talk about this for generations. You'll become a legend the way Narayani Satimata is now."

A woman entered the room with a metal glass in her hand. "This is for you, Parvati. Drink this! Sunset is approaching. You must get ready." She handed the glass to Parvati.

Kumud felt sick to her stomach at the sight of the glass. She wanted to snatch it from the woman and throw the liquid at her face.

Parvati took a sip and stared at the woman and Kumud's angry face.

"I'll watch her. You can leave. I'm sure you have things to do," Kumud said to the woman.

"I'll bring the empty glass back. You can trust me," Kumud said trying to be gentle.

The woman reluctantly left, and Kumud bolted the door behind her. "Don't drink that!" Kumud warned.

"What should I do with it?

"Let me take it," Kumud said. She looked around the room in vain for a place to dispose of the liquid. "I'm going to leave you for a while, but don't be afraid!" She looked at her watch. "There are two hours before the sun sets. Just before that, a woman will bring another glass of potion for you. Don't drink it! I'll dispose of this one and return." Kumud held the glass close to the chest and wrapped her long scarf over it. "Don't go anywhere, Parvati. Wait for me!"

Chapter Thirty-One

Nisha

Kumud cautiously closed Parvati's door behind her. That minute, no one was in the corridor. Without attracting attention to herself, she paced through the overcrowded porch and front of the house. Once out of their sight, she poured the concoction on the sand and watched the dry earth absorb it. She scooped out the wet sand with the empty metal glass and buried it. And stomped the spot with her sandaled feet.

If she didn't come up with a solution within two hours, she would end up watching Parvati on the funeral pyre with her dead husband's head on her lap. The thought made her sick. She felt frozen by feelings of hopelessness and helplessness, like she was in a jail cell whose key had been lost.

At the same time, she wanted to feel confident, determined to do something. But what? How could a powerless person change someone's mindset when a town was hell bent on the gruesome, morbid, and insane ritual? A heinous crime was about to be committed, yet no one's heart pulsated in pain.

Who could she trust at this moment? Perhaps the widows who opposed the *pratha*. But they would be too afraid to voice their thoughts. Some of them may already regard Parvati as a manifestation of Narayani Satimata.

Parvati Satimata! The two words together sounded strange, incongruous.

Not knowing what to do, she decided to go to Umraodeo's mansion. The only glimmer of hope she saw emanated at that moment from that house. Running up the serpentine cobblestone path she pushed the front doorbell repeatedly. Nisha opened the door.

"Are you all right? You look frazzled," Nisha said.

"Kundan Singh has died!" Kumud said, "They tried to drug Parvati with milk concoction but I drained it in the sand!" She confessed.

"I know. I know. Come in."

Nisha remained composed. With gentle persuasion and an affectionate tug, she led Kumud inside.

"My husband and I had a long chat after you left the other day. He is out in the fields. He has been informed about Kundan Singh."

"Nisha, Parvati does not want to commit suttee! She has changed her mind. I have come to plead with your husband to stop this mayhem. The young woman must be saved, Nisha. I can't do it alone. I need your help…. Please!" Kumud begged.

"Listen to me, Kumud! My husband's mind has been molded by centuries of tradition and a lifetime of belief. We can't change him overnight," she said. "I was at Saubhagya's suttee. No widow since her has met the same fate. Not a day has gone by since that fateful evening that I have not regretted not using my position as the wife of an influential Elder to stop the ritual. But in vain."

Nisha was overcome with emotion. She continued, "When that happened, I was perhaps the same age as you are now. A tradition firmly embedded in people's mind takes time to shift. Eradicating it completely seems impossible. What can we do?"

Kumud felt enraged by Nisha's word. She stood abruptly.

Nisha took her hand and said, "Please Kumud! Sit down and listen!

"I do not have time for this! Will you or won't you help me?" Kumud asked bluntly.

Nisha, still holding Kumud's hand, turned to face her. "What I'm saying is that before you can assert your beliefs on the people of this town, you must know the history, the worldview, the environment of this town. Why and how the Elders rule. The townspeople don't want you here. They hate your presence and want you out. How do you expect to successfully assert your ideology?"

This is no time for respect. I need action, Kumud's thought. She pulled her hand from Nisha's grip. "I must go to Parvati."

"Listen to me for one more minute, and then you may go. You have accomplished something in Ambayu, Kumud, but it has taken fifteen years to do it. If you want to bring meaningful changes to this town, you must live here—as Guruji does. And immediately announce your intention."

At the mention of Guruji's name, Kumud stopped to listen.

"He and Shyamli believe no one can fight deep-rooted tradition from outside," Nisha continued. "That's why they are dedicated on educating children. With knowledge as weapon, children can discover what is right and what is wrong."

She is not making any sense. Does she realize the emergency of the situation? The two women were quiet. A servant offered cold lemonade. Kumud refused the drink. In the cool silence of the room, she had an epiphany. She may not be able to change a whole community and its customs overnight, but she could help Parvati stay alive.

Kumud felt a powerful presence within that made her abruptly turn around and run down on the cobblestone path. A thought floated in her mind. What if she is able to convince Jabbar Singh and his wife to replace a straw effigy of Parvati? Instead of Parvati, her straw image would sit with Kundan Singh on his pyre.

Kumud had studied about ancient rituals where believers replaced heads of sacrificial victims with coconuts or pumpkins. Why wouldn't a straw effigy be appropriate? The more Kumud thought of this, the more sense it made. She had read that centuries ago in some farming communities, the decapitation of a young man was believed necessary for summoning rains to fertilize parched land. The Elders of such communities, after long deliberations and much debate had arrived at the conclusion that sacrificing young men was ineffective. Eventually, they had replaced dry coconut heads for the rituals that they had believed required human sacrifice.

Substituting an effigy would keep the custom of suttee intact and avoid taking a widow's life. Those who believed in the ritual may feel gratified, and those who abhorred it would feel satisfied. If she could convince Jabbar Singh to substitute an effigy for Parvati that would be transformational.

And if he agrees? What would become of Parvati? What would she do with her life? She would prepare her God-given youth for a greater purpose. Perhaps even remarry.

Was she getting ahead of herself? First, how would she convince Jabbar Singh and his wife of this? He would surely find the idea ridiculous. They would be offended. Suttee was an emotionally charged fest. People's passions peaked as they watched a body burn. A blazing bundle of straw would douse their frenzy.

Her idea was far-fetched, but she had nothing else. She had to give it a chance. As she turned back, she thought of how she would convince Parvati of the logic behind the idea.

Chapter Thirty-Two

Parvati's Suttee

The sun set was an hour away. Kumud was anxious. She looped her chunni around her neck twice and knotted the ends in front, then ran as fast as she could. Panting, she whispered repeatedly, *I can't let it happen again. I can't let it happen again.*

In the distance, she saw the deserted home of Jabbar Singh. *Why had they left early? How far had they gone? Was Parvati forced to drink two more milk potions? Was there still time?* She kept running. Drops of sweat collected on her forehead and dripped down her spine. She remembered a short cut through the maze of the blue houses. First left, then right, then another left to the suttee site. Leaving the zigzagging road, she ran along an unpaved lane flanked by the *kiker* trees. The suttee site was beyond the homes, the kiker trees, and the fields, hidden behind a thicket of trees. Her heart raced. At the edge of the open fields, she looked up the sky and shouted, *He Bhgawan! Oh God, please help me. I can't let it happen again. I can't let it happen! Please, please God, help me!*

She continued running, wiping her face with her

311

chunni, cleaning her nose.

"Oh, my God! I am too late!" she said, coming to an abrupt stop. Her body stood still, like the trunk of a pipal tree. An ominous cloud of smoke appeared from behind the trees. A signal of doom. Wide-eyed, she stared at the gray-black blemish on the horizon, bloodied by the red sun. "You bastards! You changed the time!" she cried, stomping her foot on the ground. Her sight blurred behind tears, which streamed down her face. "You bastards!" She shouted, "What have you done!"

She slouched and continued to walk toward the smoky black cloud. And then forced herself to see what had transpired.

The air reeked of burned flesh. The pyre smoldered. Kumud's body stiffened in shock. She saw individuals surrounding the pyre, the Elders, including Umradeo and Jabbar Singh and his wife, and priests. There were twenty or more people she did not recognize. She turned to the Elders, whose heads pivoted towards her with surprised expression.

Feeling a complete failure, Kumud stared at the darkening earth, pondering, thinking. She suddenly straightened herself and strode in the direction of the crowd. Facing Umraodeo, she shouted, "How can you call yourself wise elders? How can you go back home after this and eat and love and sleep? How can you live such lives? You are not blind, you simply can't see! Your mind is dark. It is shut and locked. The key to it lays at the bottom of a vast ocean where it will never be found. In my life, I have met savage brutes and insensitive and cruel people, but never any as heartless as you. I wish I had not met you. . . . But there must be a reason why fate brought us together." Spit spewed from her mouth; tears streaked her cheeks.

She turned to Jabbar Singh, "Now, this man and this woman," she said, pointing to Singh's wife, "should receive an award for being the most cowardly couple in the town. With their cold hearts, mute mouths, and cruel words, they are content leading their meaningless lives. They exemplify mob mentality." She threw a piercing look at Umraodeo, "I pity you, Umraodeo, Neela Nagar's mouthpiece! Weren't you distraught when they burned a woman the same age as your granddaughter? I had hoped you would be different. Your wife said you are introspective. That you think before making decisions. But she, too, was wrong this time. You didn't mull *this* over, did you!"

Two hefty men paced towards her. Umraodeo gestured them to stop.

"I wish nothing but doom for people like you! I hate all people like you! I hate this never-changing blue town!" The corners of Kumud's mouth frothed as she screamed.

"I did mull things over!" Umraodeo said.

"Like what?"

"I thought about what you had said." Then his voice changed. "Turn around and see who is coming!"

At the edge of the cremation ground, Kumud saw Guruji, Shyamli, and Nisha emerge from a taxi. The Taxiwalla who had driven her from Madhya Shahar to Neela Nagar waved to her from the driver's seat. The rest paced lifelessly towards her. There was nothing to say, nothing to do. Her feet felt glued to the ground. She waited for them to reach her.

"She is right, Umraodeo! This brave lady is right!" Guruji said. "You so-called high caste have behaved like thugs, fearful that police will be called or ministers and politicians informed if the town knew what was about to happen. You are cowards for changing the time of the suttee. Times have changed, Umradeo! Your granddaughter is to attend the high school. She will learn what her grandfather was privy to. What are you going to tell her?"

"It is a somber time, Guruji. Shouldn't we have this conversation on another day?" Umraodeo said without sorrow or empathy.

Guruji nodded in agreement. Shyamli and Guruji embraced Kumud. Bending to her, Guruji said, "My dear Kumud, you did all you could. Your ideals and determination will change the world for the better, if not today, some day in future."

Kumud sat on the front steps of Guruji's home. The sole reason she had come to godforsaken Neela Nagar was to stop suttee. She had failed, and she couldn't do a thing about it. She had failed before, and now she failed again. She was not who she thought she was and could be.

Parvati! Beautiful Parvati turned to ash, just like Sau Massi. She had not witnessed the young woman's suttee the way she had Massi's, yet it had happened. Poor, poor Parvati! She had become entangled in the religious web of a false ideal that had been passed down to her—the allure of being a faithful wife, a *Sativratta*.

Nisha was right. One cannot bring about change by coming to a place like this as a tourist and demanding change. Only its members, the insiders can change a community. One reason she had left this town was its passive people. Changing the psyche of a community is a slow process, like forming or melting of a glacier.

She felt desperate to return to the haven she had created for herself and left behind. She needed the emotional balm of Ambayu to help heal her failure and disappointment. It would bring her numb body back to life. She needed to feel worthwhile again.

Shyamli and Guruji called to her to come inside, but she needed to be alone. She said she would like to go for a walk.

Chapter Thirty-Three

The Second Vision

Once again, Kumud found herself at the foot of Chamunda Hill. She walked briskly to the third spiral where she thought the entrance to the goddess' cave would be. There was an opening! She bent to peek inside. The inky blackness blinded her. Once again, the awe and fear she had experienced the first time overcame her. Not wanting to pollute the enclosure with her shoes, she left her sandals outside. Inside, spaciousness surrounded her.

The floor was smooth and cool to her feet. The mica reflected a silvery glow on the walls and ceiling; it radiated the interior. A presence emanated from the stillness. The wall she faced moved. The silvery black mica cracked. From the wall emerged the same divine female she had seen before——sensual, stunningly beautiful and effulgent.

The essence had manifested as a goddess. Kumud was spellbound.

Her chiseled face haloed with black hair, the goddess was dressed in black and decked with pearls and diamonds. In her presence, Kumud felt unmasked, naked. This was no ordinary female. Yet she looked strangely familiar, as familiar as Kumud was to herself. Even if she wanted to, Kumud could not hide anything from this lustrous apparition. The sudden realization that this divine female knew her completely made Kumud simultaneously shrink away and surrender. Yet she was magnetized by her indescribable presence.

"Are you afraid?" the Goddess asked.

"Are you a chimera or are you real?" Kumud said nervously.

"Do you see me?

"Yes."

"Then, I am real! I am as real as your dreams, your imagination, and your intuitions. Do you think they are real?"

"Perhaps! Or I'm going crazy, which I might be," Kumud said candidly.

"There's only a razor's edge between sanity and insanity. Imaginative individuals like you walk that edge! Are you that sort of a person?"

"Maybe. . . ."

"Why are you here?"

"Don't you know?"

"Still I'd like to hear it from you; Believe me!"

"Believe you? Trust the one responsible for crimes committed in your honor?"

"Is that what you think is happening?"

"What else! If you are the miraculous and marvelous power your followers believe you to be, why didn't you stop the mayhem that occurred today?"

"You forgot mysterious!" the goddess chuckled.

"You find this amusing?"

"As serious or as lighthearted as you take it to be."

"Lighthearted?"

"Not much difference from where I stand! Faith and belief make people who they are. What the people of Neela Nagar believe to be beneficial has come to them through centuries of tradition. Until something traumatic happens, they will not question their view of the world. Religious tradition has power over them. They are not remotely aware of your viewpoint."

"They are unaware that they are burning a young woman, even if it is only once every hundred years? They have muted her voice, curbed her freedom, and nipped her life in the bud. Why can't you rid a society of this evil, a society that worships your omniscience and omnipresence?"

"All have eyes, but only a few can see. You can see! I am in each one of you. I'm the energy within and around you. People like you can bring about change and cause revolutions."

"Why can't you appear to Umraodeo's and Jabbar Singh's the way you appear to me?"

"I also dwell at the core of their hearts but they have not yet awakened to it, that is not my fault. I come only when one calls sincerely, when one's purpose is true and focused. Your frantic desire, your relentless determination summoned me. Your irrepressible resolve forced me to appear."

"Where were you when my wounds smarted?"

"You were not ready for me. Deep wounds are not enough. Suffering prepared you to ask questions, made you wonder who you really are. Made you ask the meaning of your existence."

319

"So you have to suffer your wounds to understand life's purpose?"

"In a way, yes. I warn everyone, nudge them to do right. I give them cues and clues to become conscious of sensations in their body, feelings in their heart, thoughts in their mind. These hints are trying to say something about their inner landscape. Almost all tend to ignore this inner voice becasue it does not agree with what their ego desires.

"Wounds, physical or emotional, have their own merit. They allow light to enter and heal you. Kumud, you have been struggling to excavate your own self for decades, to understand the purpose of your life. I have emerged from the depths of your memories, dreams, and reflections. They have been now cleared away. And you feel me in you."

"Why have you appeared as a manifestation?"

"For your pleasure."

"I don't belong to any religion. Why did you appear to me as a goddess?"

"Because the only association you have with the 'religion' is goddesses, and lately Narayani Satimata. You abhor her. You seemingly have nothing to do with religion. But my child, people's taboos, traditions, and beliefs are not religion. Your determination to redeem your guilt is religious; your belief in equality and the enlightenment of women is religious; your unstoppable urge to reform a society and compensate Sau Massi's sacrifice is religious. If you resolve to strengthen that belief, you can move mountains."

"But it is too late. The woman I came to save has turned to ash. I don't know what to do!" A sob escaped

THE LAST SUTTEE

Kumud.

"Your work of redemption has already begun. Since the day you arrived, your focus was to stop Parvati's suttee. The intensity of your purpose echoes like waves of reform in Neela Nagar."

"What's the use? People's minds are set, padlocked by traditions that no one wants to change. They hope to live a paradisiacal life in heaven while leading miserable lives on earth. The funny thing is, in their minds they imagine a life after death exactly as it was here—husbands ruling their illiterate wives and wives serving them faithfully. What kind of paradise is that?"

"Thinking of Sau Massi's suttee turns you emotionally into a nine-year-old. You feel helpless, entrenched in fear and condemnation for the people of Neela Nagar. But some of them think as you do."

"How do I get rid of this awful feeling I carry around?"

"The pain you feel from your life experiences—the rejection of your gender, your parents' death, your husband's lie—bleed sorrow and pain. By excavating deeply, you have linked to that which is beyond sorrow and pain—to absolute calm. Finally, you are ready."

"For what?"

"To stop blaming yourself. To stop feeling guilty! Allow the people of Neela Nagar deal with their own problems. Unless the women themselves do not rebel, unless men do not wake up from their slumbering ignorance, the transformation you desire will not happen. Major change comes from within an individual, a family, a community. Not from outside. Go back to Ambayu and focus on the good work you are doing. No one else can take care of those orphan girls the way you do. You have not birthed them, but you are their mother. You are doing more there than you can ever do in this town. Leave that for people like Guruji. All is good."

"All is good?"

"Yes, all will be good if you allow the Kumud hidden beneath that armor emerge."

"And let the culprits go free?"

"If I teach a lesson to those who destroy, maim, and kill the innocent, I will be like a puppeteer. People have been granted free will; they must use it. The saints of the world shake up people, but people must wake themselves up. You don't have to follow a religion if you pay close attention to your instincts and intuitions. Cues, clues and insights are constantly being bestowed upon you."

Kumud bowed to the personage who spoke to her in a soothing voice, folded her hands, and closed her eyes.

"Don't loathe yourself for something that happened today. Forgive yourself! Forgive yourself for not saving Sau Massi and for running away from Neela Nagar! Acknowledge the feelings of the man in Ambayu who loves you deeply."

A gentle touch on her head and eyelids soothed Kumud. A current of vitality and bliss passed through the pores of her skin. She opened her eyes to express her gratitude but found she was alone in the inky black womb-cave.

Filled with effusive joy, Kumud walked to the temple entrance, exited the cave and put on her sandals. It was as if no time had passed since she entered the womb-cave. Yet, seeing the darkened sky, she knew several hours had passed.

The wind sang in harmony with the rocks and the trees, breaking into cascading currents and drumming through rock hollows—clouds, wind, rocks throbbed as one. The wind flew over Kumud's face, freeing her mind.

The day she arrived in Neela Nagar—enraged, guilty, and an unbeliever—she called the town a howling desert. But in this dull and forbidding place was a crystalized cave with a shimmering presence. At that moment, Kumud knew that every crevice in every rock, every tree, every field, every grain of sand, and every house and person reflected the divine. She felt intense love in her heart. The burdensome emotions she had carried for the past seven days had been swallowed by the moment. Her newly awakened love in her heart overpowered her guilt, shame, and fear. A silent vitality imbued the hills, the sky, the earth. Insects, birds, animals near and far came alive. She saw the intrinsic beauty of the wind, the sand, and the rocky landscape she once considered barren. The love they emanated was real.

As she descended, the rocks she treaded upon thrived, and the trees that sheltered her swayed in hymnal joy. Why do we hew rock and fell trees to build temples? she wondered. Mother nature is holy, joyful as it is.

The eternal time that Kumud wished would never end began to fade as she stood on Chamunda Hill looking in every direction. The Tapasya River was not dividing Neela Nagar and Apna Gaon, but joining them and then flowing freely to the ocean. It moved at will as she did when she was at Save Girls Souls Orphanage in Ambayu. The sky turned dark and the streetlights came into sight. She walked past the village and crossed the bridge, from where she could see the homes of Neela Nagar.

Outside the door to Guruji's home, she heard voices. The door was unlocked, and she let herself in.

"Is it you, Kumud?" Shyamli called from the drawing room, "Where have you been? You worried us."

"I went to Chamunda Hill to have a last look," Kumud said.

"Come and see who is waiting for you!"

Kumud took off her sandals and walked in.

"Shekhar!" She looked with delight at the man she loved. He stood there, as comforting and charming as ever. She ran to his open arms. His touch sent a shivering pang through her. As they held each other, she imagined herself merging into him. Savoring the moment, she felt everything around her fade and a sense of relief envelope her.

Kumud suddenly became aware that Guruji and Shyamli were watching them. She quickly stepped away from Shekhar and sat on a nearby chair. Teary eyed, she looked at him and said, "Oh, Shekhar, I failed to accomplish what I came here for."

"That's not what I heard. Guruji and Shyamli tell me that you did more than anyone possibly could have imagined against a long-established tradition. You had the courage to try," he said, gently squeezing her shoulder.

"I let a beautiful young woman burn. I couldn't save Parvati! Burnt to ashes, just like Sau Massi! I failed miserably, Shekhar!" she sobbed.

"You did not fail, Kumud," Guruji said

affectionately and patting her back said, "We, the people of Neela Nagar, failed ourselves! Your struggle to bring change to this town has opened a new path for many of us. You awakened people with your concern. We'll reform this town, trust us! Next time you visit, you will see how it has changed."

Shyamli returned from the kitchen with four cups of steaming sweet tea on a tray.

"I agree with your Guruji," Shyamli said, handing her a cup. "Kumud, you have given us courage, more than you realize."

"What good am I if I didn't make a dent?" Kumud had stopped sobbing.

"You have been trying to make a change since you were a child. Nisha read your book and believes that you can actually do something. You care, child! And, you are already doing much good. Every person is allotted to do something good. You at the Ambayu orphanage and some of us here, in Neela Nagar. Believe it or not, your presence has made people aware that what they call a religious ritual is not pious after all. You have put a crack in dark minds, which will allow doubt to enter. This is a good thing," Guruji said.

There was some truth to what Guruji said. Perhaps Sau Massi's suttee led Kumud on a path that uplifted women who had no one else to lead them. The girls at the orphanage needed her, and she wouldn't have been in a position to help if she was not traumatized at nine. Thinking of the girls, she felt at peace. She was content with her work. Did destiny bring her to Neela Nagar to discover this truth?

"Perhaps to redeem myself I needed to leave my

world so I could heal from the painful wound at the place where it had been inflicted," she said more to herself than others.

Chapter Thirty-Four
The Proposal

"If Guruji didn't make the phone call, then who did?" Shekhar asked.

"We had forgotten about that. We really don't know," Shyamli said. "Must be one of the families from the town who knew about Kundan Singh and is vehemently against suttee."

"But how did they get Kumud's telephone number?" Shekhar asked.

"Where there's a will there's a way," Guruji said. "Fate intervenes when good things have to happen."

"I suppose so. Whoever it was, I am thankful to him," Kumud said. Turning to Shekhar, she asked, "Why did *you* come to Neela Nagar?"

"Guruji asked me to come."

"Why? Because I couldn't handle this myself, Guruji?" Kumud blurted.

"No, Kumud," said Shekhar. "Guruji admires and respects your independence. When he called, I asked him if I could come. I wanted you to come home."

"I was going to return. I was not going to stay

here."

"I came because Ambayu is barren without you. I cannot live without you. May I ask you now? Are you ready to hear what I want to say?"

"I think I am."

"I want to marry you, Kumud. Will you marry me?"

Although Kumud remained quiet but she was deeply pleased. The room fell silent. She stood to hug Guruji, then Shyamli as Shekhar watched with great interest.

"For the past few days, these wonderful people have made me feel like their daughter. I have nothing to hide from them." Then she turned to Shekhar and said, "The first time I met you, I thought the woman who spends her life with this man would be fortunate. I didn't dare imagine myself to be that woman. I did not tell you this because I felt unworthy—rejected once in love, married, widowed and middle-aged. Why should he settle for someone like me?"

"Settle?" Shekhar, Guruji, and Shyamli said in unison.

"You know what I thought?" Shekhar said as he approached her. "I thought how fortunate would be the man Kumud agrees to marry!"

"I let myself quietly love you," she said and sat down.

"Then, why did you reject me each time I gathered the nerve to propose?"

"I wasn't ready. I'd been married before. Sau Massi was married. Marriages in my world did not end well. Becoming a wife seemed unimaginable."

"Kumud, nothing matters in my life but you. You are the only woman I have really loved."

Kumud put her head on her knees and sobbed.

"Please don't cry!" Guruji said.

"Don't, Kumud," Shekhar said.

"Don't be silly; she is not sad! Those are tears of joy. Let her be," Shyamli said.

They sat in silence.

Then Shekhar walked to her and said, "Get up!"

She stood. "Shekhar . . . ."

He put his arms around her. His hand on the small of her back: gentle, firm, desiring. She felt his want: warm, arousing.

"I have always and will always love you, Kumud!"

Chapter Thirty-Five
Mystery Caller

The next morning, Kumud and Shekhar were packed and ready to leave for Ambayu. Shekhar's presence helped make Parvati's death bearable. After breakfast, he suggested they take a walk near the fields, and the two excused themselves.

As they left the house, Kumud said, "What kind of a life was that! Her sixteen-year-old body must have turned to cinders in minutes!" Kumud still felt deep regret at what had happened. Shekhar squeezed her hand.

As they walked hand-in-hand towards the moong and barley fields, Kumud pointed out Umraodev and Nisha's mansion on the hill. She told Shekhar about meeting Nisha before she had met her husband, Umraodev. She said that within a day of her arrival, Guruji, Shyamli, and Nisha had become her closest allies. She shared with him the many discussions she'd had with her hosts and Nisha and her husband.

Shekhar listened attentively. He couldn't help admiring the setting and architecture of Umraodeo's ancient *haveli*. "Who is that woman in white? Nisha?" he asked.

Kumud caught a glimpse of a woman. As a young girl, Kumud had been mesmerized by the haveli. Its beauty haunted her, and now the ghost-like figure intensified that feeling. The out-of-reach allure of the mansion captivated the imagination of the town. People simultaneously coveted it and held it at bay. In that regard, she was no different from the townspeople. Blind faith in the Elders' ability to manage the town created an aura around them that enslaved the minds of the masses. A man with that kind of power could utilize it for good of all or, like Umraodev, allow it to go to his head.

He had the personality of a charismatic Rajput prince. It was as if his piercing eyes held the same mysterious aura as the mansion where he lived. You couldn't tell whether they were cursing or blessing you. No wonder the townspeople admired him, almost devotionally, but also felt terribly afraid. He talked gently but his actions were cautious. He seemed to listen to people who did not agree with him, but did whatever he thought held fast with tradition. He argued that if everything were equal between castes and genders, what sort of world would it be? Chaotic! Who would take responsibility for what? What about samsara and dharma? What would become of this world?

"Don't you want to know what is going on at the orphanage?" Shekhar said, jolting her out of her thoughts.

"Yes, please fill me in with all the news. How is everyone?" Kumud couldn't believe Shekhar was walking beside her. She kissed his hand holding hers.

"You are missed terribly, Madam! You will be glad

to hear Vinod came to see Veena the day after you left. He may not be a courageous man but he loves her. And he loves his job. It seems at some point they will get married."

"Is Veena sure? In any case, we can't afford another marriage celebration."

"They said thay don't want a traditional marriage. Whenever they marry they want to get married by a justice of the peace."

"Hmm."

"The day Vinod returned to ask for Veena's forgiveness it didn't take her long to foregive him. He seemed to genuinely regret his behavior."

"I'm glad to her that. Still, she needs to give it more time."

"I agree."

"Anyway, How is Radha holding up? Is she still working?"

"She is. She said she would like to retire when you return. Her legs have given out. She never complains, but I asked her to take it easy. I promised her that when she retires we will arrange for a pension. She is nearing eighty. She should be resting at home, not working for her living."

"Oh, my! How will we manage without her? She is two in one. Overseeing the girls and managing the kitchen."

"Right now, Christina and the cooks are helping her do her work. Some of the girls volunteer their free time. But we'll have to hire at least two people unless we find someone who is as capable as Radha."

They walked silently for a while.

"I sympathize with Umraodev," Shekhar abruptly said. "I find him the most intriguing of all the people you met. He seems stuck between the demanding voice of his ancestors and modern thinking. He cannot decide if he should uphold his ancestral beliefs or fight for progress. He is caught between the nineteenth and twenty-first centuries."

"I suppose so. Shekhar, if you don't mind, I'd like to go and say goodbye to Nisha."

"You go ahead; I'll go back to Guruji's."

Nisha welcomed Kumud with open arms and a smile dancing on her lips.

"Dear Kumud!" she said. "What vivre you have! You did what I could not do for twenty years!"

"What are you talking about?"

"You didn't suspect? I didn't either."

"Suspect what?"

Nisha thought for a moment and then asked, "Didn't you meet my husband on your way up? He drove to Guruji's home to tell you something."

"What was so important that he would drive to Guruji's home himself to tell me? You talk in riddles, Nisha."

Nisha's face flushed. Kumud felt that she wanted to tell her something but could not. "Please, Nisha, tell me. Don't keep me in suspense."

"Some thing I want to tell you is that I was the one who ordered the telephone call that brought you here."

"The man posing as Guruji?" Kumud was flabbergasted.

"Yes, that was my husband's assistant. After

reading your book, I believed that you were the one who might be able to do something about what is happening in our town. Maybe even live here and infuse some sense into townspeople."

At that moment, from the corner of her eye, Kumud saw someone enter the room. She turned, and, lo and behold, there was Parvati, dressed in white and standing like Sarasvati, the goddess of knowledge.

Was an apparition or real, thought Kumud. She stood as Parvati walked to embrace her.

"Oh Parvati! Oh, Parvati! Am I dreaming?" Kumud's voice cracked.

She felt Parvati's sobs on her shoulder. Nisha spoke on her behalf. "No, Kumud, you're not dreaming. My husband saved her and saved face with the townspeople. He was so affected by what you said to him—so innocently, so frankly, and with such passion—that he felt he wouldn't be able to live with himself if he didn't do something.

"After you left, Jesso peppered him with questions. She had also heard you speak at the school inauguration. She couldn't stop talking about you. She echoed many of your concerns. He must have mulled over Jesso's concerns for a long time because later that day he tried to answer them but didn't seem satisfied with them himself. After that he sat for a longtime thinking. Then he suddenly got up and said, 'I've a plan.'

"Kundan Singh's litter was not brought to the designated ground but was taken to a different location two hours earlier. The people waiting for the ritual were told that the site for the suttee had been moved at the last moment because the Elders learned that police and politicians knew about the suttee and would interfere with the ritual.

"In the meantime, at a location, not too far, an effigy of Parvati was placed next to Kundan Singh's corpse. The straw effigy, dripping with ghee, was thrown onto the pyre. It turned the logs into a roaring blaze. My husband tricked Jabbar Singh and his cohorts into coming fifteen minutes late. When they arrived, they believed they were watching the sacred flames burn. Kundan Singh was cremated according to Hindu tradition. Parvati was at the mansion all along."

Kumud was astounded by all that had happened. She listened half-heartedly to Nisha's story and stared at Parvati, alive and whole and as beautiful as she had been on the day they met.

She had accepted the fact that Parvati had perished on the flaming pyre of her dead husband. Walking towards the suttee site, she felt she was on fire when she saw smoke in the sky. She had mourned for Parvati. Hated herself for not being able to save her. She had been overcome by a tremendous sense of failure. And suddenly, in a moment, all that anguish turned to joy. What a beautiful sight! What a beautiful feeling!

"Where will I go, Kumud Didi?" Parvati said breaking her reverie. "Where will I hide?"

"Are you sure you can't stay with your parents until we think of something?" Kumud asked, unsure of what to say to make her feel safe, give her purpose. *She could join a college, stay in a dorm. I can pay her tuition. . . .*

"She can stay with me until we come up with a plan," Nisha said. "Even her family believes she has been cremated. They are not going to like it if she suddenly comes back to life. They would be shamed and ridiculed. People would make their life hellish."

Kumud could not imagine a meaningful life for Parvati in Neela Nagar or any town nearby. What if she doesn't want to study? Kumud thought deep and hard; she decided on a path that Parvati could follow. She said, "Would you like to go to Ambayu with me, Parvati? You could live with my girls at the orphanage."

To Kumud's surprise, Parvati said, "This is my town. I'd like to stay here! I don't know how, but I'll figure it out."

Chapter Thirty-Six
Return to Ambayu

Seated at a window seat with Shekhar facing her, should have made Kumud feel ecstatic. But her mind wasn't on him or the girls eagerly waiting for her at the orphanage. It was on Parvati. What would she do? Where would she go? Who would accept her? Her parents had brought her up to be married. Being a married woman she was *parayi*, "an outsider, the other." Now she was a widow. As a widow, she was nobody, a possession like a cow who belonged to her in-laws. She would be a constant reminder of their dead son, the woman who betrayed her husband at the last moment. She was the ultimate unfaithful wife.

Shekhar did not interrupt Kumud's thoughts.

Fifteen years ago, she had escaped to Ambayu. Her life's purpose became helping young women. She made them believe in themselves, in their abilities and potential, and in working proudly shoulder to shoulder with men. In the process, she found purpose and beauty in her life. Living became meaningful.

Her journey from Ambayu back to the "Town

339

Under the Dome" seemed to empower her, make her wiser. However, failing to chart Parvati's future left a dark cloud in the now clear blue sky of her own life.

What began as Kumud's exasperation, loathing, and rebellion towards Neela Nagar's ancient practices had turned into a lesson in self-knowing. She had to make peace with her past and use this experience to strengthen her relationship with the residents of the orphanage.

With Shekhar on her side she can do anything. At that moment, a feeling stirred in Kumud—something wonderful was about to happen. She didn't know what, but it made her warm all over.

The train's departing whistle sounded twice, then a third time.

"Look at that couple racing to get in!" Shekhar said as the train began to inch forward.

Kumud turned and saw Parvati waving and running towards them; Taxiwalla followed carrying a suitcase.

"Shekhar, that is Parvati! Get her!"

Shekhar rushed to compartment door, and Kumud followed. Holding on to the post, he stepped down, extending his hand and pulling Parvati onto the train. He grabbed the suitcase and hoisted it inside.

"I'm so happy to see you. You *are* coming with us!"

Taxiwalla held onto the side of the window and ran with the train.

"Taxiwalla! Oh, Taxiwalla, what a good man you are!" Kumud said.

"I knew you would be happy to see her, sister. You are a good woman! We may worship Satimata, but we admire our courageous daughters more. Don't we, Parvati?"

The train picked up speed. Kumud slipped a roll of rupees into Taxiwalla's hand, "Let go of the window! You'll fall!" she said.

He handed her Parvati's ticket as the train picked up speed. Still he held on to the window.

"How did you know where we were?" Shekhar asked.

Taxiwalla shouted, "Early this morning Raja Umraodev appeared at my front door with Parvati in his car." He let go of the railing and ran panting alongside the train. "He paid me to take her to the railway station." His voice began to fade. ". . . Safely in your custody. . . . you had left. . . the bus station . . . so I came here. . . " He stopped running and waved, a wide grin breaking across his face.

The train was at full speed, and Kumud turned to Parvati. They both faced Shekhar. Tears rolled down Parvati's cheeks. Kumud and Shekhar exchanged happy and sympathetic glances. She lovingly rubbed Parvati's back as her own worries receded into the dry Neela Nagar landscape, until they were absorbed by the sand.

Boundless joy welled within Kumud. She was as light as a swallow— Shekhar and Parvati were by her side, Veena would marry Vinod, and Alka and all the girls awaited her return. She was already whole; she just hadn't realized it until now.

The train shunted and squeaked its way forward, then whistled again.

Acknowledgments

I dedicate this book to my husband, Manoj K. Wangu, who has intimately shared my writing life from the day I decided to leave the academia until the present day. Thank you, my dear husband and best friend for your attention to detail, authenticity, and unconditional love!

Deep gratitude to our friend Ajit Kumar Bansal from Jaipur. Without Ajit's help, I could not have met and interviewed the members of Roop Kanwar's husband's family.

I am most grateful to my editorial team: Sue McClafferty, my concept editor, Linda Schmitmeyer, my copy editor, and my cover designer and editor Jenny Quinlan. I am thankful to them not only for their thorough editing but also for their interest in the subject matters I write about.

My endless gratitude to all members of the Mindful Writers Groups. Writing with these wonderful groups of writers always inspires me.

Eternally and from the bottom of my heart, thanks

to my inner guide for nudging me, in good times and bad, to be my authentic self, and for rousing me to become a better writer.

Finally, to my readers, thank you for choosing to read this book! Your thoughts and voices matter to me. If you enjoyed this title, please leave a review on Amazon, Barnes and Noble, Goodreads, or any other book site of your choice.